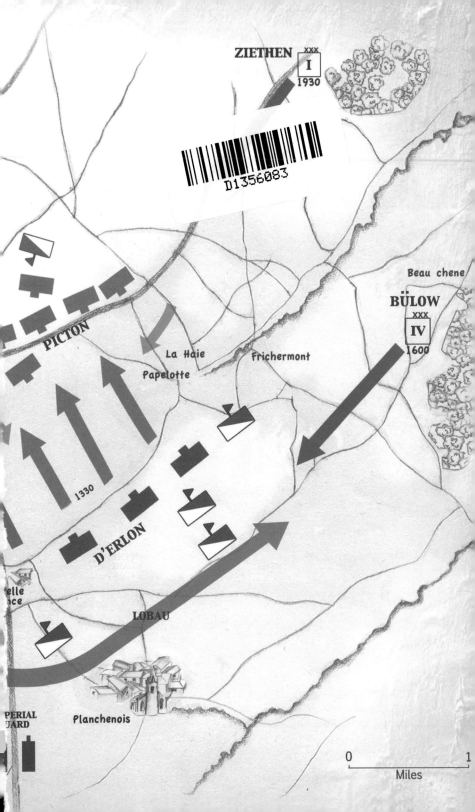

ZIETHEN
XXX
I
1930

BÜLOW
XXX
IV
1600

Beau chene

PICTON

La Haie
Papelotte
Frichermont

1330

D'ERLON

elle
ce

LOBAU

PERIAL
UARD

Planchenois

0   1
Miles

WATERLOO
THE BRAVEST MAN

By Andrew Swanston

Waterloo
The Bravest Man

WATERLOO
THE BRAVEST MAN

ANDREW SWANSTON

Allison & Busby Limited
12 Fitzroy Mews
London W1T 6DW
allisonandbusby.com

First published in Great Britain by Allison & Busby in 2015.

A CIP catalogue record for this book is available from
the British Library.

First Edition

ISBN 978-0-7490-1950-1

Typeset in 11.5/17 pt Adobe Garamond Pro by
Allison & Busby Ltd.

The paper used for this Allison & Busby publication
has been produced from trees that have been legally sourced
from well-managed and credibly certified forests.

Printed and bound by
CPI Group (UK) Ltd, Croydon, CR0 4YY

For my family

AUTHOR'S NOTE

Although this is a fictionalised account of the role played by James Macdonell and the Guards regiments in the battles of Quatre Bras and Waterloo and of the vital defence of the farm and chateau at Hougoumont, most of the characters in the story existed and much of it is true.

Accounts, even contemporary accounts, of the battles vary. Where I have had to choose, I have chosen that which best suited the narrative. Where there are gaps in the accounts, I have tried to fill them with something plausible. I have also used a little licence where it was necessary to the story.

If there are any errors of fact, they are mine alone.

'Our battle on the 18th was one of giants; and our success was most complete, as you perceive. God grant that I may never see another.'

CHAPTER ONE

1815

14th June

To James Macdonell's expert eye the two were evenly matched. One huge and powerful, the other quick and clever. James had been taught to box by his brothers at home in Glengarry. He had fought at fairs in Fort William and Inverness – indeed, had defeated more than one local favourite – but at thirty-four and a lieutenant colonel, he no longer took to the ring. He did pride himself, however, on being able to pick the winner within half a minute of a bout starting. This time he could not choose between them.

Corporal James Graham, the biggest man in the Coldstreams, taller and heavier even than Macdonell himself, was built like a cavalry horse. He had never seen the flame-haired Irishman defeated. But five minutes into the fight and his opponent, a wiry young private from the 3rd Foot Guards, was more than holding his own. He was quick as a snake and had been landing three or four punches to every one of Graham's. He ducked and weaved under Graham's guard, jabbed fast, twisted his knuckles as they met cheek or nose, and skipped back out of range before Graham could respond. He did not carry Graham's weight of punch but if he could avoid one of his thundering blows to the chin, he might just wear his man down.

Macdonell leant over to Francis Hepburn, his equivalent in the 3rd Guards – both regiments belonging to General Byng's second battalion. To see over the heads of the spectators in front, Hepburn, a good head shorter, was standing on an upturned crate. 'Good man of yours, Francis. On the balls of his feet and fast hands. What did you say his name was?' He had to speak loudly to be heard.

Hepburn turned and grinned up into his friend's face. He put his hand to his mouth and spoke into Macdonell's ear. 'Joseph Lester. Private. Fancy a guinea on your man?'

Despite his misgivings, Macdonell did not hesitate. 'Make it two, Francis, and payment in full before supper, if you please.'

For its discreet location behind the town hall, the yard was the favoured place in Enghien for regimental prize fights and wrestling bouts. Since the guards had arrived in the town there had been many such bouts. Soldiers had to be kept busy. Today, for the match between the champion of the Coldstreams and the champion of the 3rd Guards, it was overflowing with spectators, not one of them impartial, and most shouting themselves hoarse.

The yard was formed on three sides by the tall houses that were typical of the town – three or even four storeys, brick-built, substantial – the houses of prosperous Belgian town officials and merchants. Their residents leant from every window, cheering for their favourite and hissing at his opponent. In the yard, small boys sat on their fathers' shoulders or crawled between uniformed legs to get a view. Everyone liked a good fight.

Guards of both regiments in their red jackets and stovepipe shakos had linked arms to form a rough circle within which the fighters were obliged to keep. If either man was forced against the ring he would be shoved roughly back. If he left the ring he would be disqualified. A sergeant from each regiment stood behind the crowd, ready to restore order if it became too unruly.

In the warm evening sunshine sweat splattered off the bare chests and arms of the fighters, spraying the front row of spectators and making the cobbles treacherous. Above them a layer of pipe smoke hovered in the air, the sweet aroma of tobacco mingled with the sharp smells of effort and excitement.

Lester danced forward, thrust his left hand into Graham's eye, anticipated the counter aimed at his head and ducked under it. He jabbed again with his right and drew blood from Graham's lip. The 3rd Guards loved it. 'Joe, that's the way, man. Put the big ox on his arse.'

Graham grimaced and spat out blood. He jabbed out a huge left fist but landed only a glancing blow on his man's shoulder. Lester's knuckles were already red and raw from the punches he had landed, Graham's barely marked. It looked to Macdonell that he was about to see his man lose for the first time and, what was more, be obliged to hand over two guineas.

Sensing a result, the crowd became even more raucous. The Coldstreams yelled at their man to land a punch that would end it, the 3rd Guards roared with delight every time theirs landed a blow or cleverly avoided one. Graham's hair and chest were plastered with sweat. His nose was bleeding and his lip was split. Lester was unmarked and showing no sign of slowing. Very much a light company man, thought Macdonell. Quick, clever, elusive.

The Coldstreams tried to rally their man. 'Imagine he's a frog,' yelled one. 'Wipe the grin off his froggy face.' But hard as he tried, Graham could not land a telling blow. Lester was in and under his guard before he knew it, landing a punch, stepping back and never taking his eye from his opponent. The 3rd Guards sensed victory.

Among the red and white uniforms in the crowd was a scattering of bonnets – wives and sweethearts who had travelled with their men from England and local mademoiselles who had attached themselves to one of the English officers who had been flooding into the country for nearly three months. Enghien was but one of a dozen towns in which a British regiment had been billeted. At home no respectable lady would attend a prize fight. Here it was different. Belgian society had its own rules.

A young woman detached herself from the crowd and made her way to where Francis and James were standing. She wore a pink bonnet and a flowing cotton dress embroidered with tiny blue violets and tied under the bosom with a white ribbon. 'Colonel Hepburn, I wish you happiness,' she greeted Francis with a curtsey.

Francis grinned and stepped down from the crate. 'And I you, Miss Box. I had not thought to find you here.' It was an effort to speak over the hubbub without shouting.

'Indeed not. I would not have come had some of the ladies not pressed me. And who is this gentleman?' She indicated James with her fan.

'My colleague, Colonel James Macdonell of the Coldstream Guards. James, may I present Miss Daisy Box?'

James inclined his head and took the outstretched hand. '*Enchanté*, Miss Box. I wonder how it is that we have not previously met.'

'I have not long been in the country, Colonel Macdonell, and came to Enghien only a few days since. My father is employed in the embassy in Brussels. I came across to visit him and have stayed a little longer than planned.' She glanced at Francis, whose handsome side whiskers could not quite conceal a blush. 'I have found the city most agreeable.' Miss Box's blonde curls peeped out from under her bonnet and when she smiled a dimple appeared in each cheek.

'Then we must hope that the sun continues to shine and the country to amuse you,' replied James, hoping he did not sound too pompous.

There was a huge roar from the crowd. They looked up. At last Graham had landed a worthwhile blow. Lester was down on one knee, wiping blood from his mouth. He spat out a tooth and pushed himself unsteadily to his feet. 'Now we'll see how good he is,' said James quietly.

As if he had heard the remark, Lester advanced to within striking distance, changed his angle of attack at the last second, and landed a solid punch on Graham's nose. More blood gushed forth and Graham snarled. He wiped away the blood and snarled again. It was the sound of a wounded beast turning on its attacker. The direct hit on his nose had given him new purpose. The crowd sensed it and went quiet.

He circled his opponent, his eyes fixed on his target, feinted twice, saw that Lester's reactions had slowed very slightly, took a long step forward, brushed aside his guard and smashed a huge fist into his face. Lester wobbled but did not fall. A fearsome uppercut jolted his head backwards. For a second a look of utter astonishment came over him. Then he did fall. Prostrate on the cobbles, he was not going to get up again.

The crowd cheered and groaned in equal measure. But when Lester did not move, it went silent. Two guards detached themselves from the ring and crouched over him. One of them used a towel to wipe blood from the stricken man's mouth and nose. The other called for water, which came in a bucket and was tipped over Lester's head. Still he did not move. Another bucket was fetched. A guard slapped him gently on the cheek and spoke quietly. 'Up you get, Joe. It's all over now.'

Lester opened his eyes and blinked. He spluttered and retched and struggled up, supported by a guard on either side. Vomit ran down his chest on to the cobbles. He shook his head like a dog with a rat and cursed. 'Lucky Irish bugger. I slipped. He was all but done for.' The crowd laughed with relief. It was a fight they had come to see, not a death.

James Graham, who had stood quietly watching his stricken opponent, went over to help him to his feet. One of his eyes was swollen and closed and his nose was still bleeding. A cloth was held out to him. He wiped his face and hands and threw it into the crowd. 'The luck of the Irish, was it?' he asked in his

16

lilting brogue. 'It's a strange thing I've learnt now – the harder I hit the luckier I am.'

Lester held out a hand. 'And that's the hardest I've ever been hit. I'll take more care in future.'

'You do that and you'll be a champion,' replied Graham with a painful smile. 'Although not in Ireland.' He took the proffered hand, put an arm around Lester's shoulders and led him through the crowd. 'Now, come and we'll spend some of the purse.'

James and Francis watched the two men go. 'Stout fellows, both of them,' said Francis.

'Stout indeed. And we shall need plenty like them when Boney arrives,' agreed James, holding out his hand. 'Two guineas, was it not?' Francis produced two coins from his pocket and passed them over. 'Perhaps Miss Box would care to join us for supper?'

'How gallant, Colonel Macdonell.' Daisy beamed at him. 'I should indeed care to.' She slipped an arm through his. 'Come along, Francis, all this excitement has given me quite an appetite.'

They were about to leave the yard when there was a yell of pain from behind them. They stopped and turned. A scuffle had broken out. A punch was thrown and a woman shrieked. In a trice, guard was fighting guard. A sergeant swiftly rounded up the ladies and ushered them away like a shepherd with his flock. Macdonell recognised two of the brawlers – both Coldstreams and both cut from the same shabby cloth – frequently drunk and forever in trouble. There were rotten apples in every orchard and Privates William Vindle and Patrick Luke were as foul and maggoty as any. He was on the point of stepping in when Francis tapped his elbow and turned away. 'Time for our supper, James. The sergeants will sort it out.' He strode off, leaving James to escort Daisy.

Since arriving in Enghien, Macdonell had had ample time to explore. A man could not spend every hour training and studying. He had discovered a town of fine avenues and narrow streets, tall houses and ancient churches. Twenty-two or so miles south-east of Brussels it was close enough to attract visitors but distant enough not to be overwhelmed by them. Town officials made sure the streets were clean and petty crime was swiftly dealt with, so shopkeepers and merchants prospered. Much as he missed home he had come to like the place.

The avenue down which they strolled ran from north to south almost the length of the town and was lined with stalls selling cakes, cheeses, chocolate and sweet drinks. In the shade of a plane tree, they drank punch. 'Now, then,' said Francis when their glasses were empty. 'To the Grand Café, I fancy. For a few francs we shall have a good supper and another glass of punch. Advance.'

The Grand Café, a favourite with British officers and Enghien burghers alike, was a short walk down the avenue. Outside it, tables and chairs – mostly occupied – had been set for those who preferred to dine in the evening sunshine. Waiters in aprons, carrying plates and trays, bustled about trying to keep their customers happy. Wine flowed and voices were raised. James and Francis nodded to officers they recognised and smiled at their admiring glances. Daisy pretended not to notice and led them to a table. 'Today

I shall eat veal,' she announced. 'I do so enjoy it and we seldom see it at home.'

They ordered their meal and more punch. The food was good and the punch strong. James did not have to make much of an effort at conversation, leaving Daisy to chatter away happily. She was born in Hampshire, her mother had died when she was a girl, her father was a senior official in the embassy, and she had insisted on crossing the Channel to visit him and to see a little of the country. She hoped there would be no fighting to spoil her visit. Francis Hepburn assured her that there would be no fighting for some weeks, if at all, and that she should concentrate on enjoying herself.

She waxed lyrical about Brussels restaurants, its elegant squares and parks and the courtesy of its people. 'Such a change from England,' she declared. 'I had not before realised how uncouth we English can be.' She put a hand to her mouth. 'I do not mean to offend, Colonel Macdonell. Although you of course are from Scotland, are you not?'

'I am, madam, and I rather agree with you. The Englishman is a rough type, unlike his cousins to the north. We can only hope he is not found wanting when Buonaparte arrives. The Corsican comes from much the same sort of stock.'

'And will he arrive, do you think, Colonel?'

'Despite what Francis has told you, I fear that he will. But we shall be ready, shall we not, Francis?'

'Naturally, we shall. If he comes anywhere near the border, he will find us blocking his path. I daresay he will turn his army around and run back to Paris.'

Macdonell raised an eyebrow. 'Let us hope so.' He rose and

excused himself. He was duty officer the next day and must be up soon after dawn. He left Francis to entertain Miss Box and returned to his billet in the Château Enghien.

Supper had been good, the evening was agreeably warm and the town was quiet. Yet he found as he walked that neither the prize fight nor Miss Box had lifted his spirits. He was sick of waiting, sick of trying to find ways of keeping the men occupied and out of trouble, sick of the tedium. For three months Wellington and Napoleon had been building their strength. Now, surely, they were ready. Napoleon would cross the border and the Allies would march to face him. Very soon they would be at war and Francis Hepburn knew it as well as he did.

CHAPTER TWO

15th June

Macdonell was woken by his servant with a mug of sweet tea and the regimental order book. He rubbed sleep from his eyes and checked his pocket watch, a gold hunter made in Paris by M. Lepine, and of which he was uncommonly proud. It was five o'clock. He had slept little. He had still not adjusted to a bed which was six inches too short for him – at three inches over six feet, most beds were too short for him – and just before he retired a galloper had arrived to report that Napoleon's Armée du Nord was on the march and seemed to be heading for Charleroi on the River Sambre. If the French attacked the town and crossed the river they would have committed an act of war and would be on their way to Brussels, a city that Wellington had vowed to defend. Major General Sir George Cooke, commander of the 1st Infantry Division stationed at Enghien, had immediately sent a despatch to the Duke, summarising the news and requesting orders. As a reply would take several hours

21

to arrive, James had retired in the vain hope of sleep.

He swallowed a few mouthfuls of tea and took the order book from the servant. 'Any news?' he inquired hopefully.

'None that I know of, sir.'

'Shouldn't be long.' In a neat hand he entered the first order for the day. The light companies would parade at eight o'clock in marching order. Sixty rounds to be issued to each man and all horses to be thoroughly exercised and fed. He signed the order Lt Col J Macdonell, Coldstream Guards, and handed it back.

'Sick to report to the infirmary as usual, Private,' he said. 'We shall not want any stragglers. And ask Captain Wyndham to have every musket cleaned and tested. Every one, especially the flints. The last batch was useless.' Faulty flints supplied by unscrupulous dealers were a constant source of complaint.

'Yes, Colonel. There is one other matter, sir.'

'What is that?'

'Vindle and Luke, sir. Fighting. Sergeant Dawson instructed me to tell you.'

'For the love of God, not again. Drunk?' The very pair who had been at the prize fight.

'Yes, sir.'

'Tell Sergeant Dawson that I will see them before parade.'

'Yes, sir.' The private saluted smartly and left. James hurriedly drank the remains of his tea, splashed water over his face, ran a comb through his mop of sandy hair and struggled into his new uniform, already brushed by the servant. It was as fine a uniform as any in the army. A red jacket with a high blue collar and blue cuffs, white breeches, cross-belt from right shoulder to left hip and calf-length black boots. The jacket was laced with gold braid. He checked his appearance in a mirror. He was ready. And if the French were on the Sambre, he would need to be.

On the first day of March, Napoleon Buonaparte had landed with about a thousand men at Golfe Juan on the southern French coast. Ironically, the Duke of Wellington had been in Vienna, discussing with the other European powers how best to ensure peace and stability for all after twenty years of conflict. Boney, not for the first time, had caught them napping and by the sound of it he might be about to do so again.

Macdonell had been with the regiment in Brussels when the news arrived. At first, some of his fellow officers did not take it seriously. They thought that Boney would get no further than Lyon. They did not believe that the veterans who had left their wives and families to fight for him and had seen so many of their comrades die in Spain and Russia would dust off their uniforms, sharpen their swords and make ready to follow him again.

Others did not accept the threat Napoleon posed because they did not want to. They were enjoying themselves too much in the glittering hotels and salons of Brussels to want to go to war, and so persuaded themselves that the little Corsican would simply go away.

James knew they were wrong. The highlander's instinct that had served him well on battlefield and Scottish hillside alike told him that it would not be many weeks before they were at war again. He had fought in Italy and with Wellington in the Peninsula. He had seen French Lancers destroy an infantry line in a matter of minutes, he had watched helpless as French artillery had turned an infantry square into a mess of blood and bodies, and on dark nights he could still hear the remorseless drumming that signalled the advance of the French Imperial Guard.

Napoleon would not have left his exile on Elba without being confident that these tough veterans of his Russian and Spanish campaigns would follow him once more. Macdonell had even bet a guinea on it with Francis Hepburn. The guinea was paid the day they heard that Marshal Ney, commander of the Imperial Guard, and so-called 'bravest of the brave', had declared his support for the Emperor. If Napoleon's beloved 'immortals', complete with their pigtails and earrings, were with him, not a man in France would entertain the remotest possibility of defeat.

Within two days of Ney's declaration, King Louis XVIII had fled with his family to Bruges, and their emperor, to the joy of the people, had entered Paris. The Allies declared war on France and Wellington made haste to Brussels. Macdonell had heard the Duke say that he wished a more distant island had been found for Napoleon. St Lucia in the Caribbean, perhaps, where yellow fever or malaria might have done for him, or even the lonely island of St Helena, stuck out by itself in the middle of the Atlantic. And the Duke had been proved right. For Napoleon, Elba in the Mediterranean had been no more than a stepping stone back to France.

The Château Enghien stood at the north-eastern edge of the town beside a heart-shaped lake fringed with willow and oak. Once a magnificent building with a grand park, it had long ago fallen into disrepair. Nevertheless it had provided the officers of the 2nd Brigade with more than adequate accommodation. The walls might be peeling and much of the furniture broken, but it was dry and comfortable enough. James had tried, and failed, to imagine it as it must have been in its glory days – the scene, surely, of lavish banquets, grand balls and glittering musical gatherings. Just the things Napoleon was known to hate.

He strode out of the chateau, down a broad flight of stone steps and set off around the lake. A good walk before joining General Sir John Byng for breakfast and to be briefed on the night's news would help clear his head. It was Sir John's habit to take breakfast with his senior officers. Unlike Major General Peregrine Maitland who commanded the 1st Brigade, Byng liked to extol the merits of a good breakfast. The fastidious Maitland dismissed it as an unwelcome new habit and insisted that a man should do at least two hours work before breaking his fast.

Macdonell worked better on a full stomach. He had more energy and thought more clearly. And if they were to march, a clear head would be needed. Mobilising troops who had been in quarters for as long as they had would not be easy.

Among the rows of tents the first stirrings were apparent. Grizzled heads appeared, sniffed the air like hunting dogs, relieved themselves and retreated back inside. Fires were being lit and water boiled for tea. Most would breakfast on their ration of boiled beef and biscuit. A few might have scrounged an egg or some bread. In front of a tent at the head of a line, two large figures and an unusually small one were busy preparing their food.

'Good morning, gentlemen,' Macdonell greeted them. All three immediately snapped to attention. Macdonell grinned. He could not help grinning when he saw the Graham brothers together. They were so alike that they could have been twins, although today James bore the marks of the fight. One eye was swollen and both cheeks bruised. Six and a half feet tall, broad-shouldered, ruddy-faced, hewn from the hardest Irish granite, and inseparable. Macdonell often thought that if the army had just ten thousand like the corporals Graham, Napoleon would be wise to turn tail and run.

In appearance, the third man, Sergeant George Dawson, was rather different. Barely an inch over five feet, pug-nosed and barrel-chested, he might have been about forty years old. No uniform had ever quite fitted him, however skilful its maker. He was a tough borderer from the town of Hawick who carried his lack of height with a certain panache. Dawson, too, had been at Maida and in that odd, short battle, had fought bravely and by word and deed had encouraged others to do the same. That was why he now wore a sergeant's crimson sash.

'Good morning, Colonel,' replied the sergeant. 'You find us making ready for the day.'

'Joy of the morning to you, Colonel,' added James. 'Mug of fine Irish tea?'

'No thank you, Corporal. Good fight. Well done. How are the wounds?'

James raised a hand to his face. 'Wounds, Colonel? Just a few scratches and my hands are good as new. Joe's a fine mess, poor fellow. Hope he can hold his musket.'

'So do I. How was the night?'

'Long, Colonel. We expected news.' This time it was Joseph.

'Will we be marching today, Colonel?' asked Dawson. 'The men are asking.'

'I expect so. Full parade at eight. Be sure to kick the drunks and dreamers awake and in to line.'

The corporals smiled their lopsided smiles. 'That we will, sir,' replied Dawson. 'Are you aware of Vindle and Luke fighting again?'

'I am, Sergeant, and I will deal with them after breakfast.'

'Very good, sir.' Macdonell nodded and went on his way.

A cloudless sky and already he could feel the warmth of the coming day on his face. God willing, the order to march would come that morning. If they were off to fight, the men should not be kept on parade for too long. Knapsack, blanket, sixty balls, powder, musket, bayonet and three days' biscuit weighed nearly sixty pounds. As a young ensign he remembered finding the load heavier when standing still than when marching or fighting. Mind you, when it came to battle, the light companies he commanded would carry nothing but their guns, ammunition and a light oilskin haversack. Speed and stealth were the skirmishers' best weapons.

Beyond the rows of tents the park stretched out towards distant woods. Sweeps of grass, close-cropped by the horses, were fringed with lines of poplars. All semblance of a garden had long disappeared, although there were paintings in the chateau of what had once been spectacular beds of roses and tulips. Macdonell made his way towards a stream that ran through the park and into Lac d'Enghien. On the banks of the stream grew willows, their branches draped over the water and, here and there, stooping so low that they might have been trying to drink. Just once he had seen a kingfisher there. It had swooped so fast to spear its prey that it had been no more than a blur of green and red; it was only when it emerged with a stickleback in its beak that he had been sure of what he had seen.

Macdonell liked that spot. He went there to watch dragonflies and waterboatmen and, occasionally, to take off his boots and dangle his feet in the cool water of the stream. Although no more than a few hundred yards from the noise and bustle of the camp, it was peaceful. It was a good place to think. Army life allowed little time for private thought. And it reminded him of home – Glengarry, where the river ran down to the loch and on to the Great Glen above Fort William. He had been born there, grew up there with his brothers, learnt to catch salmon, stalk deer and shoot pheasant there. At school in Douai he had missed the lochs and glens of Scotland almost as much as his family. And he missed them now. He stooped to pick up a pebble and threw it into the stream. He watched the circles it made in the water as they expanded outwards, eventually to be swallowed up by the current. He used to do the same in Glengarry when the river was slow.

For him, the Netherlands and Northern France were too flat to lift the heart, too much of a muchness. He craved the wildness of the highlands, snow on the peaks, icy streams, crofters' cottages, the sweet smell of burning peat, yellow gorse and purple heather on the slopes. God willing, it would not be many days before he saw them again.

As the third son of a Catholic highland family, his father dead, he had chosen a military life for himself. The family estate had passed to the eldest brother Alasdair, the second was content with his writing and his books, which left James. He had considered the Church, politics, travel, exploration, and had settled on the army. It had been a wise decision. The discipline and order suited him. He enjoyed the company and fellowship of soldiers. And he had acquitted himself with distinction in battle, enjoying the irony of a member of a staunch Jacobite family serving a German king who sat on a throne in London.

A knot of tension was growing in his stomach. He had felt that same knot in Italy and in the Peninsula. Not fear, not excitement, more a sharpening of the senses, an acute alertness that presaged action and danger. Today, surely, they would march. The Duke of Wellington would give the order and they would march to meet Napoleon. Napoleon, who could not acknowledge defeat, had risen again and, if he were not stopped, would sweep through the Netherlands to the coast where he would gaze across the Channel to England. And then what?

Dragging himself from his reverie, he turned and walked briskly back to the camp. The camp stirrings had taken on a new energy and he knew at once that the tension was not his alone. He could see it, hear it, even smell it among the men. It was there in the urgency of their movements, it was there in their gruff voices and it was there in their faces. They were going to war and they wanted to get on with it. Wellington had called them, admiringly, the scum of the earth – scum who had taken the King's shilling rather than see their wives and children starve, or to avoid the horrors of Newgate or Bridgewall. It worried the Duke and his officers that so many had never hefted a sword or fired a musket in anger, but they were at least survivors, scrappers who the army had trained to fight as a unit and had turned into proud members of a proud regiment. Like as not, Macdonell's light companies would be first into battle and first to draw blood.

Unwilling to face more questions, Macdonell skirted the camp and returned to the chateau. General Byng was a man who insisted always on exactness and accuracy. Breakfast at seven o'clock meant just that and woe betide the officer who was late.

CHAPTER THREE

That morning they were ten – Byng, Lt Col Alexander Woodford, who had command of the 2nd Battalion and was thus Macdonell's immediate superior, Francis Hepburn, Captain Charles Dashwood of the 2nd Battalion, Harry Wyndham, four other captains and Macdonell. At seven exactly, Byng entered the dining room and invited them all to be seated. Fortunately, the long mahogany dining table and twelve curved-back chairs had survived the demise of the chateau.

Sir John Byng, veteran of Vittoria, Pamplona, Ireland and Toulouse, was the most courteous of men. 'Before we eat, gentlemen,' he began in his gentle, almost scholarly manner, 'I know you will be wanting news.' At the table there were murmurs of assent. 'The position this morning is as follows. Ney's Armée du Nord is still on the eastern bank of the River Sambre, facing the town of Charleroi.

The three main bridges over the Sambre are, we understand, intact. The Duke expects Ney, in due course, to cross the river and advance towards the town of Mons to our south-west but he will not commit us until he is sure. We are to be ready to march at short notice, although it may be days, even weeks, before we do.' He looked around the table. 'I see the disappointment on your faces, gentlemen. I, too, would prefer to wait no longer, but you will see the sense in the Duke's strategy. He wants Napoleon to show his hand before acting. Are there any questions?'

'Can we still count on Marshal Blücher?' asked Woodford.

'Marshal Blücher and his Prussians are guarding the eastern approaches to Brussels at Ligny and Liège. The marshal may be over seventy but there is no more gallant commander. He will not fail us.'

'What is his strength now, General?' This time it was Francis Hepburn.

'About the same as our own, some seventy thousand. The French, His Grace estimates, number one hundred and twenty thousand. The Russians and the Austrians will advance from the east but are unlikely to arrive before the end of the month.' Byng looked at Macdonell, seated next to him. 'What do you think, James?' he asked. The general had a habit of seeking the views of his officers, not always having regard to their rank.

'If I were Napoleon,' replied Macdonell, who had lain awake thinking about just this, 'I would rely upon the element of surprise. I would move quickly to drive a wedge between the Prussians and ourselves. I would attack Charleroi and advance without delay on Brussels. Surprise has always been a tactic he favours.'

'You would not go west to Mons or east to Ligny?'

'I would not, General, especially if it meant splitting my force.'

For a long moment, Byng gazed at Macdonell. 'And perhaps that is just what he will do. We shall know soon enough. And how would you respond to this threat?'

'I would march at once, join the Prussians and seek to take the initiative.'

Byng looked doubtful. 'Hm. Would you now? Defender turned aggressor, eh?' He paused and looked around the table again. 'Does anyone else agree with Colonel Macdonell? No, on second thoughts, do not answer that. The Duke has decided and that is that. Now let us take our breakfast.' He rose and went to a sideboard on which silver pots of tea and coffee, plates of brioches and French bread and slabs of pound cake had been laid out. The officers followed him, loaded their plates and returned to the table. None of them would start the day on an empty stomach.

When they were all seated again, Byng turned to Woodford. 'My carriage will be departing at seven this evening for the Duchess's Ball, Alexander. Would you care to join me?' The rule against carriages in the town had been lifted for the evening.

'That would be most kind, General,' replied Woodford.

'Excellent. You, too, Harry. We have room for three. General Cooke, I understand, will be leaving earlier. He has an afternoon engagement in Brussels.' The officers suppressed smiles. Wellington himself was known to be fond of afternoon engagements. In Paris he was even rumoured to have conducted simultaneous affairs with an opera singer and an actress, both of whom had previously been lovers of Buonaparte. 'I am unhappy at leaving Enghien at this time, gentlemen, but the Duke is insistent that we attend the Duchess of Richmond's Ball. It has been weeks in preparation and he does not wish Her Grace to be disappointed.' He smiled kindly. 'And I know I shall be leaving matters in the most capable hands.'

Harry Wyndham, second son of the Earl of Egremont, had received an invitation and, a little to Macdonell's surprise, had accepted. The product of a grand English public school, determinedly independent in spirit and inveterate wag, Harry was twenty-five years old, and a captain in the light company of the Coldstreams. Despite the differences in age, rank and background, he and James had become friends. In fact, their ranks were not as different as it might have appeared to anyone not familiar with the strange ways of the Guards because James held not only the rank of lieutenant colonel but also the lesser one of major and Wyndham that of lieutenant colonel in addition to captain. To anyone outside the regiment, double-ranks were utterly confusing. Harry was always good company, an important quality in times of dreary inactivity, and found it difficult to take life seriously. Whenever James erred towards self-importance, Harry could be relied upon to find the *mot juste*. All he lacked was battle experience. It would not be long before he got it.

James feared that he too might be included in the Duchess's guest list because of his family connections and had been greatly relieved when he found that an ancient Scottish lineage was not enough to warrant an invitation. From the Coldstreams, Woodford, Wyndham and three young ensigns from distinguished families would be joining General Byng. Macdonell disliked all dancing other than a good Scottish reel, and would be very much happier at Enghien. True, a highland regiment was due to give an exhibition of sword dancing, but the guests would be gavotting and waltzing and quadrilling well into the early hours.

At fifteen minutes before eight, Byng carefully wiped his mouth with a linen napkin and rose from the table. 'Good morning, gentlemen. I will leave you now to be about your duties. If there is more news I will, of course, send word.'

James left the dining room with Francis Hepburn. 'What did you make of it?' he asked quietly.

'I agree with you, James.' replied Hepburn. 'The peer is being too cautious. We should dictate terms by marching to join the Prussians and crushing Napoleon once and for all.' He paused. 'Still, His Grace is the field marshal and we are not. We'd best do as we are told.'

Macdonell laughed. 'As we always do.' At the bottom of the chateau steps, Sergeant Dawson was waiting for Macdonell. Another colonel might have left the matter to the company captain. Macdonell insisted on dealing with all disciplinary offences himself. 'Very well, Sergeant,' he said, 'where are they?'

'At the stables, Colonel. Corporal James Graham is with them.' Macdonell had considered promoting one of the Grahams to make distinguishing between them easier but had decided that would not be fair on the other.

'Good. Let us hear what they have to say for themselves this time.'

The Enghien stables, at the back of the chateau, were enormous, another legacy of bygone days. Graham and the two privates were waiting at the far end of the cobbled yard. 'Thank you, Corporal,' said Dawson, as they approached. 'I will take over now. You make ready for parade.'

'Very good, Sergeant.' Graham saluted and marched off, leaving his charges to their fate. Privates William Vindle and Patrick Luke were as nasty a pair of ferret-faced, thieving, good-for-nothing drunks as could be found in any regiment of the British Army. Macdonell had never quite understood how any recruiting sergeant could have taken them into a Guards regiment and, had he been able to, he would long ago have thrown them out or, better still, hanged them from a Dutch elm. Between them they had caused more trouble than the rest of the battalion put together. 'Right, Sergeant. What have they done?'

'Drunk on watch, Colonel, and fighting.'

'Fighting each other or some harmless old woman?'

'Each other, Colonel.'

'Why?'

Vindle, who might never have told the truth in his life, cleared his throat and rubbed his almost hairless head. His face was filthy and pockmarked. 'It was nothing, Colonel. A little argument.'

'Were you drunk?'

'No, Colonel,' replied Luke, in his slimy, weedly voice. 'No more than a glass of rum to wet the throat.' Macdonell stared

36

into the narrow eyes set under a low brow and either side of a twisted beak of a nose. They were red and rheumy from drink.

'Sergeant Dawson says otherwise.'

'Sergeant Dawson is wrong, Colonel,' growled Vindle.

Macdonell took a step forward and bellowed into Vindle's face. 'No, Vindle, Sergeant Dawson is not wrong.' He sniffed. 'You stink of rum. You were drunk and you were fighting. Over who had stolen what from whom, I daresay. If I could, I would shoot you both myself. But we are going to war and you will be needed as targets for the French sharpshooters. I hope their aim is true.' He turned to Dawson. 'In the meantime, Sergeant, half rations, remove every bottle they have hidden in their tents and put the wretches to clearing out the stables. They can spend the day shovelling muck. Let me know if they stop for so much as ten seconds. And count yourselves fortunate, you two. If we were not about to fight the French you'd be locked in the cellar and left for the rats. No more chances. Next time it'll be a whipping. Take them away, Sergeant, before I lose my temper and crack their heads together.' Macdonell disliked public whippings but these two had used up all their lives.

'Very good, Colonel,' replied Dawson.

Macdonell turned on his heel and strode off. It was time for the light companies to parade.

In appearance, Wellington's army had changed in the few years since it had chased the French around Spain and over the Pyrenees. Then officers wore whatever they liked and soldiers whatever they could find. A dead Frenchman's trousers were as good as any if they were intact. Wives and daughters were kept busy darning and sewing and making up whatever they could from bits and pieces into shirts and jackets.

The three hundred men of the Coldstream and Third Guards Light Companies, however, had done no fighting for over a year and new uniforms had not long arrived from London. In their red jackets, white trousers, stovepipe shakos and good leather shoes, they had been formed up in four lines and looked as fine as if they were in Horse Guards Parade. The shoes, especially, were a godsend. The flimsy things they had worn in the Peninsula had lasted no time on rough Spanish roads. Each man held a musket and carried a bayonet, a pouch of cartridges, another of balls, a wooden canteen and an oilskin knapsack. Only the pattern of buttons on their jackets told the two companies apart.

These were the skirmishers, the ghosts and spirits who would work their way close to the enemy by hiding in fields and behind trees, and would pick off as many Frenchmen as they could before withdrawing quietly whence they came. Macdonell was proud of them and, in the expectation that they would march that morning, had prepared a few words of encouragement. Nothing grand, nothing Agincourt-like, just a quiet reminder of the great traditions of their regiment. But all he could tell them was that they were going nowhere until further orders arrived from Brussels. As he spoke, faces dropped and shoulders slumped. Another day hanging about with little to do, they were thinking, and he could hardly blame them. Three months in Enghien, not a Frenchman in sight and fingers itching to pull triggers. Last night, the news that the frogs were at the Sambre would have been around the camp like the plague. Why were they not being sent to meet their advance? Would they have to wait until the frogs were hopping around the gates of Brussels before attacking?

James Macdonell, their colonel, who had fought in Spain, France and Italy, who wore the Gold Medal for Maida, could not tell them. He could only instruct Captain Wyndham to dismiss the parade and to find what work he could to keep them busy. It was not what he or they had expected.

Nor was it what the two young ensigns attached to the Coldstream Light Company had expected. Superficially alike – smart, ambitious, hard-working sons of well-to-do families – in temperament they were as far apart as beef and mutton. Henry Gooch, seldom lost for a word, boasted of being impatient to 'make widows of a hundred French madames'. Thoughtful, devout James Hervey, when pressed, would say only that he prayed he would let neither his regiment nor his family down. Very different, yet perhaps no more than two sides of the same coin. A coin minted in fear of what was to come – one side braggadocio, the other prayer.

The two of them had been standing with Captain Wyndham during the parade. 'Why are we not marching, Colonel?' asked Gooch, as the men dispersed.

'It is not for me to say, Mister Gooch,' replied Macdonell, 'nor for you to ask. We shall await orders.'

'But, Colonel, if the French—'

'Enough, sir. Your leadership skills will be tested today.'

'I daresay the order to march will come soon enough,' ventured Hervey, 'It sounds like Buonaparte means to fight and

I wonder that the Duke did not receive earlier warning from his agents in Paris. Surely they would have known?'

'An interesting point, Mister Hervey, and another to which I have no answer. Now, kindly be about your business, gentlemen. Find work for your companies and for yourselves. Muskets, drill, packs. Check and check again. Keep them busy.'

The ensigns saluted smartly and marched off towards the camp. Macdonell watched them go. Neither had seen battle and he doubted they had much inkling of what it was like to see the head of the man next to you blown to splinters of bone, or to face ranks of cheering cavalry whose sole intention is to slice you in half, or to stand in square and face artillery round shot without flinching. They would have heard stories but they would never know the awful horror of it until they experienced it for themselves. No one did.

The day dragged on. He walked again around the park. He watched the Coldstream band at practice. He had no ear for music and could only just tell the French horn from the serpent. Pipes and trumpets and drums and cymbals – the instruments of battle – were more to his liking.

He made another circuit of the camp, exchanged a few words with the Grahams and some of the men, made a show of checking musket barrels and boots – reminding the new recruits that an infantryman's boots could kill him as readily as a French sabre – before retiring to his room to rest and to write to his mother in Glengarry.

He was not an artist or a diarist, as some were, preferring to hold images and words in his mind rather than commit them to paper, but he was a dutiful correspondent. He wrote of his pride in his men and of the frustration of waiting. He wrote of the coming battle and his certainty of victory. He wrote of his friends, Harry Wyndham and Francis Hepburn, and he wrote of little things – Belgian bread, the kingfisher at the stream, a good claret. He inquired after his brothers and promised he would see them soon. The letter would go with the next despatch rider to Brussels and thence to Dover, London, Glasgow and Fort William. By the time it arrived, word would probably have already reached Glengarry that Napoleon had been defeated, but the Macdonells would have to wait a little longer to discover if James had survived.

He passed the afternoon by walking slowly around Lac d'Enghien, dozing in his room, and trying with little success to read his battered copy of *Waverley*. His mother had assured him that Walter Scott's splendid Fergus MacIvor was modelled on his mercurial brother, Alasdair. Perhaps. After a light supper he wandered down to the north gate of the chateau to watch the carriages and cabriolets departing for the Duchess's Ball.

Francis Hepburn, puffing at an enormous cigar, was there before him. He was raising his shako in salute to every carriage that passed and wishing its occupants a glorious evening. From General Byng's open cabriolet, Colonel Woodford and Harry Wyndham, in sparkling dress uniforms, gleaming buttons and gold lace everywhere, waved happily to them. The general himself, all in black, looked rather miserable. 'I don't think Sir John will be dancing much, do you, James?' asked Francis. 'Looks like he's off to a funeral.'

'I do not blame him. He'd rather be killing Frenchmen than attempting one of their impossible dances. By the way, is it true that the ball is to be held in a coachmaker's workshop? Seems an odd place to me.'

'Not a workshop, a coach house, I believe. It's probably the only place in Brussels big enough to accommodate all the guests. Everyone but us seems to have been invited. It is an odd place for a ball, though.' He raised his shako to Major General Maitland, commander of the 1st Brigade. 'Good man, Maitland,' he said as Maitland's carriage passed. 'And a fine cricketer. Plays for the Marylebone Club.'

'Is Miss Box attending the ball?' asked Macdonell innocently.

'She says not. Her papa is not senior enough. I shall be damned cross if I find she's deceived me.'

By half past seven all the carriages had departed. 'Ah well,' said James, 'there'll be a few thick heads in the morning. Let us hope Napoleon does not have a spy at the ball to send him reports on the state of the generals.'

'I would not put it beyond the wily little Corsican. Intelligence officers dressed as servants and furnished with something nasty to slip into the peer's glass. We had better hope not.'

At the chateau, Francis went to his room. For a few minutes Macdonell stood at the steps enjoying the warm evening air and listening to the muffled sounds of soldiers preparing to sleep. Two familiar figures approached from his left. 'Corporals,' he greeted them. 'An evening stroll?'

'Yes, Colonel,' replied James Graham. 'Not quite ready to sleep. We've been talking and we agree.'

'Agree about what?'

'That we'll march tomorrow,' said Joseph. 'We are sure of it.'

'Then let us hope the ball is over before we do. Goodnight.'

'Goodnight, Colonel.' It was said in unison.

CHAPTER FOUR

16th June

The news arrived by galloper an hour after midnight. The French had crossed the Sambre, taken Charleroi and were advancing rapidly towards the town of Ligny. Having delivered his report to Francis Hepburn as the duty officer, the galloper changed horses and sped on to Brussels. A second galloper had taken the direct road there but a message of such importance was commonly carried by more than one man. The Duchess's Ball would be ending rather earlier than planned.

His servant had no need to rouse Macdonell who had been awake since retiring soon after eight. Five hours of anxious tossing and turning had done little for his humour. With a flood of relief that the waiting was over, he barely touched the mug of tea on his writing table and was up and out of the chateau within minutes. Francis Hepburn was waiting for him by the steps.

'Bonjour, James,' he greeted Macdonell. 'It seems you were

right. Boney has caught us napping. I have ordered the drums to beat to arms but I suppose we had better wait for the dancers to return before marching.'

'Let us be ready when they do.'

A bugler sounded reveille. The drummers thumped out the call to arms. In moments, the camp was awake and about its business. Torches were lit. Sergeants and corporals shouted orders and half-dressed men scurried about, getting in each other's way and tripping over tent ropes in their haste to make ready. Red-jacketed guards poured from outbuildings, hoisting up trousers, struggling into overalls and fumbling with buttons.

By the flickering light of the torches Macdonell watched Joseph Graham help a nervous young private do up his jacket buttons. The boy was one of the many who were about to face their first battle. For every veteran of Spain or Italy, there were four or five in General Cooke's Division who had never fired a shot in anger. Corporals strode up and down the lines urging the slowest to hurry. Sergeant Dawson aimed a kick at Private Vindle's backside and received a gratifying yelp in reply. Campfires were lit and water boiled. It was over thirty miles to Charleroi. A long enough march, too long without beef and tea in a man's stomach.

Within the hour, chaos had turned to order and purpose. Every man had eaten, checked his musket and cartridges, packed a clean shirt and linen into his knapsack and strapped his blanket to it. Sir John Byng's Second Brigade, the light companies at their head, formed columns outside the chateau and were ready to go to war. It needed only the return of the general himself and they would march to meet the French.

For another hour, they stood ready. Just after three, as the first glimmerings of a summer dawn began to lighten the sky, carriages started arriving from Brussels. Byng, Woodford and Wyndham were in the first of them. Their cabriolet came to a halt outside the chateau and they jumped out. 'I see you have made ready, James,' said Byng. 'Good. We will march in ten minutes. I do not care to fight in dancing shoes.'

'Nor I,' agreed Woodford, before taking the steps two at a time and disappearing into the chateau.

'My apologies, James,' said Harry Wyndham, sounding not in the least apologetic. 'Perhaps I should have stayed here. And the ball was tedious. Too much talk of Buonaparte and very little waltzing. Not to my taste at all.'

'No more than you deserve, Harry,' replied Macdonell with a grin. 'Be off with you and get ready.'

When the officers reappeared, the trumpets sounded, the drums rolled and the columns moved off, the regimental colours of the Coldstream Guards and the Third Guards held proudly aloft. Light companies at the front, line infantry and artillery in the middle, quartermaster and his long train of carts and fourgons at the rear. From the direction of the stables, a private, his pregnant wife hanging on to his arm, came hurrying to catch the last wagon. He bundled her in and ran to join his company.

To the beat of the drums and cymbals, the deep bass of the serpents and the cheerful trill of the flutes, nearly two thousand men, horses, wagons and camp followers trundled into the town. Boots thumped down on the cobbles, wagon wheels clanked and rattled and nervous horses kicked and snorted their displeasure, their breath hanging briefly in the morning air. Along the way, they collected men and women from their billets, the men taking their places with their companies, the women joining the supply train. On street corners and from upstairs windows, ancient Flemish women in their strange long-sided caps gaped in awe and young ones, some still in their shifts, waved fond farewells from doorways and street corners. The most daring of them darted forward to thrust a cheese or a pie into a grateful hand or for a fleeting embrace. Many wore squares of orange silk or cotton over their hair.

In the town square a score of latecomers, bleary-eyed and bad-tempered, appeared and found their places in the line. Down the Grand Avenue they marched to the steady beat of the drums. The town had woken and the going became slower through the crowds. By the time the light companies reached the edge of the town, the sun had risen in a cloudless sky. The day would be hot. They passed farmers bringing their fruit and vegetables to market and milkmaids returning from the fields. Any man who tried to grab a cabbage or an onion from a barrow or a dog cart risked the wrath of his sergeant. Macdonell, like Wellington himself, had let it be known that he would not tolerate theft from the local people. Everything must be paid for. Dawson and his corporals ensured, as far as they could, that the rule was enforced. Unlike the soldiers, small boys scrambled about grabbing whatever they could before scurrying home with their booty.

It was the best part of an hour before the entire 2nd Brigade was safely out of the town and on the road south. A mile on they joined General Maitland's 1st Brigade, which had been billeted on the other side of the town. Four thousand men of the 1st Division of Foot Guards were, at last, on their way to war.

CHAPTER FIVE

As the morning grew hotter, they marched on through hamlets, across shallow streams and past farms and cottages. The road was seldom more than baked earth, broken by short stretches of embedded flint and chalk or a thin layer of gravel. Farm workers, traders and innkeepers stopped their work to watch them go by. Most simply stood and stared. A few waved orange flags and shouted enouragement. At the front of the column the 2nd Battalion light companies set the pace. Macdonell, riding at their rear, made sure it was not too fast. Exhausted men would not be much use when it came to fighting.

Before taking up his commission in the Coldstream Guards, Macdonell had served as a captain in the 17th Dragoons. He was comfortable on a horse. Many infantry officers, Francis Hepburn among them, were not. For the march he had chosen a handsome grey who knew him well, beautifully turned out by the grooms. His saddle glowed, and his stirrups sparkled in the sun. In clean overalls, he could almost have been a cavalry officer. At his side he wore his sword encased in a black leather scabbard. It was a fine weapon, given to him by his late father. At almost a yard of straight, pointed steel, with a bone handle covered in fish skin and a heavy brass guard engraved with his initials, it needed a strong man to wield it. James Macdonell was a strong man.

They marched between fields of corn and rye as high as a man's shoulder. In grassland red and yellow poppies and blue cornflowers danced in the breeze, and in low hedgerows mallows and loosestrife took shelter from the sun. Flat the land might be, but fertile and pretty enough.

Outside the village of Braine-le-Comte the Division halted. They had marched twelve miles in four hours and needed food and rest. Seven men from the 2nd Battalion had already fallen by the wayside and Macdonell did not want to lose more. He had ordered them to be left with sufficient water and instructions to rejoin their companies when they could. If they were malingerers intending to disappear, they would not be missed.

While the men boiled their kettles and ate their beef and biscuit, he trotted back down the line to find General Byng. The further back he went the thicker the dust and the greater the number of men who had succumbed and been left to fend for themselves. Behind them, General Maitland's 1st Division must have been suffering even more.

He found Byng with Colonel Woodford. 'I have halted the light companies, sir,' he reported. 'Are we to enter the town or await orders?'

'I wish I knew,' replied Byng gently. 'We believe that the Prince of Orange has set up his headquarters in the town but General Cooke has as yet received no orders from him. The general is becoming impatient.'

'A party has been despatched to find the Prince,' added Woodford. 'They should have returned by now.'

'Shall I return to my battalion, sir?'

'Might as well stay here until we know more, James,' replied Byng. 'How is morale?'

'It is good, sir, but if we are to fight today, it will be with tired men.'

From the rear of the column, a party of riders trotted towards them. One of them carried the 1st Division's standard. 'Ah,' said Woodford, 'here is General Cooke.'

Whether mounted or on foot, Major General George Cooke was a man of formidable presence and looked a good deal less than his forty-seven years. Square-jawed and broad-shouldered, he would not have been out of place in a prize fight. He had found time since leaving Brussels to change into his usual black jacket and white breeches. As he approached, he leant forward in his saddle and thundered, 'Does anyone know what the devil's going on? Because I certainly do not.'

'Can the Prince not be found, General?' asked Byng.

'No, dammit, he cannot. My scouts report that the Hôtel du Miroir, where he is supposed to be, is deserted. The locals say that men and artillery have been passing through the village all night and the streets, I gather, are still full of them. But not a word from the young frog.' Prince Willem Frederik van

Oranje-Nassau GCB, old Etonian, friend of the Prince Regent and Commander of 1 Corps of the Allied army, was known variously as His Royal Highness, slender Billy or the young frog.

'Where has he gone, General?' asked Byng.

'He and his aides left on the Nivelles road, but whether I'm supposed to follow him or stay here, I am at a loss to know. Two Brigades, four thousand men and equipment, and no orders. It's as bad as Flanders twenty years ago. What do you recommend, gentlemen?'

Macdonell cleared his throat. 'If I may, General, if the streets are blocked it will take us some time to get through, but the men need rest. If we are ordered to make haste to Nivelles, it would be better to be on the other side of the town.'

General Cooke stroked his chin. 'Very well. We will march on through Braine-le-Comte and then rest until noon. By then the Prince might have remembered to send us his orders. If not, we will go on to Nivelles. Proceed, gentlemen.'

At the front of the line, Macdonell found Harry Wyndham drinking tea with Sergeant Dawson. They jumped up when they saw him. 'We're on the move again, Harry,' he said. 'We're to rest on the other side of the town until noon.'

'Is the view better from there?' asked Wyndham, grinning as broadly as ever.

'I doubt it. It seems the town is blocked so we had best get through in case we are needed in a hurry. Get them moving, please. Quick as you can.'

Wyndham emptied the remains of his tea on the grass. 'Thank you for the tea, Sergeant,' he said. 'Very good, it was. But now we must be off. Rouse the men, please, and we'll find a way through the town. Pass the word that we'll rest on the other side. That should lift their spirits.'

'I will, Captain,' replied Dawson, straightening his jacket around his midriff, 'although a barrel of gin would lift them more.'

The battalion was soon on its way again. This time Macdonell rode at the head of the column. If the town was really blocked, he wanted to assess for himself how bad it was.

It did not take him long to realise that it was very bad. He ordered Harry to halt the column on the edge of the town, dismounted and tethered his horse. The main street was a melee of men, horses and wagons on their way to Brussels, the lanes and alleys off it entirely blocked by carts and animals whose owners had taken refuge from the lines of retreating and advancing soldiers. Local carters and shopkeepers bawled and cursed and jostled the retreating soldiers. Just as in Enghien, carts were overturned and urchins crawled about in search of plunder. Further north the shouts had been shouts of encouragement. Here ancient crones shouted insults, accusing the cowardly British of leaving them to be robbed and raped by the French. A small boy darted forward to kick an infantryman's bandaged leg. Another threw a handful of stones at a wagon carrying the wounded. Both disappeared down dark alleys before they could be caught.

These were the troops who were stationed near Charleroi and had taken the full force of the French attack. Among the wounded, the lucky ones were being comforted by their women. Most had to suffer alone. There was little sound of distress, as if all energy had been expended. Instead, those who could be propped up sat and stared blankly into the distance. The rest lay silently, many curled up like babes asleep. Very few of the bloodied faces and shattered bodies looked capable of surviving the journey to Brussels. Beside them the walking wounded struggled to keep up, some holding on to the side of a wagon, others, their eyes bandaged, with a hand on a comrade's shoulder. Among the British were Nassauers, Germans and Netherlanders in their black and green uniforms.

There was a sharp shove in the small of Macdonell's back. He lurched forward and narrowly avoided colliding with a limping lieutenant wearing the badge of the 3rd Infantry Division. The exhausted man was using his musket as a crutch. His left trouser leg was red from waist to ankle. Macdonell apologised and asked where they had come from. 'East of Nivelles,' the lieutenant mumbled, where, he said, there had been heavy fighting. The wagons were taking the wounded and the women back to Brussels. 'The Hanoverians are behind us,' he added. 'They have had a bloody time of it. They were caught in the open by Lancers before they could form square. The devils were hiding in the woods.' He was slurring his words and looked ready to drop. 'God be with you if you are heading that way, sir.' It was little more than a whisper. The wretched man was wounded not only in body but also in mind. He would not reach Brussels.

Macdonell had seen French Lancers at their murderous work at Maida. Deceptively elegant in their blue uniforms, often with yellow collars and facings, they had ripped the heart out of an entire infantry battalion before it could form defensive squares, spearing the fleeing men with their lances, cutting and slashing with their sabres and butchering the wounded as they lay helpless on the ground. They had revelled in their ferocity, sparing not a man and shrieking for joy as they hacked at arms and faces. He had hoped never to witness such slaughter again.

The division should wait, of course, until the town was clear before entering it. The road was not wide enough to allow two columns to pass and the side streets were blocked. But if the Hanoverians were also coming, it would be some time before the division could proceed. And if the French cavalry were on the rampage, it was time they did not have.

Macdonell recovered his horse and made his way back to where Harry Wyndham was waiting for him. 'The town is blocked, Harry,' he reported, 'but we cannot wait. Take twenty men and see what you can do to clear a way for us. Don't mind too much about the locals – they seem to have turned against us, fickle buggers. Bundle them all into side streets if you have to. Ought to try a bit of fighting themselves. Take Hervey and Gooch and the Grahams with you.'

Harry, as ever, grinned. 'Eighteen men and two Grahams makes thirty. Should be plenty, sir.'

'Good. Off you go. We'll wait here. Send word when it's clear to march on. Oh, and Harry, they've had a bad time of it, but we must get past.'

'Right, sir.'

While they waited, Macdonell ordered his men to lie down. Eat when you can, rest when you can. In the heat and dust of Spain it had been Wellington's mantra. It was an hour before a light company private trotted back from the town with a message from Captain Wyndham that it was safe to proceed. Macdonell thanked the man and sent him straight back to report that they were coming.

In the town it was as if the entire population had been swept off the main street and crammed into the alleys and lanes running off it. Light infantrymen stood shoulder-to-shoulder across each junction, their muskets held across their chests, their backs to the main street, blithely ignoring the howls of fury and protest. An enormously fat man brandishing a leg of pork tried to push his way past a guard. He was sent crashing backwards into a cart by a sharp blow with the butt of a Brown Bess. The infantryman stepped nimbly forward, grabbed the leg of pork and stuffed it into his haversack before anyone else had moved.

The two ensigns were busy keeping an angry group of women armed with cooking pans from launching an attack from the town hall. James and Joseph Graham were marching up and down the street, lending their weight where it was needed. They nodded a greeting to Macdonell. 'Just like herding the cows for milking,' called out James.

'Only cows do not throw cabbages,' added Joseph, bending down to pick one up. He lobbed it to his brother. 'Keep that for the pot, shall we?'

Macdonell found Harry at the far end of the town. Somehow the captain had managed to halt the retreating column outside it, clear the street, and pen the locals in the side streets. 'How did you do it, Harry?' asked Macdonell.

'Bit of luck, Colonel,' replied Wyndham. 'Bumped in to an old friend in the Cambridgeshires, asked him to speak to his colonel. He did and the colonel was happy to oblige, even though he has lost an eye. Said he was not going to get it back in Brussels, so he might just as well wait for us to pass. He is halted outside the town until we go through.'

'Are they badly cut up?'

'Pretty bad,' he said. 'Netherlanders and Hanoverians took the worst of it. South of a crossroads called Les Quatre Bras. Outnumbered and short of cavalry. Charlie is escorting the wounded. Hopes reinforcements will reach the crossroads before they are all wiped out.'

'Right, let us get through as fast as we can. We'll halt beyond the town and wait for orders to march on.'

With the street clear, both brigades marched quickly through the town, ignoring missiles and abuse, until they emerged into the countryside on the southern edge, where the Cambridgeshires were waiting. Macdonell found Colonel Hamilton, his face swathed in bandages, lying in a wagon, apparently asleep. 'He has lost his right eye,' said a medical orderly. 'The left is also in danger.'

'Artillery shell?' asked Macdonell.

'Yes, sir. Killed four officers.'

'Get him back to Brussels, if you can. And thank him for his cooperation.'

'I will, sir. And good luck. Give the frogs what they deserve.'

The fields in which four thousand men gratefully threw off their packs, laid down their weapons and lit fires for their tea, sloped gently up from either side of the road. There was no shade and in the full glare of the sun it was burning hot. Jackets were unbuttoned and shakos removed. On the march, the buttons would be done up again and the shakos replaced. They left the wagons and artillery on the road rather than laboriously manhandle them into the fields. The horses were left in their traces with their nosebags strapped on and given water and fodder by the grooms. While they ate, farriers came forward from the rear to check their hooves and repair damaged shoes as best they could.

Enterprising traders, resentment apparently forgotten, appeared from the town with bottles of wine and loaves of fresh bread and moved among the resting men peddling their wares.

From a vantage point halfway up the slope on the left side of the road, Macdonell saw General Byng arrive at the rear of the 2nd Brigade. Byng dismounted, sat down on a camp stool provided by an aide and mopped his brow. Macdonell waited until the general had a glass in his hand before walking down.

'Ah, James,' Byng greeted him. 'We are all through the town. Did you encounter any problems?'

'A vegetable or two, sir, nothing more. Has the Prince sent orders?'

'He has not, dammit. General Cooke has worked himself into a rare fury and I cannot say that I blame him. A poor chain of command almost guarantees failure.' Byng lowered his voice. 'And between you and me, I am not at all sure of the Netherlanders. They've seen the mess their militia battalions are in and some of them, we should not forget, were fighting for Napoleon not so long ago.'

'We can hardly tell them to go home, General,' replied Macdonell. 'So I suppose we must hope for the best.'

'Hope for the best. It's about all we seem to do at the

moment. Orders. That's what we need. Orders to march and bloody some French noses.'

Macdonell had seldom seen the general so exercised. It must have been the heat. He spoke gently. 'The men do need a rest, sir, and food. Doubtless our orders will arrive shortly.'

The general raised an eyebrow. 'Go and drink your tea, James. I'll send word.'

Harry Wyndham had brewed tea in a Flemish kettle. He handed Macdonell a mug. 'Hot and sweet, James, just like those highland lassies. Any news?'

'Still awaiting orders. Have you made a count? Has the battalion lost many?'

'Thirty, I think.' Out of nearly nine hundred, that was better than might have been expected. 'Exhaustion, mostly, and foot sores.'

'Morale?'

'Up and down. The wagonloads of wounded shook the new men. No one is sure about the Netherlanders and there are voices of dissent.'

'Dissent?'

Harry affected the voice of a borderer. 'If His Grace had not spent the night dancing we'd be among the frogs by now, not sitting in a field dripping with sweat, hungry and parched and not knowing where or when we're going. Something like that.'

'Make sure the new men are mixed in with the older ones. Don't let them form their own little groups. And tell them to sing. Singing's good for the spirit. How are Gooch and Hervey faring?'

'Well enough. I think they'll do.'

At noon the trumpets sounded and the drums beat to arms. Hastily they packed up, made ready and, under the watchful eyes of Captain Wyndham, Sergeant Dawson and the Corporals Graham, marched down the slope and on to the road south. General Byng was waiting to join his 2nd Division. He saw Macdonell and beckoned him over. 'Still no orders, James, but General Cooke's patience has run out. We are heading for the town of Nivelles – ten miles or so east. We'll bivouac there tonight.' James could only hope the general was right about a bivouac. Ten more miles of heat, flies and dust, and half the division would be beyond fighting.

CHAPTER SIX

Unencumbered by artillery and wagons, the light companies drew steadily ahead of the rest of the division. After two hours' march, they came to a cluster of farm buildings with a narrow stream running between them, where Macdonell ordered a halt. Judging by the dust cloud behind them, the wagons and artillery were a good mile behind and both men and horses needed food and water.

While the troops rested by the side of the road, Harry Wyndham led a party to buy whatever he could from the farmers. Macdonell handed him a small bag of coins, issued that morning by the quartermaster. 'Offer them a fair price, Harry,' he said, 'but not too much. Hay for the horses and I see turnips and cabbages in the fields. Fresh meat if they have any. Might be a pig or two hanging in a barn.' While Harry went in search of food, a second party was sent with buckets and kettles to fetch water from the stream.

All afternoon they had passed small groups of transports and wounded men heading west. As at Braine-le-Comte, they were mostly from Dutch and German regiments and had made way for the Guards to march past. They had obligingly hauled wagons and herded cattle off the road and even pushed the wagon carrying the Prince's personal equipment to one side. A few words were exchanged but there was no time to dally.

Macdonell was holding the bridle as his horse munched tufts of dry grass on the edge of a field when another party appeared from the direction of Nivelles. This one was different. Twenty or so blue-coated and unarmed Frenchmen under the guard of four Brunswickers. He led his horse down the road to meet them.

'Colonel James Macdonell, Second Battalion, Coldstream Guards,' he announced himself. 'Who here speaks English?'

A lieutenant in the black of the Brunswickers stepped forward. 'Lieutenant Franz Mezner, Third Battalion, Brunswick Corps, Colonel. We are escorting these prisoners to Braine-le-Comte.' Brunswickers, unlike the Dutch and Belgians who used dogs to pull their carts, ate them. A useful taste if food was short, although Macdonell had never had occasion to try it.

'Prisoners, Lieutenant? I am surprised you and your men could be spared.'

'They are deserters from the French army, Colonel. The general ordered them to be taken for interrogation.'

'Who is your general?'

'The Duke of Brunswick, Colonel.'

Wellington was not the only duke on the Allied side. His Serene Highness the Duke of Brunswick was another. What a waste of four fit soldiers, thought Macdonell. 'What news do you bring, Lieutenant Mezner?' he asked.

'When we left, Colonel,' replied Mezner, 'we were holding a defensive position at the crossroads at the village of Les Quatre Bras. Our light companies had advanced further south.'

'At Braine-le-Comte we saw many wounded men. There was talk of artillery fire and cavalry.'

'Yes, sir. The French artillery has been pounding our positions all day. Their cavalry make sorties on the flanks in the hope of catching our infantry before they can prepare to meet them and then retire back to their lines. The casualties have been high.'

'No infantry attacks?'

'Not yet, Colonel, but it cannot be long. Our intelligence is that they are massing for an attack up the Charleroi Road. But reinforcements have been arriving since noon. General Picton's division may be there by now and also General Kempt's. And the Duke of Wellington himself, of course.'

'And Napoleon?'

'He has not been seen. These men say that Marshal Ney commands their army. They think Napoleon has marched east in search of the Prussians.' If so, there would be no French advance through Mons, although Buonaparte had split his force. He must be confident of disposing quickly of the Prussians before rejoining Ney. Perhaps the Duke had underestimated his strength.

A thought occurred to Macdonell. 'Why did they desert?'

Lieutenant Mezner smiled. 'They claim to support their king, Colonel. It is more likely, however, that they do not care for British bayonets.'

'Thank you, Lieutenant. Carry on while we are halted.' The lieutenant saluted smartly and returned to his prisoners. Macdonell watched them go. Why send them to Braine-le-Comte? He would have taken their weapons, stripped them naked and told them to fend for themselves. In any army, deserters were deserters, whatever the reason.

Harry Wyndham and his party had returned. They were not quite empty-handed, but little better. 'Not the friendliest of farmers, James,' he reported. 'Some turnips, a cabbage or two, but no meat, although he has ducks and chickens. They wouldn't sell them and I had to pay far too much for these.' He waved a hand at a small heap of vegetables.

'Ah well. Hand them out as best you can. We'll just have to make do with what we've got. We're not going to wait for the quartermaster and he probably won't allow us anything anyway. Have the horses been watered?'

'Horses and men, both.'

'On our way, then.' From behind him, Macdonell heard voices raised in anger. He turned sharply. 'What the devil? Oh, dear God, not again.' Privates Vindle and Luke, each held by a Graham brother, were being dragged up the road. It was obvious that they were drunk. 'What is the story this time, Corporal?' he asked.

'Drunk, sir,' replied James.

'On what?' asked Harry. 'There has been no gin ration.'

Joseph held up a green bottle. 'This, sir. It's some sort of local brew. Schnapps, I believe. Tastes like gunpowder and must be as strong.'

'Where did you get it, Vindle?' demanded Macdonell.

'Found it, sir.'

'Where?'

'Same place they found this,' said Joseph, producing a dead chicken from behind his back.

Macdonell stared at him. 'Drunk and thieving. I could have you shot. You too, Luke.'

'Not worth it, Colonel. Waste of ammunition,' said Harry.

'What do you suggest?'

'We haven't time for a whipping. Front of the line where Sergeant Dawson and I can keep an eye on them, four kettles and a pack full of stones each and not a sip of water until I say so.' The unlucky fourth man in each company usually had to carry the kettles.

'Very well. Empty their packs and find good homes for whatever there is.' Macdonell turned to Vindle and Luke. 'With luck, the march will kill you. If not, it should sober you up. Take them away, Corporals, and make sure they keep up the pace.'

'That we will, Colonel.' Once more it was said in unison.

In mid-afternoon, having marched well over twenty miles since dawn, they reached open land on the western edge of Nivelles, where General Cooke sent forward orders that they were to halt and set up camp. 'Looks a good enough place to spend the night, Harry,' observed Macdonell, pointing to a copse of oak and chestnut. 'Plenty of wood for cooking fires and there might be a stream in those woods. Send out watering parties and get fires lit. Let us hope that is it for the day. I'm worn out and I've been sitting on a horse all day.'

'Pity there's no pond around,' replied Harry. 'I'd strip off and jump in.'

'Well, at least we're spared that.' While Harry organised watering parties and wood collectors, Macdonell stretched his legs by wandering among the men. Like them, he was plastered in dust and sweat. He ran his hand over the stubble on his cheeks and scratched his groin where his trousers, damp with sweat, had chaffed the skin. The muscles in his back and thighs were shaking from ten hours in the saddle and his throat was on fire. Unlike them, he had not been on his feet carrying sixty pounds of weapons and equipment. No wonder many of them had thrown off their cumbersome wooden-framed packs, unbuttoned their jackets and stretched out on whatever strip of grass they could find. A few looked actually to be asleep. William Vindle and Patrick Luke were among them. Macdonell kicked them awake and told them to fetch wood for a fire. Muttering bitterly, they struggled to their feet and staggered off in the direction of the wood. No matter if they never came back.

Some of the younger men had taken off their shoes and were busy washing sores and picking at blisters. The older and wiser of them had left their shoes on, knowing that if they took them off their feet would swell from the heat and they might not be able to get them on again. If by chance they did have to move on that evening, they did not want to do so in bare feet.

The Grahams had lit their fire and were preparing to eat. From their packs they had retrieved the scraps of meat and biscuit distributed at Enghien and were occupied in making them edible. James cut out the filthiest bits and handed the rest to Joseph who swilled them in a cup of water and laid them out on the grass. All around, groups of men were doing much the same. 'It's a fair way off, Colonel,' said James Graham, 'but that is cannon fire I can hear, is it not?'

'I believe it is, Corporal. But do not let it spoil your supper. I doubt we'll be needed today,' replied Macdonell, not believing it. They were upwind of the cannon, which would make the guns seem further away than they really were. He reckoned they might be no more than two miles off.

Macdonell walked on, greeting the men he knew by name and offering a word of encouragement to the youngest. He accepted a sip or two of gin and a mouthful of weevily biscuit and when the first group returned with water, drank a cupful and splashed a little on his face.

At last they could eat and rest properly, and he would try to find out what was happening beyond Nivelles. General Cooke would have sent a rider forward to announce their arrival. He would bring back news.

What the rider actually brought back, however, were orders to advance at once through the town. The general, much invigorated, in turn sent orders out for the drums to sound the call to arms and for the battalions to fall in. Miserable, complaining soldiers doused their fires, packed up their knapsacks, buttoned up their jackets and prepared to march again. Under instructions from the corporals, they checked their flints and counted off ten rounds of ammunition.

Every one of them knew that the time had come. They had marched all day and now they were going into battle. If they had not been needed, they would have been allowed to rest. The

Emperor's troops, hard, well equipped and impatient to avenge past defeats, awaited them.

Macdonell watched old soldiers encouraging new ones to take a swig of gin. He listened to throats tormented by the heat and dust, retching and coughing as if fit to rip themselves open. He listened to prayers spoken aloud and snatches of hymns croaked tunelessly out. And, in the distance, despite the wind, he caught the unmistakeable smell of cannon. And of a battlefield.

As at Braine-le-Comte, the Nivelles streets were choked with wagons, artillery pieces and the wounded, pleading pitifully for water, help, or their mothers. Many had lost an arm or a leg, some both. Others held their hands to their stomachs, as if trying to keep their guts from falling out. There were no surgeons with them. They would be too busy further forward to accompany the wagon train. Carriages, ambulances and fourgons, left behind by Netherlanders and Belgian Jägers in their rush to reach Quatre Bras, added to the confusion. The light companies scrambled over and round them as best they could.

A company of Highlanders seeking temporary respite from the battle taunted them as they went by. 'What's your hurry, laddie? The Frenchies will wait for you.' 'Remember your manners and say bonjour to m'sieur.'

'Hop on my back, man, if you're tired. I'll take you to meet m'sieur,' shouted back Joseph Graham.

The wind shifted and suddenly the cannon sounded very close. A number of men fell back, and from exhaustion or fear collapsed onto the roadside. Harry Wyndham, in a fine tenor voice, belted out the first verse of a song about the lovely ladies of London Town. Those with the energy joined in with the chorus.

On the other side of the town the watering parties caught up with them. Macdonell, his throat still burning from the dust, took a gulp from a bottle offered to him by a Foot Guard. It was not water but ale. 'Kind lady outside the inn,' grinned the private. Macdonell took another gulp and handed the bottle back. A stray shell whistled overhead and landed in a field. 'Nearly there,' he croaked.

The air was becoming so thick with dust that it was difficult to see or breathe. Carts carrying more wounded trundled towards them. Clouds of flies buzzed around open wounds. A company of Belgians lay in a ditch, trying to scoop its filthy water into their mouths. They had little to say except that Wellington himself had arrived that afternoon and that it had been bloody work. They had been battered by French artillery and had narrowly survived several cavalry charges by hastily forming square or dashing into nearby woods. They did not know if the crossroads were still held or what was happening further south.

Macdonell urged the light companies on. More overheated and exhausted men fell by the wayside. They were left where they fell, Captain Wyndham quickly ordering the columns to close ranks. Surprisingly, Vindle and Luke were still going. For all their thieving and drunkenness, they were a tough pair of weasels.

They found the crossroads and the buildings around it still held by companies of Jägers, Nassauers and Brunswickers.

But the French artillery had been at its terrible work and the defenders had paid a terrible price. Hundreds of bodies were strewn in all directions. Many were headless or in bits. Medical orderlies scurried about doing what little they could for the wounded. A field hospital had been set up in a house on the Nivelles road. Inside and outside it, blood-soaked surgeons amputated limbs and stitched up stomachs. In German, Dutch and English men pleaded pitifully for water. Mutilated horses lay still attached to overturned gun carriages. Dogs sniffed hopefully at corpses and black crows circled overhead. The stench of death – a stench like no other – filled the air. And from the south, French artillery, not yet satiated, hurled more death at them.

In the fields to their left, British cavalry had been deployed in line. Macdonell took a glass from his pack and put it to his eye. Unless he was mistaken, General Picton's cavalry division had indeed arrived and the general himself, easily recognised in blue coat, white stock and black hat, was at their head. Despite the carnage around him, he could not help smiling. If there was a fight to be had, General Thomas Picton would be among the first there.

General Byng summoned Macdonell and Hepburn. 'I have just received orders from the Prince,' he told them, spreading a map on the ground. 'We are here,' he said, pointing with a twig to Quatre Bras. 'The centre of our line is on and around the Charleroi Road.' The twig ran down a line southwards from Quatre Bras. 'On our right, the Bois de Bossu, seething with Frenchmen and a threat to our right flank. Colonel Hepburn, you will take the 3rd Foot Guards into the wood with the 1st

Brigade. Lord Saltoun's 1st Foot Guards have already entered the wood. Clear out the enemy and secure it.' He turned to Macdonell. 'Colonel Macdonell, take your light companies up this slope.' He pointed to fields on their left. 'If this map is right, you will come to a farm.' Byng peered closely at the map. 'La Ferme de la Bergerie, with fields and more woods beyond it. There has been heavy fighting there and the wood and farm are also full of Frenchmen. Drive them back. I will send Captain Tanner up with the light cannon after you. Further south there is another farm.' Again the general peered at the map. 'La Ferme de Gemioncourt. It was taken by the French this morning and is now sheltering the artillery that is bombarding us.' He coughed lightly. 'The 69th took the brunt of it and were then cut down by a cavalry charge.'

'Were they not in square, General?' asked Macdonell.

'Alas, no. I am told that the Prince was concerned at the artillery fire they were taking.' Macdonell shook his head in disbelief. Ordering infantry into line with cavalry nearby was tantamount to murder. 'Your task is to prevent the French from getting around our left flank. I will send more intelligence when I have it. Any questions?' There were none.

Macdonell ordered flints and powder checked again. He put on a light pack, specially made for him in London, in which he kept a spare shirt, a woollen blanket, a razor and a sharp knife. If his mule was lost or killed, he would need them. He left his horse with a groom, knowing that the beast would be no use in wooded areas and anyway preferring to fight on foot.

Harry Wyndham was at his shoulder, Gooch and Hervey just behind. They took neither a drummer boy nor a medical orderly. If they were to push the French back they would have to move quietly and fast. No drums, no shouting, no stopping for the wounded. Just what light company men were trained for. With a glance behind him, Macdonell signalled the advance and four hundred men, muskets primed and loaded, followed him up the slope.

There was to be no surprise. French sharpshooters were hiding in a copse of trees on the right-hand side of the slope. The guards were no more than halfway up it when shots began whistling about their heads. Men screamed and fell. Macdonell felt a ball touch his shoulder and nearly stumbled. They were in the open, taking fire from a hidden enemy – the worst possible position and the very opposite of what light company men were used to. He yelled an order to lie flat and threw himself to the ground. The mounds and hollows on the slope offered a little protection and a man lying on his belly was a much smaller target than one standing up.

Harry wriggled up alongside him. 'Saw us coming, James. Lucky they did not wait until we were closer before firing, stupid clods. What now?'

Macdonell grunted. He was angry with himself for not having guessed there would be voltigeurs about. They would be ahead of the main body of French troops, scouting the land and picking off the enemy when they had the chance. 'Spread the men out, Harry, a good five yards between each pair, and in broken line. We'll make it as hard as we can for them.'

'I'll shout when we're ready,' replied Harry, slithering away down the slope.

With luck the voltigeurs would fire their next volley as soon as they saw their targets. At eighty yards, the casualties should be light. They would take the volley and charge up the slope to the copse of trees. That should scare the foxes from their den.

The moment Harry shouted, Macdonell was on his feet and running up the slope. He did not run in a straight line but weaved this way and that in the hope of confusing the voltigeurs. At six feet and three inches and above seventeen stone, he was not the most nimble Guards officer but he ploughed on towards the copse. Behind him, nearly four hundred men took his cue, yelling and firing into the trees. The French volley came almost at once. Twenty or so shots in all. Macdonell did not look round but from the few cries he heard, knew that it had not been effective.

He was no more than thirty yards from the trees when twenty blue jackets ran out from the side and made for the top of the slope. The Guards' fire took down three of them, the others scuttled off. Macdonell halted his men. He had caught sight of a farmhouse roof over the ridge of the slope. There would be more frogs there. He did not want to lead the Guards headlong into a trap. But his orders were to clear the farm of the enemy. They would advance cautiously.

They moved slowly around the trees, keeping low and watching the farm. For the new men, this was their first fight. Macdonell knew how nervous they would be. Charging flat out at an enemy was one thing. Advancing slowly towards muskets they could not see was quite another. There was a risk that one would panic and run. If that happened, the panic would spread. He found he was holding his breath.

This time the voltigeurs waited until their attackers were

almost at the low farm wall before opening fire. Then they let loose. There were more French in the farm. From windows and doors a storm of bullets hit the guards. A dozen fell, dead or wounded. Fifty reached the wall and crouched behind it. The rest lay flat and fired at the windows. Macdonell peered over the wall. A shot fizzed past his head. A blue jacket was hanging out of a window. Another was on his stomach by a door, blood seeping through his uniform. He could see no others.

He vaulted over the wall and ran for the farmhouse. There were no shots. He called to Harry who signalled the fifty men to follow him and the rest to stay where they were. They skirted the house and turned up the side. Around the farmyard at the back stood a small barn, sheds and an empty pigsty. There was a haystack in one corner and a gate beside it.

Macdonell led them through the gate, which opened into another, larger yard. They stopped and stared. This yard was strewn with bodies, mostly Brunswickers in their black jackets and Nassauers in green. Many of the dead were twisted into grotesque shapes, their stomachs ripped open by sword or sabre. A dead horse lay in one corner, its legs buckled under its body and blood covering its flank. Another, headless, lay beside it. Carrion crows had lost no time in beginning their feast. They hopped on and around the corpses, pecking at eyes and squabbling over scraps. Even when they were disturbed, they carried on gorging themselves. The sight of the birds and the smell of blood and death were too much for some. They fell to their knees and emptied their stomachs on to the bloody ground. Henry Gooch was one of them.

The French had left the farm but they would not be far

away. Macdonell sent James Hervey back to bring the Guards forward. Stepping carefully over bodies, he led the fifty men into a vegetable garden enclosed by a thick beech hedge. Without warning they were under fire again. Beyond the hedge there was a small field sloping up to another wood, this one much thicker and larger than the copse on the slope. The French were firing from it.

They ran doubled up to the far end of the garden. James turned and looked for the Graham brothers. They were there. He beckoned them forwards. 'Make a gap in the hedge about here. Just big enough for a man to get through.'

The brothers took out their bayonets and hacked at the branches of the hedge. They heaved on the roots and bent the branches back but the beechwood was thick and did not yield easily. They exchanged a look. 'You push,' said James. Joseph nodded. James took off his shako and stood with his back to the hedge, his arms folded over his chest. The moment he said 'ready', Joseph lowered his shoulder, charged forward and knocked him backwards through the hedge. James was back on his feet and safely on the right side of the hedge in a trice. He bent over to catch his breath. Joseph put an arm around his shoulders. 'Not too hard, was it?'

James coughed and stood up straight. 'Away with you. Our mother hits harder than that.' Led by James Hervey, the remaining Guards had joined them. Through the hole, Macdonell took them into the field of rye beyond. They formed two ranks facing the enemy positions in the wood. The French fired again. There were shrieks of pain and two men went down. One was holding what was left of his nose, the other's shattered arm hung uselessly from his shoulder. The Guards got off a volley but they were firing uphill from close on a hundred paces. A direct hit would be more luck than marksmanship. Macdonell hesitated. The wise course would be to withdraw back behind the hedge and wait for the cannon to arrive. But if they did and the enemy chose to attack the farm, the cannon might be intercepted and they could be trapped. They would have to stay where they were.

He called for the wounded to be taken back to the farm and for two lines to re-form in pairs and spread out to give the French muskets less to aim at. It was a manouevre they had practised in the dull days at Enghien and they carried it out perfectly. He sensed relief among them. They were light infantrymen, skirmishers, will o' the wisps, unaccustomed to fighting in lines. He took a position from where he could observe the accuracy of their shots and watch the reactions of the enemy.

A competent infantryman could get off three shots a minute as long as he had a pouch full of prepared cartridges. The drill was always the same and they had practised it a thousand times. Make sure the barrel and breech were clean, bite off the end of the cartridge paper, hold the ball in your mouth, set the hammer to half-cock, tip a little powder in, shut the hammer, pour the rest of the powder down the barrel, follow it with the ball and the paper for wadding, ram it home with the ramrod, cock and fire. After half a dozen shots a man's mouth was dry as tinder from the powder and his head throbbing from the smoke and noise. It made no difference. He was trained to go on loading and firing, reloading and firing again until he had run out of cartridges or was dead.

The pairs worked together, one loading, the other firing. After every six shots they moved to a new position – a little back, a little forward or to the side. It made a Frenchman's aim just a bit more difficult – a bit that might save their lives.

The cannon soon arrived – four six-pounders that had been hauled up the slope and around the house. Within a minute, the gun teams had loaded, primed and fired. The first salvo was short. The second landed among the French, sending bodies and muskets flying into the air. They watched the blue coats turn and flee, and Macdonell signalled the advance. Shrieking and yelling, through the smoke and the rye they ran, most of it trampled and lying flat. Yet more bodies lay everywhere – infantry and cavalry, French and British and Brunswickers. And horses, dozens of them. Men and beasts alike had suffered and died here.

On the far side of the field, they came to another house and garden surrounded by a fence. There corpses were piled high and covered in a black cloud of flies. The headless torso of a young infantry officer in bright-scarlet jacket with crimson lace lay slightly to one side. Highlanders had fought there too. Kilted bodies lay about, some obscenely exposed.

They skirted the house and garden and carried on through the rye, crouching low and making themselves as small a target as they could. They stepped over more mangled bodies and more blood-soaked limbs. 'Eyes on the enemy,' shouted Macdonell. 'We can do nothing for these souls now.' There were no wounded. Either they had managed to crawl to safety or they had been despatched by the point of a bayonet.

A cannon roared and a six-pound shell whistled over their

heads. The French had brought up artillery. Another landed a little to their right, sending up a spray of earth but doing no damage. Instinctively, the men moved left and spread out. Almost immediately there was a shout of 'cavalry'. The French also had cavalry and had anticipated their manoeuvre. Macdonell yelled the order. 'Form square. Prepare to meet cavalry.' The troops ran towards their appointed leaders and began to form irregular-shaped but tightly packed squares around them, with the front line kneeling and bayonets pointing outwards. It was another manoeuvre they had practised and practised until they could do it blindfolded and it was all that stood between them and death at the point of a lance or the edge of a sabre. No horse would run in to or try to jump a line of bayonets.

The French cavalrymen, in their fine plumed helmets and green jackets and breeches, were expert and ruthless. Two of the slowest of Macdonell's men were caught in the open and cut down with scything swipes of a sabre. The remainder had scrambled into the squares when the first of the French cavalry reached them, the last of them diving head first over a kneeling front line. Sure enough, the horses shied away and their riders were forced to bear off. But as soon as they were clear, more artillery shells exploded around the square. A phalanx of stationary soldiers made a tempting target for a Gunner.

A shell landed just in front of the first rank, broke into pieces and killed two men instantly. Their bodies were dragged aside and the gap they left closed. From the middle of his square, Macdonell shouted an order and it crabbed sideways and forwards. The others followed suit. The French cavalry stood a hundred yards away, waiting for the squares to break.

If they did, they would be on their prey in a trice, sabres held in extended arms, ready to thrust and hack at defenceless heads and bodies.

The next shell fell harmlessly in the place they had vacated. Another shouted order and again the squares crabbed sideways. Macdonell had the strange sensation of acting out a play in front of a mounted audience. Receive cannon shot, move, keep the square tight, more shot, move again. Hold the square. Never give the audience a chance to attack. More like a dance, perhaps, than a play. Men went down, blood streaming from their heads and chests. One called pitifully for his mother. Another looked Macdonell in the eye, swore mightily and died. No one moved to help the wounded. The square must be held or they would all die.

There was a break in the cannon fire and the cavalry came closer, shouting insults and daring the infantrymen to fire at them. When they retreated, the French artillery started up again. Macdonell, keeping an eye on the cavalry, tried to gauge the moment to form line and charge at the infantry. Too soon and the cavalry would reach them before they were among the enemy and into the woods behind them, too late and they would be easy meat for the French muskets.

He was spared the decision. Captain Tanner's artillery teams had dragged their cannon over the field and around the charnel house of the farm. The captain's first shot was aimed at the cavalry. It sent horses and riders, earth, debris and bodies cartwheeling into the air. The survivors did not wait for a second shot, but turned their mounts and galloped for cover. The light companies' charge was instant, so fast that Macdonell did not know whether the men had waited for his order or not. Screaming their battle cries, they ran at the French line, driving it backwards into the wood. Fifty yards short of the treeline, he halted them and called for them to spread out in their pairs in the tall rye. They would give the French something to think about in case they were considering another attack.

Of French cavalry there was now no sign. The artillery volley had spooked them and rather than attack the guns they had gone in search of easier prey. And the French artillery was as good as useless against skirmishers their gun captains could not see. It was tempting to seize the opportunity and charge straight at them. But Macdonell did not know their strength and a headlong dash into the woods might prove disastrous.

Off to their right, he knew from the remorseless crash of cannon that the fighting in the centre of their lines was ferocious. Wellington would have demanded reinforcements for the beleaguered troops at Quatre Bras and would have thrown everything in to his defence of the crossroads and the road to Brussels; Ney would have used his heavy artillery, followed by his cavalry, to break it. Macdonell could only hope that the defence had held and that he and his light companies were not cut off. There was no time to dwell on it. He had his own battle to fight.

From their left a small company of black-clad Brunswickers arrived. Their captain presented himself to Macdonell. He was a man of about Macdonell's age, almost as tall and fair-haired. 'Captain Hellman, Colonel. We saw you from our position and thought you would appreciate some help.'

'Pleased to have you with us, Captain. How many are you?'

'Forty, Colonel.' Despite their taste for dog meat, the Brunswickers were good soldiers who hated the French. Many Brunswick families had suffered greatly from the deprivations of the feared Imperial Guard, to whom Napoleon always gave free rein after a victory. Forty of them would make a difference.

'Our orders are to clear the area of the enemy and push them back beyond the farm at Gemioncourt.'

Through the rye and up the slope they went, heads low and muskets held across chests. Macdonell had placed Captain Hellman on his left wing. Harry was on the right and he in the centre, Gooch and Hervey with him. He had been too occupied to keep an eye on the ensigns but they were still standing and appeared unharmed. Advancing in an irregular line made life more difficult for the French marksmen, but if the cavalry reappeared, they would be in trouble. It was a calculated risk.

A few shots whistled over their heads, mostly to Macdonell's left where the Brunswickers were impatient to get at the French. They advanced ahead of the line, drawing sporadic French fire but never wavering.

At the top of the field they came to a low, straggly hedge. Beyond the hedge was a sunken track. In the hedge and on the bank of the track, flies swarmed over yet more bodies of dead and wounded men. There were dozens of them. The wounded spoke of the battering they had taken that morning. Macdonell ordered them to be moved into the shade of the oak and birch that grew along the side of the track and to be given water and blankets. Firing from the wood had ceased and the cannon had gone. Either the French were up to one of their tricks or they had withdrawn through the wood.

Macdonell found Captain Hellman and his company well placed on the bank of the track where the undergrowth was dense. The captain was intent on the wood. 'Any sign of movement, Captain?' he asked.

'None, Colonel. But they might be in there waiting for us.'

'Indeed they might. What do you suggest, Captain?'

'I could take some men and try to get round the side of the wood without being seen. If we see any movement, we'll know they are in there.'

'Very well, Captain. I'll give you twenty minutes.'

Captain Hellman grinned. 'Leave it to me, Colonel. We'll soon see what they're up to.' He gathered four men and set off. Macdonell returned to his place in the middle of the line, where he found Harry waiting for him.

'Orders, James?' he asked.

'Captain Hellman has slipped round the wood to see if there are any Frenchies still lurking in it. I'll send word when he returns.'

Away to their right around the Charleroi Road, artillery started up again. The crash of heavy cannon reverberated through the trees, hammering eardrums and blocking out all other sound. Rooks shrieked in alarm. The men on the bank of the sunken track lay down their muskets and covered their ears.

When Captain Hellman returned he had to cup his hands and all but shout into Macdonell's ear to make himself heard. 'The devils have withdrawn but they might have left a small party to cover their retreat. If you were to hold back your centre, Colonel, and allow both wings to advance through the wood at an oblique angle, we should take any ambushers by surprise.'

Macdonell considered. It was a sensible plan but he did not like the idea of holding back. 'No, Captain, we will all advance together, making as much noise as we can. We'll beat them out of the wood like pheasants. If the main body has withdrawn the rest will surely follow.'

If Captain Hellman was surprised he did not show it. 'I had forgotten the British penchant for frightening birds half to death before shooting them,' he said, 'It will be an interesting experience for us.'

Macdonell ordered the men to be lined up in a crescent formation with instructions to yell, scream, rattle their swords and beat their muskets against their kettles. Anything to make enough noise to frighten an enemy who could not see them into thinking there were thousands of them and running for the safety of their own lines as fast as they could. Anything, that was, except fire their muskets. The risk of accidents and ricochets in woods was too great.

Macdonell gave the signal and off they went. The light companies of the Coldstream and 3rd Guards, trained to move silently in any terrain, crashed into the trees and through the undergrowth, shouting, hammering and rattling into the wood. Rooks shot into the sky like black rockets, squawking and screeching in fury.

They followed the trails left by gun carriages being hastily dragged back through the undergrowth, until, in the middle of the wood, they came across the remains of campfires. Macdonell held his hand over a small pile of ashes. They were warm. The French had camped there, but there was now no sign of them.

Further on, they came to a clearing. In the middle of it

lay the body of a Nassauer infantryman, face down, his back covered in congealed blood. Thinking it might be some sort of French trick, Macdonell halted the line and approached the body cautiously. A thick cloud of flies rose briefly from their work before settling back down on the corpse. He waved them away and turned the body over. The man's face was covered in burn marks. Macdonell swore. The demands of war he understood. A soldier killed because he had to. It was his duty. But here a captured soldier had suffered for the amusement of the French and his body had been left as a warning to others. That was beyond his understanding. Damn them to hell.

They carried on through the wood until they reached its southern edge where trees gave way to open land and, a little further on, a field of corn. They had seen neither Frenchman nor pheasant, just gruesome evidence of the enemy's barbarity. Captain Hellman found Macdonell peering through his glass at the cornfield. 'Any sign of them, Colonel?' he asked.

Macdonell shook his head. 'Can't see any, but the corn is high. They might be in there.' On three sides of them, cannon continued to hurl their deadly charges at enemies seen and unseen, explosions ripped through the morning air and men would be dying in their hundreds. Macdonell did not give it a thought. All his attention – his eyes and ears and mind – was focused on the field in front of him. He searched in vain for movement in the corn. There was none. The French infantry had withdrawn still further. He signalled the advance.

In a ragged line, the men of the light company and the Brunswickers moved forward into the open. If the French were hiding in the corn they would flush them out. If not, they would take up a position at the far end of the field and await orders. Beyond it a low hedge separated it from another wood.

The line had covered about fifty yards when there was a shout of warning from the left. Macdonell turned. Sergeant Dawson was bellowing at the top of his voice. From somewhere French cavalry had appeared. They were Lancers – probably the same troop they had encountered earlier – and must have been hiding in one of the many sunken lanes that criss-crossed the area, waiting for the light companies to emerge from the wood in line. A ragged, extended line at that.

It was a trap. Twenty horseman, lances extended, galloped towards them. There was no time to form squares. They had been caught in the open and would be slaughtered.

'Run!' Macdonell shouted, waving his arms and pointing back to the wood. The men needed no urging. The sight of French cavalry who would soon be close enough for them to see the grins on the riders' faces and the bared teeth of their mounts was enough to send even the slowest of them running like rabbits back to the trees.

Most of them made it. Some, Macdonell among them, did not. He had lagged behind to encourage the stragglers and was five yards from safety when the first of the Lancers reached them. The leading lancer must have seen his colonel's epaulettes because he ignored the others and charged straight at Macdonell. He held his lance on his right side, his arm fully extended and ready to thrust its point into his prey's face or chest. Macdonell turned towards him, stood with sword raised and watched him bearing down. To turn one's back on a lancer was to invite certain death. The lance was no more than six feet from him when he hurled himself across the path of the horse. So late did he leave it that he felt the outside of the horse's hoof touch the sole of his boot. He rolled over once and rose to his feet, the sword still in his hand. The lancer, with no time to react, galloped on until he could rein in his mount and turn back for the kill.

Macdonell saw two men slain by merciless strikes of French sabres, one almost beheaded, the other speared through the back. Three others, including Sergeant Dawson, were desperately trying to reach the woods. He ran after them and would have made it had he not stumbled and fallen a few yards from the treeline. He was on his knees when he heard a shot and a lancer landed beside him. A bullet had entered the lancer's head just above the left eye. A little dazed, Macdonell was struggling to his feet when two strong arms hoisted him up and dragged him to safety. 'Now that was a trifle close for comfort,' said a lilting Irish voice.

Lying on the ground, Macdonell peered up into the man's face. He could not tell. 'Joseph?' he muttered.

'Bless you, sir, no. Joseph would more likely have shot you, his aim is so bad.'

'James, then. My thanks. Help me to my feet, please, and we will see what is to be done.'

Still dazed, Macdonell managed to stand. Harry Wyndham emerged from behind a tree. 'Very acrobatic, Colonel. Are you hurt?'

'I am not.' The Lancers, doubtless disappointed at not catching more of the Guards, were milling about a hundred yards from the wood. They knew that was the extreme limit of a musket's accurate range and the risk of a lucky shot was slight. 'Tell them to hold their fire unless the brutes come closer,' ordered Macdonell. They were quite safe where they were – trees and cavalry did not mix well.

Macdonell could not be sure but he thought that the lancer who tired of doing nothing and trotted forward to within fifty yards of the treeline was the one who had first charged at him. He was shouting angrily and gesticulating with his sabre. He did not, it seemed, approve of their strategy of hiding in the woods. 'Stupid frog,' muttered Harry, raising a musket and firing. The lancer's horse, shot through the neck, fell to the ground, shuddered and died. The lancer, beside himself with fury, ran towards them, shaking his fists and yelling something about '*mon empereur*'. Another shot rang out and the lancer fell. The man was a fool. Nor was he much good to his emperor now. 'Now what, Colonel?' he asked. 'Wait for help to arrive or charge the bastards?'

'I need half a dozen of our best sharpshooters,' replied Macdonell. 'Vindle was a poacher, if I'm not mistaken. Make him one of them.'

Harry raised an eyebrow. 'Even Vindle won't hit anything at this range.'

'Then we shall have to make it easier for him. And have a hundred men hidden on the edge of the treeline, muskets cocked and ready to fire.'

Among the six who presented themselves to Macdonell were Vindle and two others who had been convicted of poaching and sentenced to hang, only to escape the noose by joining the army. Poachers were good shots. Macdonell instructed them to check their muskets and to follow his orders exactly. 'We will advance into the open, form up and, on my command, fire a volley. Aim for the horses. As soon as you have fired, run back here. Do not stop to help a fallen man, and if your musket slows you down remember that a wild-eyed Frenchman with a bloody great sabre is right behind you. Clear?'

It was clear. Ignoring Vindle's look of pure venom, Macdonell took the musket that Harry had prepared for him, lined up the six of them behind him, took one look round, let out an ear-shattering highland cry and dashed out into the field. The French cavalry simply sat on their horses and stared in astonishment. The volley, which brought down two horses and one rider, galvanised them. Macdonell and his shooting party were no more than halfway back to the woods when the Lancers charged.

He had judged it nicely. As the seven men dived into the trees, a hundred musket balls struck their pursuers, bringing them down in a screaming heap. Ten men died instantly, and as many horses. The wounded, legs and arms lacerated and broken by musket balls and falling horses, did their best to scramble out of danger. It was as Macdonell had hoped. The French Lancers, true to their reputation for pride and impetuosity, had brought death upon themselves.

From the safety of the trees they watched the Lancers turn their mounts and canter back through the cornfield towards the woods beyond. 'Well, Colonel,' said Harry Wyndham, standing beside Macdonell. 'Fancy Lancers running away twice in one afternoon. Perhaps they feared you were about to sing one of your Scottish songs.'

Macdonell pointed to a party of horsemen cantering towards them from the west. Their jackets were blue and gold and their blue shakos were adorned with red cockades. They were British Light Dragoons. 'There is your reason, Harry. My tuneful singing had nothing to do with it.'

As they approached, Macdonell stepped out of the trees. The Dragoon captain rode up to him. The flanks of his mount were glistening with sweat. 'Colonel Macdonell?' he inquired, holding his long, curved cavalry sword upright.

Macdonell nodded. 'I am Macdonell, Captain, and pleased to see you.'

'We were told we might find you here, Colonel,' said the captain. He pointed with his sword to the dead Lancers and horses. 'Although it does not look as if you need our assistance.' There was a thunderous explosion from the direction of the crossroads at Quatre Bras. The captain's mount started in fright and did its best to throw him. It took the captain a good minute to bring the beast under control. 'He's been skittery all day,' explained the captain. 'And that must have been a shell hitting a powder wagon.'

'Then let us hope that the powder was French.'

'Indeed. Colonel, General Byng's orders are for you to push on through the cornfield and into the woods. The 90th and a company of Jägers will attack the farm at Gemioncourt from the south and west. You are to clear the woods on this side of the farm.'

Macdonell thanked the captain and wished him luck for the day. Harry was standing at his shoulder. 'Ten minutes rest, check muskets, and then it's more work for us, Harry. Pass the word. And find Captain Hellman.'

Away to their right, the roar of cannon had intensified and another monstrous explosion ripped through the air, sending flames towering into the sky. With his musket slung over a shoulder and his hands over his ears, Captain Hellman appeared. 'Colonel, you sent for me?' he asked.

'I did, Captain. We are ordered to cross the field and enter those woods, where the French are hiding. Would you and your men care to join us, or will you return to your battalion? It sounds as if you might be needed there.'

Captain Hellman shook his head. 'My men are foresters and farmers. They are at home in fields and woods. We will accompany you, Colonel.'

'Very well. Five minutes more and we will advance.'

They crossed the field at the double, every man keeping an eye open for French cavalry and ready to form square instantly. Much of the corn had been trampled by men and horses, making their advance easier. Where the corn ended, they came to a low hedge which concealed another narrow, low-lying lane. Macdonell led them along it, keeping one bank of the lane and the wood on their left.

A thin stream ran alongside the lane. Forgetting how close they were to the enemy, the men took turns to lie on their stomachs and used their hands and shakos to scoop water into their mouths. Biting the ends off powder cartridges turned a man's mouth and throat to burning sand. Macdonell made no attempt to stop them. He had not fired many rounds, yet his own throat was as rough as pine bark.

The worst of their thirst slaked, they moved on. At a point where the bank had crumbled, Macdonell sent Captain Hellman and his Brunswickers up and into the trees. In the gloom of the wood their black coats rendered them almost invisible.

Further on he found another place where access to the wood was easy. He left half the company in the lane with Harry Wyndham with orders to stay there to cover their backs, and led the other half into the wood. At the top of the bank they spread out, crouching low and moving as quietly as the undergrowth allowed. At first the trees were widely spaced and thin, allowing light to penetrate the canopy and offering scant cover. Further in they became thick and dense. In the gloom, shapes and shadows danced among them. Here a man might easily fire at nothing or, more worryingly, at a friend.

Macdonell was nervous. Very few men of the light companies had served in the American War. Like him, they had fought on plains and in mountains but never in woods like these. He hated fighting in the dark or where he could not see his enemy and these woods were dark and forbidding. And full of Frenchmen. Voltigeurs and tirailleurs would be lurking behind trees and in the undergrowth, eyes accustomed to the dark and muskets poised to spit a bullet into an enemy face. For all Macdonell knew, they were watching him now, waiting for a certain kill shot, just as he would have waited for such a shot on a Scottish hillside. A finger of fear ran down his spine. He took a deep breath and moved cautiously forward.

They were fifty yards into the wood when a musket fired, echoing among the trees and bringing a howl of pain as it struck home. Then another, this time from a little behind and to the left. So the French were not evenly deployed but were scattered around the wood. Another musket fired from somewhere in the gloom ahead of him and a ball slammed into a tree no more than a hand's breadth from his head. Voltigeurs, like light company men, always looked for the officers first. Suddenly the whole wood was alive with musket fire. Men yelled warnings and screamed in agony. Bullets tore into flesh and ripped bark from the trees. The voltigeurs had allowed them to enter deep into the wood and were now all around them. Shadowy blue figures slipped through the trees, using the smoke as cover, always on the move, pausing only to reload and fire. Outside the wood, where the sun still beat down on exhausted soldiers, cannon crashed and thundered, bringing instant death to unseen enemies. Inside it, in the shade of the trees, muskets cracked and spat and killed just as surely.

Macdonell cursed. He should not have led them into this trap. He sensed a man at his shoulder. 'It's like shooting at ghosts, Colonel,' said a lowland voice. Another shot whistled over their heads, close enough to make them duck behind a fallen oak.

'It is, Sergeant. Any ideas?'

'Yes, Colonel. Get among them with our bayonets. Slice a few faces and fillet some bellies. They'll squeal like babes.' Dawson was right. Hand-to-hand fighting would give them a better chance than waiting to be picked off by invisible sharpshooters. The problem was how to get among them. As if he had read his colonel's mind, the sergeant continued, 'If you call for a retreat, we could run back towards the edge of the wood where it is more open and hope they chase us. If they do, we will let them get close, then turn and charge.' He paused and grinned. 'Bayonets fixed, of course.'

'And if they do not, at least we will have regrouped for another go at the brutes. Do your best to pass the word. Rapid retreat on my call in two minutes. Fix bayonets. Let them get close. Shriek like stuck pigs. Fear and panic. Halt at the lane. Turn and face them. One volley and charge.'

Macdonell filled his lungs and shouted. 'Fall back. Light companies retreat.' Twice he shouted the order before clattering back through the undergrowth himself. He kept shouting to encourage the men to do the same and in the hope that the French would hear him and take an officer's flight as a signal to give chase. All around him men sped back through the woods. Some stumbled and fell, others ripped their jackets on brambles, one stepped on a snare and howled in anguish when its iron teeth bit into his ankle. He managed to prise it open and hobbled after the others, cursing French poachers, French farmers and anything else French he could think of.

Macdonell passed a man on his knees, fiddling with his musket. 'Leave it, Private,' he ordered. 'Get back to the lane.' The private looked up, startled. It was Vindle. Macdonell ran on. Idiot. If the French chopped him in half, it would be his own fault.

A few yards further on he came to a small clearing. He had almost crossed it when a musket ball thudded into his back and sent him flying. Lying dazed on a heap of fallen leaves, he was aware of feet running past him. He struggled to his knees. There was no pain and no sign of blood. His pack had saved him. The charge must have been weak and the shot had buried itself in his blanket. He ran on.

At the southern edge of the wood, all but a handful halted.

A few, having either not received or having misunderstood the order, jumped into the lane. The rest halted, turned and waited for blue coats to appear.

They soon did. Muskets flashed and men fell. The blue coats were everywhere but they used the thin trees as cover and did not come close enough. Macdonell wondered fleetingly if the plan was going to backfire. For a charge to be successful, they must lure the French nearer. If not, they would be back in the lane where the French would use them for musket practice.

Some way to his left, he glimpsed movement in the trees. More dark coats. Beside him, James Hervey had also seen them and aimed his musket in their direction. As he pulled the trigger, Macdonell grabbed the barrel and pulled it skywards. The shot went high into the trees. Hervey looked at his colonel in astonishment. 'Look again at those jackets, Ensign,' said Macdonell.

Hervey peered through the smoke. The jackets were not blue but black. Captain Hellman and his Brunswickers burst out of cover and charged through the trees. A second later, Macdonell and the light company did the same, followed by Harry Wyndham's men who had scrambled up the bank to join them.

Some of the French turned to face the threat to their flank. The others stood to take the full force of the light companies' charge. None of them ran. They were brave men, well trained and proud.

Macdonell held his sword extended, ready to slash or slice. He ran at the French and with a thrust of his long arm skewered a voltigeur, twisted his hand and pulled the sword from the man's stomach. Blood spurted out. The Frenchman clutched the wound and collapsed. A backhand slash almost cut the next man's arm in two. Around him, the light companies used bayonets, swords and their hands to kill and disable. The Graham brothers were fighting back-to-back, protecting each other's rear, killing and wounding with bayonet and musket butt.

A man beside Macdonell went down holding his shoulder. Another cursed as his musket misfired before taking the force of a French bullet in his mouth. A third leapt at a Frenchman who was struggling to reload. He drove his bayonet into the man's throat and screamed in triumph. A moment later he too was dead, his neck half-severed by a French sword.

A shout of warning from his left made Macdonell turn sharply. A French sabre was poised to split open his head. He ducked to one side and thrust the point of his sword into the man's eye. The sabre fell to the ground but the Frenchman, to Macdonell's astonishment, remained standing. He reversed his sword and smashed the handle into the man's face. Bones broke and he too fell. He turned to see Henry Gooch, his face ashen white, staring at the dead Frenchman.

Steel clashed on steel, men screamed and fell and blood splattered on the woodland floor. Macdonell saw Harry block a cutting slash and chop his sword down on his attacker's neck. For a while the outcome hung in the balance. The French, attacked from two sides, fought bravely. But when the Brunswickers got round behind them, they were doomed. Their captain lay down his sword and called for his men to do the same. Reluctantly, they did.

Macdonell took a moment to catch his breath. When he could speak clearly he ordered Harry to have all French muskets and ammunition collected and the wounded attended to. Those who could walk set off down the lane where they would come to the road back to Quatre Bras. Those who could not were given rum or gin and made as comfortable as possible. With luck, they would be found by medical orderlies.

The French captain was waiting patiently to learn his fate. Macdonell scratched his head. What he was to do with a clutch of French prisoners when the light would soon be fading and he had no idea where the Guards would be spending the night, he did not know. 'We could shoot them all,' suggested Harry cheerfully.

'Then we could eat them,' added Captain Hellman, licking his lips and patting his stomach. 'I expect they taste like poodles.'

'I would rather you did not,' said the French captain in perfect English.

'*Vous parlez bien*, Captain,' said Macdonell, taken by surprise.

'*Merçi*, Colonel. However, we are your prisoners and I expect you to treat us honourably, just as we would treat you honourably if our roles were reversed.'

'Like the poor wretch we found in the woods?' asked Joseph Graham. 'Tortured and murdered, he was, and by cowardly frogs.'

The captain looked horrified. 'I can assure you that my men would never commit such an act.'

'Well someone did,' growled James.

Macdonell made a decision. 'Captain Hellman, kindly escort the prisoners back to the crossroads. I believe it is in our hands all the way there. If you pass a medical wagon, tell them there are wounded here. And my thanks for your assistance.'

'As you wish, Colonel. I will do as you say. Perhaps we shall meet again tomorrow.'

'Now what?' asked Harry when the Brunswickers had gone.

'Now I'll send word to General Byng and await further orders.' From a pouch attached to his belt, he took a stick of graphite pencil and a small notebook. His report to the general said simply that they had cleared the wood and would shortly be encamping for the night. He tore out the page, folded the paper and peered through the last of the light for a man to take it back down the hill. A young private who looked no more than twelve was trying in vain to scrape blood off his jacket. He jumped up when Macdonell approached him. 'Take this to General Byng, Private. You'll find him at the crossroads.' He tapped the private on the shoulder. 'And no dallying in the inn.'

The private took the paper and gave his colonel a gap-toothed grin. Despite having marched nearly thirty miles that day, having eaten little and faced French cavalry and artillery for probably the first time, the boy seemed pleased to be given the task. 'Leave it to me, sir. I'll be back before you know it,' he said, smiling through a face streaked with powder and dirt. Macdonell watched him jump into the lane and trot off towards the road. The boy was as likely to carry out the task as anyone.

They followed the line of the wood to the road, passing three dead French cavalry horses and their riders spreadeagled in a ditch. The sounds of war were gradually dying. Macdonell could not be sure that the 90th had retaken the Gemioncourt farm or where their front line was. To the east of the Charleroi

Road he had been immersed in his own part in the battle. He had received one message from the Light Dragoon captain and knew from Captain Hellman that the crossroads were secure – or at least they were when the Brunswickers were sent to help him – but that was all. He badly needed accurate intelligence, or, better still, orders. Until they arrived, he would have to wait and hope.

On its western side, the road was separated from the Bossu wood by narrow fields of rye. They chose a flat area near the wood to bivouac for the night. Here, too, lay the bodies of the dead. Macdonell ordered them cleared and pickets to be posted. Beside him, Harry glanced at the darkening sky. In the last of the light, black clouds were gathering. 'If those are rain clouds, it won't be a very comfortable night,' he muttered.

'No, Harry, it will not. And God knows where the enemy are skulking – in the woods, at the farm, in the next field – but we need rest. A wet night it will have to be. Post pickets, get fires lit and use blankets for bivouacs. Usual procedure – two blankets for four men. Muskets ready. No stacking in case we have to move quickly. Send a watering party back to the stream. Dawson was a butcher. Tell him to take the Grahams and cut what he can off those horses.' Harry nodded and went to find the two corporals.

Wriggling out of the straps that held his pack was always a pleasure. Macdonell stretched his back and sighed. Then he remembered the soldiers' saying: 'Every bullet has a billet'. He found the hole and put his index finger through it, opened the pack and rummaged around among his spare shirt and blanket. There it was. He pulled it out and squinted at it by the light of the fire. At first he did not notice. But then he realised. It was a British bullet, larger than a French musket could take. A French bullet could be used, at a pinch, in a British musket, but not a British one in a French musket. Could the French in the wood have been using captured guns?

He sat cross-legged in the bivouac, tossing the bullet in his hand and trying to remember. Had he not passed Vindle on his dash out of the wood? Despite having been told to run for it, the idiot had stopped to reload. Vindle of all people. Why would he do that? You would expect him to be first out of the wood, not last.

Unless he had a reason. Unless, for example, he had spotted an opportunity and wanted to get behind Macdonell. His haste to reload might explain the weak charge. He might have spilt some powder. Macdonell would not have entertained the thought of any other man, even Luke, being guilty of such an act, but Vindle . . . He had cause and it would not have been the first such incident in the army.

The storm arrived with sudden and monstrous force. Thunder crashed and forks of lightning lit up the sky. Rain poured down and within a minute every man and every piece of equipment not under cover was soaked.

Harry returned to the bivouac, an oilskin draped over his head. He had ordered a roll-call. The light companies had lost sixty-four men, dead, wounded or abandoned on the march from Enghien, and now, including officers, numbered two hundred and thirty-six.

It had nearly been sixty-five lost. Macdonell slipped the bullet into his pocket. There was no proof, Vindle would protest his innocence and this was not the time to risk divisions among the men. He would wait for the right moment.

Night had fallen when the watering party returned laden with kettles of water. Macdonell swallowed several gulps, wiped his mouth on his sleeve and belched loudly. 'Sweet as a highland burn. Send another party to fill the kettles for the morning.'

Lightning flashed, thunder rolled and the rain came down in sheets. Shivering soldiers huddled under their bivouacs and did what they could to keep themselves and their weapons dry. The pickets could not even do that. Out in the rye they crouched or lay flat, watching and listening for any sign of movement. If they sensed danger they would scuttle back to the camp.

The two of them sat cross-legged under blankets stretched between branches cut from a tall beech hedge and listened to the rain splashing on the rye and on their meagre roof. 'Anything to eat while we wait for the main course?' asked Macdonell. Harry fished in his pouch and pulled out a chunk of hard tack.

'Try that. The navy swear by it.'

'So I believe.' Macdonell shook a family of weevils out of the tack and broke off a corner. It was hard as stone and almost tasteless. 'Glad I'm not a sailor.'

'If the rain goes on like this, we'll need sailors. It'll be a naval battle.'

As if the heavens had heard him, there was a break in the rain and a large figure emerged out of the darkness. 'Saved the best for you, Colonel.' James Graham handed Macdonell a chunk of horsemeat. 'Juicy slice of rump.'

'Thank you, Corporal. Is there enough for all?'

'Yes, sir. A little each. I'll save some for the sentries.'

Harry nursed their fire to life and cut the meat in half with a knife. They skewered the two pieces on bayonets and held them over the flame. Their mouths filled with saliva. The meat was still raw and bloody when they took their first bites. While they chewed, the rest went back over the fire. 'Boney was right about an army marching on its stomach,' spluttered Harry with his mouth full. 'The French always get better food than us because they steal it.'

A shriek of pure, shivering agony split the night. And then sobbing, a man calling out to his God, and silence. The voice had been French. 'They still die like us,' observed James drily, 'well fed or not.' The wretched man must have been left for dead on the roadside.

'That they do. Now, shall we share the night? You get some rest and I will wake you in three hours.'

'I fear sleep will prove elusive, but I shall try. Wake me if there is any news. And make sure the pickets are alert.'

'Of course.' Harry pushed himself to his feet and went to inspect the camp, leaving James with enough room to stretch out his legs under the oilskin. In the distance thunder rumbled, warning that another storm was sweeping in from the west.

CHAPTER SEVEN

17th June

Sure enough, James did no more than doze and when Harry shook him gently he was more awake than asleep. 'An hour after midnight, James,' whispered Harry. 'All quiet and the storm has passed. I have changed the pickets.'

Macdonell stood up and very nearly fell down again. His head ached and his stomach heaved. He retched, spat out a piece of meat and tipped water from the kettle into his mouth. It steadied him a little. 'Thank you, Harry. Time I stretched my legs. Has that private returned yet?'

'I'm afraid not. Lost, deserted or dead, I fear.'

'Damn. I thought he would serve. I'll send another.'

'Might be better to wait until morning.'

James considered. Harry was right. It would be light in three hours. He would send another man then.

The camp was quiet, although few were sleeping. It was a strange thing. A man could march all day carrying his musket and pack and wishing for nothing more than rest, yet, when the opportunity came, be unable to sleep. Eventually his mind and body would surrender but Macdonell had seen men go without sleep for two or three days and still be sharp and ready to fight.

He found Sergeant Dawson sitting with his back against a tree. He had taken off his jacket and was dabbing with a piece of cloth at his arm. He scrambled to his feet when he saw Macdonell and held the cloth behind his back. 'Sergeant Dawson, a wound?'

'A scratch, Colonel, no more. Probably a thorn bush.'

'Show me, please,' insisted Macdonell. Reluctantly Dawson held out his arm. A long cut from elbow to wrist was dripping blood. 'Thorn bush, Sergeant? French sword, I'd say. Why have you not had it bandaged?'

'Didn't seem worth it, Colonel. I'll bind it up myself.'

'Take it to a surgeon as soon as there's one available. Let him sew it up.'

Dawson blanched. 'I hardly like to trouble a surgeon, Colonel. There'll be many worse than me needing his attention.'

'There will. But kindly do as I say. Understood?'

The sergeant could not look his colonel in the eye. 'Understood, Colonel,' he mumbled.

The Grahams were lying back-to-back in their bivouac. They were too tall to sit or squat under their blankets and were excused having to share with two others. He motioned to them not to stand and squatted down beside them. 'Any sign of trouble?' he asked.

'None, Colonel,' replied Joseph. 'Frenchies are sleeping like babes.'

'But you are not.'

'No, Colonel,' said James. 'We are telling the stories our mother told us about imps and devils and ghostly creatures.'

'Much more frightening than a few Frenchies,' added Joseph, and laughed his gurgling laugh.

'Better tell that to the young ones,' replied Macdonell. 'Unless I'm mistaken, we're in for some hard fighting today.'

'That we are,' agreed James.

'Don't worry, Colonel,' said Joseph. 'We've good men in the company. They'll look out for the boys.'

Macdonell stood. 'I know they will.' He went from fire to fire, exchanging words with those awake and reminding them that a faulty flint or a damp charge could kill a man as surely as a French sabre.

Without warning, there was a commotion from somewhere behind them. Macdonell made his way towards it, half-expecting a scuffle or an argument over a scrap of horsemeat.

It was neither. The young private sent with his despatch to General Byng had hobbled into the camp and stumbled over a sleeping soldier. The soldier had panicked and assumed they were being attacked. Happily he had recognised the boy just in time. 'Are you wounded, Private?' asked Macdonell.

'No, sir,' gasped the boy. 'My ankle twisted in a hole in the road. I did not see it.'

'Did you deliver my despatch to the general?'

'Yes, sir.' The boy took a rolled sheet of paper from under his shirt and handed it to Macdonell. 'This is the general's reply.'

'Did you see anything of the enemy?'

'No, sir.' That was something, at least. No Frenchmen behind them.

Macdonell turned to the man who had been woken. 'Get him food and water and put him on the first wagon going north.' The private began to protest. 'Enough, Private.' Macdonell's voice was sharp. 'You're no use to us if you can't walk, let alone run.' He turned and strode back to his bivouac.

Harry was asleep. James unrolled the despatch and tried to read it. It was still too dark. He gave the fire a kick with his boot, sending sparks into the air, and exposing the ashes. When he held the paper close, they gave off just enough light.

General Byng acknowledged Macdonell's report and informed him that the French had been driven back down the Charleroi Road and instructed him to hold his position until ordered otherwise. There was no mention of advancing further. It was disappointing. James read it twice to be sure he had not misunderstood. They had forced the French back down the road whence they came. Somewhere out in the darkness, in the woods and fields and farms, Allied troops would be itching to chase them all the way back to France. Why not press home their advantage? He would let Harry sleep for another hour before waking him with the news.

But for Harry and every other man in the camp there was no more sleep. An arrow of lightning lit up the night sky and thunder again rolled over their heads. Harry jumped up and grabbed his musket. 'Only thunder, Harry,' laughed Macdonell. 'And we've had orders to stay put.' He handed over the paper.

Harry rubbed sleep from his eyes. 'What about the Prussians? Those deserters said Napoleon was after them.'

'No news, but Blücher will stand and fight. He always has.'

'What if he stood and fought and lost?'

'Old Blücher? Come now, Harry. No one hates the frogs more than the Prussians.'

'I hope you're right, James.' Another flash of lightning and the rain arrived again. It poured down in sheets and soon the camp was a muddy bog. Men scrambled back into their bivouacs and lay on their muskets.

For once, Harry's good humour deserted him. 'I'm heartily sick of this,' he said, huddled again under their oilskin roof. 'Damnable weather, damnable frogs. They could slip past us and be in Brussels before the rain stops. And we'll never keep our muskets dry. Lie on them, point their barrels at the ground, wrap them in oilskin, they'll still be wet.' The first glimmerings of dawn were appearing. 'Cup of gin all round? We're likely in for another long day.'

'Cup of gin it is. One only, mind.' James picked up their kettle and tipped water into his mouth. A few drops ran down his chin. He wiped them off and inspected his hand. 'Good God. It's red. Where did it come from?'

'The stream back beyond the farm,' replied Harry.

James sniffed his hand. 'Blood. It was not there yesterday. It must have come from upstream. Human or horse, do you think?'

'No idea. Didn't taste too bad last night but I'll stick to gin this morning.' Harry reached into his haversack and pulled out a brown bottle. He took a gulp and offered it to James who was about to take it when a man appeared out of the half-light. He was panting.

'Private Mills, Colonel, on picket duty. Heard men in the rye ahead. Coming this way.'

'How many, Private?' asked Macdonell.

'Small party, sir, perhaps half a dozen. Voltigeurs, I daresay, come to take a look at us.'

'Right. Harry, collect the ensigns and eight men and we'll give them a surprise for their breakfast.' The men were quickly assembled. 'Lead on, Private. Show us where you heard them.' They moved slowly and quietly forward into the rye, muskets primed and loaded and held across their chests, a hand over the breech to keep out the rain and taking care to keep their heads below the level of the stalks. Macdonell unsheathed his sword and held it loosely at his side. At first, he could hear nothing but the breeze. But when the private stopped and pointed a little to their left, he caught the tiniest hint of movement through the rye, perhaps thirty yards ahead.

Macdonell nodded and signalled his men to fan out. If they could work their way round the voltigeurs, they could trap them like herring in a net. The Frenchmen would have expected sentries but must have thought they had avoided them. Whatever their purpose, they were alarmingly close to the camp.

Harry led five men back and to the left, James the other six to the right. Dawn was breaking but overhead more thunder clouds were gathering. One moment it was light, the next as dark as pitch. The breeze was becoming a wind. Taking advantage of its covering noise, James risked moving faster and hoped Harry was doing the same. It would be a pity not to catch the fish.

They circled the spot he thought the voltigeurs would have reached and he peeked over the rye. Through the rain he made out the back of a man's head. He turned, lifted a finger to his lips and pointed. All six men nodded their understanding. He signalled for them to extend in line and move forward. They stood between the voltigeurs and their own lines. If Harry had managed to block their way forward, the Frenchies were as good as trapped.

Macdonell rose to his full height and charged through the rye, yelling for the others to follow. A second later, Harry Wyndham did the same. Thirteen men, muskets at the ready, ran at the voltigeurs from every direction. And stopped. They were not voltigeurs. Voltigeurs did not wear red jackets with white cross-belts. They were Guards.

Or at least they looked like Guards. At Albuera, Macdonell had very nearly been duped by a platoon of French infantrymen in British uniforms. Speaking in French, he asked the surrounded men to which battalion they belonged. There was no answer. He ordered them to put down their muskets. None of them moved. There was a lieutenant among them. 'We are 3rd Foot Guards under the command of Colonel Hepburn,' said the young man. 'And, if I may ask, who the devil are you?'

Macdonell ignored the question. 'Then you are fortunate Foot Guards. You were close to being shot by the light companies of your own battalion. What are you doing creeping about here?'

'Colonel Hepburn sent us out to check that there were no French behind us. We are camped a quarter of a mile further south at the edge of the wood.'

'Are you now? Then you may escort me to Colonel Hepburn. Captain Wyndham will accompany us. The rest of you return to camp and await our return. Tell Sergeant Dawson where we are.'

The bivouacs of the 3rd Foot Guards had been set up at the southern edge of the Bossu wood, where the Guards were lighting their fires and boiling their kettles. They found Francis Hepburn with a glass to his eye, sheltering under the branches of an oak and scanning the fields of rye that stretched south along the road to Charleroi. A young corporal stood beside him. 'Damned if I can see anything in this rain,' said Hepburn, passing the glass to the corporal, 'You have a look, Corporal.' Hepburn turned and saw them. 'Well, damn me if it isn't Colonel Macdonell and Captain Wyndham. I was wondering where you had got to. Corporal, find some tea for our guests.'

'I assume you cleared the wood, Francis,' said James.

'We did. Bloody work. Saltoun's battalion took heavy losses. At times there seemed to be a frog behind every tree. And telling friend from foe was not easy. Nasty fighting, but the Hanoverians are holding it now. No danger of the frogs attacking from there. And you, James, bloody work as well?'

'It was. Nearly fifty men lost, but the ground is secure as far as the Gemioncourt Farm.'

'Which the 90th now hold. And not a frog in sight. Do you suppose they have gone home?'

'No.' James peered into the distance. 'They're not far away and we'll see them again today.' The corporal returned with two mugs of tea. James took a sip and raised his eyebrows. 'Excellent tea, Francis. Where did you get it?'

Hepburn blushed. 'Er, Daisy gave it to me before we left. Said it would remind me of her.'

'And does it?'

'It does. Now, I suggest you strike camp and bring the light companies down here so that we are all ready to move off when the order to advance comes. It shouldn't be long.'

Far to the south a cannon cracked and moments later an eight-pound ball landed twenty yards in front of them. Had the ground been dry it would have bounced and might have killed all of them. Fortunately, it stuck in the sodden earth and did no damage. 'A shot to clear the barrel,' said Harry, wiping his brow with a sleeve, 'and the sooner we get at them the better.'

More cannon fired and more round shot plummeted into the ground in front of them or smashed against trees, sending shards of timber and bark flying through the camp. One man shrieked and fell to the ground with a twelve-inch needle sticking out of his arm. 'They are only clearing their throats,' shouted Hepburn. 'Lie flat until it's done.' He turned to James. 'And we'd better do the same.'

They lay on the ground under cover of the wood and waited for the throat-clearing to finish. 'Will you return fire?' asked James.

'No,' replied Francis. 'Waste of ammunition and the peer disapproves of what he calls long-distance duelling. Likes us to save our best for the infantry.'

For thirty minutes cannon fired, rain fell in torrents and drenched men found what shelter they could from both. It was still raining when a small troop of Light Dragoons came cantering down the road. Their captain dismounted and led his mount to the edge of the woods. Over his uniform he wore an oilskin cloak and carried a messenger bag, also oilskin. He tethered his horse and approached the camp. 'I have urgent orders for Colonel Hepburn from General Byng,' he announced, taking a packet from his bag. 'And I am told Colonel Macdonell commanding the light companies is also here.'

Francis strode up to the dragoon. 'I am Colonel Hepburn, Captain. And this is Colonel Macdonell.'

The captain handed his packet to Francis. It was rolled in oilskin and tied with cotton thread. General Byng was taking no chances with the rain. 'Your orders, sir,' said the Dragoon. 'And now we will go to the farmhouse.'

'Are the orders for the 90th the same?' asked James.

'They are, Colonel.'

That was encouraging. A general advance down the road to Charleroi, where the French would be chased back over the river. Francis unwrapped it and extracted a single sheet of paper. It did not take him long to read the order. Without a word he passed it to James. Then he swore. 'Bugger it, James. We've cleared the frogs out of the woods and fields, taken the farmhouse, sent them packing and held the road north. Why in the name of our German king are we now being ordered to withdraw?'

'Francis,' replied James with a shrug of resignation, 'I have no more idea than you. But the order is clear and emphatic. We are to return with our companies to Quatre Bras at once.'

'Damn and blast. God knows what the men will make of it. Bloody fighting, comrades killed and wounded, and now we are to turn tail and run for it.'

'It says withdraw, not run.'

'Bloody withdraw, then. What's the difference?'

Macdonell did not reply. 'I must return to my company, Francis. Thank you for the tea.'

Back they trudged, splashing through puddles, unable to think of anything to say. Harry gave the order to strike camp and make ready to march. 'Going to chase the frogs back to Paris, are we?' asked James Graham, rubbing his hands. He and his brother had come through the day unharmed.

'It seems not, Corporal,' replied Harry. 'At least not yet. We are returning to the crossroads.'

'Won't find many frogs there,' growled Joseph, 'except the green ones they eat.'

The French artillery, now fully awake, had started up again, and their Gunners were firing at the woods, the road and the Gemioncourt farm. On top of the cannonade, thunder boomed, lightning flashed and miserable soldiers packed up their bivouacs, collected their few possessions together, helped each other into their sodden packs and prepared to march. Having taken all the ground for the best part of a mile south of the Quatre Bras crossroads, they were now, it seemed, going to give it back.

The road was thronged with men, horses and artillery heading north. Behind them French guns fired at their backs as if mocking their retreat, and all along the roadside the bodies of the dead lay heaped. Blue uniforms, the black of the Brunswickers, green Riflemen, kilted Highlanders, the blue of the French Infantry and the red of their Hussars. Bodies crushed, mangled, butchered. Skin flensed from faces and hands. Horses, gun carriages, muskets, swords – the tools of war. And, here and there, a woman – a soldier's wife who had remained at her husband's side. The looters had already been out – packs lay open and discarded, pockets emptied and jackets cut from backs – rich pickings for the scavengers.

At the crossroads it was worse. The dead and dying lay together on the road, propped against blood-spattered walls, and in doorways. Exhausted medical staff were still hard at work, moving from body to body, searching for signs of life. The wounded were heaped onto wagons to be sent north, the dead piled in gardens and on patches of bare ground. A kilted Highlander whose left arm was a bloody stump sat, silent and blank-eyed, watching his leg being sawn off. Mutilated horses were despatched with a single musket shot. Soldiers trudged through the village, too weary to do more than put one foot in front of the other. Knots of infantrymen from the 28th and 32nd regiments sat, silent and unmoving, around improvised campfires. And from everywhere came the sounds of men and women weeping.

General Cooke had set up his headquarters in a room of the farm, which was also being used as a hospital. There Macdonell found him, seated, head in hands, at a plain pine table. Beside him stood General Byng, General Maitland, Lord Saltoun and Colonel Woodford. Francis Hepburn was there too, having ridden hard in his impatience to find out what was happening. A map was spread out in front of them. 'Ah, Macdonell,' General Cooke greeted him, 'I am delighted to see you unharmed. What is your strength?'

'Two hundred and thirty-six, General, including officers,'

replied Macdonell, 'Sixty-four dead or wounded. What is our present situation?'

Cooke cleared his throat. 'We have taken heavy losses, but so have the French. Yesterday, however, Field Marshal Blücher and his Prussians were engaged by the French under Buonaparte at the town of Ligny.' He pointed to the map. 'They were badly mauled and forced to retreat.'

So that was it. The retreating Prussians had left Wellington's left flank exposed. If his centre did not also retreat, it would be cut off and destroyed. 'Have the Prussians gone east or north?' asked Hepburn.

'A good question, Colonel,' replied Byng. 'We do not know. We do know, however, that Blücher has given his word to the Duke that he will wheel to join our main force.'

'And the sooner the better,' added Maitland.

'Meanwhile, gentlemen,' went on Cooke, 'you are to lead your battalions north up the road to Brussels, towards the town of Waterloo. South of the town, the Duke is establishing a strong defensive position on a ridge known as Mont St Jean. That is where we shall next meet Buonaparte.' Macdonell and Hepburn turned to leave. 'One more thing, Colonel Macdonell,' said Cooke. 'You will have cavalry cover, but I want the light companies at the rear of the line.'

'Of course, General.' The rear of the line was the most dangerous position in a withdrawal, and this would be a fighting withdrawal. Macdonell expected nothing less than that his light companies would bear the brunt of it.

CHAPTER EIGHT

For the present they were out of range of the French artillery, and the rain, thankfully, had eased. Macdonell stood with Harry and watched the sad procession heading north. Regiment after regiment converged on the crossroads and streamed back up the Brussels road. Dutch Nassauers, German Jägers, Brunswickers and Hanoverians, Dragoons and Militia, followed by General Picton's 5th Division, General Cooke's 1st and General Alten's 3rd. Thousands of soldiers heading miserably back the way they had come. Their white trousers turned pink by the dye running from their red jackets somehow made the spectacle even worse. It was as if the jackets themselves were weeping.

Once again, the road was jam-packed with men and horses, artillery and carts, the injured and the exhausted. Wagons carrying the most seriously wounded followed each regiment, clanking over the rough road and through the blankets of dust thrown up by marching feet. For all the rain that had fallen, the road was still hard and dry. Artillery pieces were dragged along by teams of tired horses. Officers dismounted to give their mounts a rest. Villagers – squat, round-faced, glum – watched in silence. The British and their allies were leaving. Very soon French soldiers would arrive, take what they wanted and march on. It had happened before.

'Did we lose the battle?' asked Harry. 'And there was I thinking we had done exactly what the peer asked of us and pushed the frogs back down the road to France.'

'Neither won nor lost, I suppose,' replied James. 'But the next battle we must win. I doubt we'll get another chance.'

'If we have to fight without the Prussians, it won't be easy. Outnumbered, outgunned and outsupplied we'll be.'

'Not to mention having an army made up of Dutchmen, Belgians and Germans as well as us. I hear that the Duke has even rounded up some companies from the Indies. Perhaps their black faces will frighten the frogs.'

'West Indies or East Indies?' asked Macdonell, who had served for a year in the Caribbean.

'No idea, James. Both, hopefully. We'll need every one of them.'

It was no time for defeatism. 'Come along now, Harry,' said James. 'We have work to do.'

The light companies had found a small stand of trees to the west of the village, in which to settle down and light their fires. As usual, the Grahams were sitting together with mugs of tea in their hands. They rose to greet the colonel. 'Tea, Colonel?' asked Joseph. 'I fear we have nothing stronger.'

Macdonell laughed. 'I'll wager you have, Corporal. But

keep it for later. You will need it.' A third man had been sitting with the brothers. He looked familiar. 'And who is this?' asked Macdonell.

'Private Lester, Colonel,' replied the man. 'Third Foot Guards, light company.'

Macdonell remembered. The man who had so nearly defeated James Graham at Enghien. 'Recovered from the fight, Corporal?'

'Yes, thank you, Colonel. Lucky punch, no more. James was beaten otherwise.'

'You fought well, Lester. As we all must tomorrow or the day after.'

'Will Boney attack, sir?' asked Joseph.

'He will, you may count upon it. The risk he took in splitting his own force has paid off. Now he has split ours by defeating the Prussians. He will march to join Marshal Ney in a full assault on us.'

'Will their strength be greater, Colonel?' asked Lester.

'It will, but in numbers only. In all other ways we will of course be superior. Shall we not, Corporals?' Given the raw inexperience of so much of the Allied army, it was a doubtful proposition, but necessary.

'That we shall, Colonel.' The brothers spoke as one.

'We are to march at the rear of the line,' Harry told them. 'We shall have cavalry cover, of course, and our job is to keep the frogs at bay.'

'We expected as much,' said James Graham. 'Someone has to do it and it might as well be us.'

'Indeed,' replied Macdonell. 'Be ready to move off by noon.

Pass the word and tell them to eat and drink what they can. There will be no stopping once we go.'

A fighting retreat was notoriously difficult to carry off successfully. Look what had happened on the march to Corunna – loss of discipline, disorder and a retreat very nearly turned into a rout. He had not been there himself but he had heard enough from those who had. Here they would not be climbing mountains and wading through snow, but with the French cavalry in hot pursuit, it would be tempting to go too fast. That was the risk. If marching men became running men, they would be lost.

Much would depend on the cavalry shielding them. Forming square would not be easy on the march, and even if they managed it, they would fall behind the main body and might be cut off. He would order it only as a last resort. And if the French brought their artillery up quickly enough, they would be sitting ducks for their Gunners. Buonaparte himself had been an artillery man and had always insisted on training, training and more training for his gun teams. That was why they were so devastatingly accurate.

Macdonell looked at his pocket watch. It was eleven o'clock. Ney's voltigeurs would soon discover that the farm at Gemioncourt had been abandoned and the woods deserted. Even Ney – the bravest of the brave, they called him, and just as headstrong – would be wary of a trick. He would, of course, know that the Prussians had been routed, but feigned retreats, just like the one the guards had conducted in the woods, were not uncommon. That would hold him up for a while, but it would not be long before his cavalry scouts came to reconnoitre.

Once Ney was sure that the Allies really were leaving, he would send his artillery forward to bombard the village. The light companies, at the rear of the column, had better be on their way before that happened.

The word came at fifteen minutes before noon. The light companies of the Coldstream and 3rd Foot Guards were to follow the 1st Battalion out of Quatre Bras and to fall back slowly on the village of Genappe, guarding the right wing of the retreating army. Two battalions of Brunswickers would be on the left. A squadron from the 2nd Brunswicker Hussars would cover them. An army that frequently did things badly was managing the withdrawal with calm competence.

Macdonell's mule had disappeared but his charger had survived and been stabled in the village. He brushed himself down, mounted and watched the companies preparing to march. Harry Wyndham, assisted by the ensigns, supervised their formation – some one hundred and thirty pairs, deployed behind and to the right of the Brunswickers. They must move forward whilst watching their backs and be ready to protect themselves and those in front of them against attacks by French cavalry – a cavalry doubtless abrim with confidence at seeing the backs of their enemies and all too anxious to get amongst them with lance and sabre. The dream of every lancer and cuirassier in the French army.

Macdonell allowed himself a moment of pride. They had marched more than twenty-five miles on little sleep or food, fought in the rye and in the woods for four hours, withstood attacks by cannon and cavalry, been fried by the sun and drenched by the rain and suffered torments of dust and thirst.

Yet few heads were down. Their work was far from over and they would keep going until it was.

Two miles on and, as if knowing that the last of the army had left the shelter of the village, the heavens opened again. Down came the rain, threatening to render muskets and cartridges useless. Every man did his best to keep them dry but until they were tested he would not know if he had succeeded. By then it might be too late. Shoes splashed through puddles and water streamed off shakos. They could not stop. To do so might be fatal.

Macdonell could see for no more than two hundred yards. He turned his mount and cantered back along the road for about half a mile. Peering through the gloom, he saw no sign of cavalry and quickly rejoined the column. 'Anything?' asked Harry, wiping his eyes.

'Nothing. How far to Genappe, Harry?'

'About two miles, I think. An hour at this pace. Keep them moving but slow and steady. No point in coming up against the traffic in front.'

It was still pouring down when they reached the outskirts of Genappe. There the Hussars rode a short way back down the road. Macdonell ordered the light companies to take up defensive positions guarding the entrances to the village. If the French arrived he could only hope that their muskets would fire.

In the village, he found the inevitable chaos. The narrow streets were crammed with men and wagons and angry officers barked orders as their horses shied at the crush of bodies around them. It would take time to clear a route. Like it or not, the light companies would have to stay where they were, keeping watch and keeping out of trouble.

Gradually the rain eased. Harry ordered muskets fired and flints checked. There was no shortage of water to wash down a dry biscuit or a scrap of meat; those who had some took a mouthful or two of gin or rum, and he gave permission for jackets to be removed and shaken out. His own trousers had shrunk so much that he feared he would have to cut them off. Sergeant Dawson went from group to group, examining muskets and counting cartridges. Macdonell saw him and remembered. 'Sergeant Dawson,' he called out. 'Have you had your arm treated?'

The sergeant jumped. 'Quite forgot, Colonel,' he said sheepishly, 'I'll do it at the next opportunity.'

Macdonell felt a spark of anger. 'I ordered you to see a surgeon, Sergeant. You disobeyed. Why?'

Before Dawson could reply, there was a cry of alarm from the rear. Macdonell looked round. A squadron of French Light Dragoons had appeared on the road and stood facing the line of Hussars. They kept their distance and showed no inclination to attack, but they were there, still and watchful. The eight miles to Mont St Jean would be harder, much harder, than the four they had covered. The Dragoons wheeled and cantered off back down the road. Their presence had somehow been more disquieting than a full-blooded charge. In a matter of minutes, Marshal Ney would know exactly where the rear of the Allied army was.

The Hussars watched them go. All but one held their position across the road. A single man cantered back and into the village. The cavalry would need reinforcements.

The sergeant's arm temporarily forgotten, Macdonell returned to the village. The main road through it was still blocked. He did not waste time finding out why but hurried back to find Harry. 'Harry, we cannot get through yet and I dare not go around for fear of exposing British backsides to French sabres. Find the best defensive positions you can and tell them to hold their fire until I give the word. We do not want to waste ammunition or shoot a Hussar. We will hope the cavalry holds them and withdraw through the village when we can.'

As if they had heard him, a larger troop of Hussars – perhaps a hundred of them – came trotting up to join their comrades. They formed an extended double line across the road and the fields.

It did not take long for the first Dragoons to appear and when they did the captain of the Hussars ordered an immediate charge. Black plumes waving in the breeze, swords unsheathed and held upright, they galloped straight at the Dragoons, giving them little time to organise themselves.

The engagement was brief and bloody. A hundred or so Hussars surrounded fifty French Dragoons and slaughtered them like cattle. Swords skewered bodies and men screamed. Macdonell stood beside Gooch and Hervey and watched. He had almost forgotten what a cavalry engagement was like. 'Wish you were in a cavalry regiment, gentlemen?' he asked, without taking his eyes from the fight. Both shook their heads.

Just one Dragoon managed to escape the circle. Alone, he galloped towards the village, brandishing his sword and shouting his loyalty to France. He was a brave man, but doomed. Macdonell took Dawson's musket, waited until the Dragoon was thirty yards away, and shot him through the eye. The man fell to one side, his foot trapped in a stirrup, and was dragged away over a field by his mount. Macdonell handed back the musket. 'Thank you, Sergeant,' he said quietly. 'A brave man. I would not have wished for anyone else to have killed him.'

The Dragoons could only have been a scouting party and none of them had escaped back to their lines. The Hussars had bought them time. But probably not much of it. The French would soon wonder where their scouts had got to, fear the worst, and send more forward. And if they brought up artillery, there would be carnage. Streets blocked or not, it was time to move.

Halfway through Genappe, they found the cause of the delay. At a sharp bend in the main street two wagons had tipped over, spilling ammunition and supplies onto the cobbles and injuring the horses. The wagons had blocked the road. They had to be unlimbered, righted and new horses found before the column could move on. Amid the confusion, that had taken the best part of an hour. Cursing himself for not having gone forward to take charge of the mess, Macdonell led the companies through and to the road beyond the village. There they re-formed on the right. Behind them, the Hussars formed a screen across the entire width of the retreating army.

The rain which had come and gone for more than a night and a day now settled in for the afternoon. Dripping and miserable, they trudged on, never far from the rear of the column and hoping that they were safe behind the Hussars. An hour passed, then another. Macdonell reckoned they had marched four miles and had four more to Mont St Jean. There were no more villages on the road, just squelching earth and puddles of mud. The rain battered the rye and filled the streams. It went through trousers and overalls like paper, it doubled the weight of a man's pack and it flowed like a waterfall off his shako.

Harry rode up to Macdonell with an oilskin over his shoulders. 'At least no one will go thirsty,' he said. 'And there has been no sign of the frogs. Perhaps they are sheltering from it.'

'I doubt it, Harry,' replied James. 'Ney will be promising the first man to kill one of us the Emperor's undying gratitude. They will be galloping up the road, sabres at the ready and dreaming of a life of ease and wealth at the Emperor's expense. I am only surprised that none of them has arrived yet.'

'I hate this, James. Retreating like this. The French at our backs and goodness knows what ahead. For all we know, Buonaparte has swept down like the wolf on the fold and torn Picton's and Alten's to shreds.'

'Showing off, Harry? I would not have taken you for a lover of Lord Byron.'

'Harrow, James. They taught us all manner of odd things. Poetry, Latin, geometry . . .' A shout penetrated the rain. They turned towards it. French Lancers. The Hussars had seen them and formed in line. But there was no point in taking chances. If the Lancers broke through, they would be on the infantry in seconds.

'Form square,' shouted Macdonell. 'Prepare to meet cavalry.' The weary men dragged themselves into squares around their officers, fumbled at their bayonets with slippery hands and prayed that the Hussars would save them from having to keep the Lancers at bay. In this weather, anything could happen. If a horse slipped and crashed into a square, it might break it open. And the exhausted men kneeling and crouching shoulder to shoulder and knee to knee knew it.

In the hands of an expert a lance was a brutal thing, needle-pointed and terrifying, its edges as sharp as a razor. A good lance was perfectly balanced and strong enough to withstand the impact of flesh or bone. There was no lancer more skilled than a French lancer and these Lancers had come to avenge their dead comrades in the Dragoons. They hurled themselves at the Brunswickers, heedless of the treacherous ground beneath their horses' hooves, heads down and lances poised to kill.

The disadvantage of the lance was that if the target slipped past its point, the lancer was as good as defenceless against a hacking sabre or swinging sword. Unmoving, the Hussars stood ready to receive the Lancers' charge.

The Brunswickers knew their business. They were there to protect the Allied army from attack from the rear or the flanks. To do that they must prevent pursuing cavalry from reaching the light companies at its rear. They met the charge of the Lancers in tight formation, deflecting the wicked blades with their sabres and thrusting under and round them into unprotected chests and stomachs. Even when a lance found its target, the lancer was as likely as not to be felled by the next man in line. If he did not pull the blade out before its victim fell, the lance would be lost and he would be at the mercy of sabre and sword. For every Hussar who fell, two or three lancers did the same.

The Lancers soon broke off the engagement and retired,

sent on their way by a volley of insults and jeers from the Brunswickers. Their captain trotted back to the infantry squares and raised his hat. He noticed that it had lost its splendid blue and gold plume, regarded it distastefully and threw it into the square. He was cheered back to his line.

Twice more over the next two hours the Brunswickers resisted attacks by French cavalry – the first by another troop of Lancers, the second by breast-plated cuirassiers. Each time Macdonell ordered squares to be formed but they were not needed. Thanks to the Hussars no Frenchman came within musket range.

As soon as the French cavalry disappeared, the squares broke up and the march continued. They had to hasten to make up lost ground on the wagons and artillery ahead. It took something out of them. Feet began to drag and heads to drop. But not for long. One of Harry Wyndham's songs, the rhythm beaten out on kettles and musket barrels, did wonders at reviving spirits.

On they marched between fields of rye and corn devastated by the rain, through puddles almost big enough to be called ponds and past exhausted soldiers huddled under hedges or prostrate on the roadside. Some were dead, others dying from their wounds or from plain fatigue. Their cries of distress were pitiful. There was no time to offer assistance. They must go on.

It was approaching six in the evening when some two hundred and sixty officers and men of General Byng's 2nd Brigade light companies reached the village of Planchenois, from where the land dipped into a shallow valley before rising gently up towards the ridge at Mont St Jean, becoming steeper nearer the top. James and Harry stopped and stared. It was like watching an army of ants on the move. Every yard of the road and overflowing into the fields on either side was alive with men and horses and artillery and wagons as far as they could see. James had to blink to convince himself that the road itself was not moving. On the ridge and its southern slope there was endless movement this way and that as if the ants were building a new nest.

'Have you ever seen anything like that?' asked Harry.

'Never. The Duke must be concentrating his entire force there.'

Harry stroked his chin. 'If Boney's strength is as they say, even this may not be enough to stop him. It would be reassuring to know that the Prussians are on their way.'

The final mile was the slowest. Men who could do no more than put one foot unthinkingly in front of the other trudged up the slope at the pace of those in front. Artillery teams urged their horses on with hand and whip. Dragoons rode up and down the ragged line calling absurdly for it to go faster. Unless it sprouted wings and flew, it could not.

Macdonell looked to their rear. There was no sign of the French, although they would be close. Their voltigeurs would be pushing forward through the cover of the rye, eager to pick off a retreating Englishman or two, and the best of Boney's infantry divisions would not be far behind. By nightfall, he reckoned the battle lines would be drawn.

Beyond Planchenois they passed an inn at the tiny hamlet of La Belle Alliance. To their left they had glimpses through copses of trees of a large farm at the base of the slope. Ahead there was another farm. When they reached this one they found

131

it being fortified with timber and stone by a company of the King's German Legion. Macdonell asked the farm's name. 'La Ferme de la Haye Sainte' he was told.

There was no doubting when they had finally reached the top of the ridge. On both sides, villages of tents and bivouacs stretched east and west, cannon were being heaved and dragged into lines and cavalry horses, safely tethered to trees or each other, were munching away at the sodden grass or at the handfuls of hay sprinkled over it. Farriers went from one to another, checking hooves and shoes. At least the animals had a feed.

At the summit a pair of mounted staff officers were directing traffic. One of them, in the uniform of a captain of the Life Guards, asked Macdonell his name and regiment. The captain consulted his list. 'General Cooke's division. To your left, Colonel, about two hundred yards.'

A single elm tree stood where the road met a rough lane. From there Macdonell let his eye rove over the landscape. To the north, arriving troops were making slow progress against a tide of camp followers heading away from danger. Wives and sweethearts, some carrying infants, others leading mules or pushing handcarts, walked alongside the baggage wagons. Macdonell knew the Duke well enough. Just as the captain of a frigate would order his deck cleared for action, Wellington would have ordered all unnecessary obstacles and impediments out of the way. And there were a lot of them. The exodus might go on all night.

To the east, regiments of cavalry – the redoubtable General Picton's one of them – were bivouacked north of the lane. A high thorny hedge separated them from the infantry on the other side. To the west, on the reverse side of the ridge and thus invisible from below, infantrymen built clusters of bivouacs or huddled around meagre fires while artillery pieces were heaved into place behind them. Further back, quartermasters' fourgons and ammunition wagons were parked in front of a dense wood. Behind them were the dressing stations. How typical of the peer, he thought, to have nature protect his rear with a wood, into which his infantry could dash for cover if they had to. On the south side of the ridge, the Duke had placed battalions of Netherlanders and Nassauers. Below them, open country was given shape and shadow by folds and hollows in the land. That would be their battleground. And how typical of the peer to have selected a ridge from which he would be able to observe the battle and issue orders. In the peninsula, he had done exactly that more than once.

He led the men in column down the rough lane to their left for about two hundred yards until he found General Cooke's Second Division, its colours, hanging limp and bedraggled, only just recognisable. As they turned off the lane and into the field, familiar faces looked up and shouted greetings. A few raised a hand in salute. Someone called out to Sergeant Dawson. Someone else lobbed a clump of grass at Lester and shouted at him to wipe himself down. 'Disgrace to the regiment you are, Joe Lester. Mud all over your new uniform. Get cleaned up.' Joseph Lester picked up the clod and threw it back, gleefully knocking over the man's tea.

They found patches of grass and earth and began to set up their bivouacs. They stuck their ramrods into the soft ground, and using the buttons and loops on their blankets to join them together, laid them across to make a roof. It was the Guards' own way – better than nothing and in the rain it allowed kettles to be boiled for tea, pipes to be lit and frozen hands to be warmed back to life. The muskets without ramrods and flints were stacked neatly among the bivouacs. Ignoring the hubbub and bustle all around, each man concentrated on his own small space and his own affairs.

James and Harry dismounted and watched. They would not settle themselves until the men had done so. Oddly, the Graham brothers were making no attempt to build a shelter or even to light a fire. Instead, they stood together, smoking their foul-smelling pipes, under a blanket draped over their heads. Harry asked them why they were not bivouacked. 'A feeling, sir,' replied James, 'that we are not yet finished for the day.'

'Not finished?' Harry was horrified. 'What else would you have us do?'

'Not us, Captain, His Grace. We've an idea he has more work for us before we get a rest.'

'What work would that be?'

Joseph scratched his beard and looked thoughtful. 'We do not know, Captain. It's just a feeling.'

'Well, I do hope you are mistaken.' The brothers sucked on their pipes and looked doubtful.

Sergeant Dawson, even with help from Joseph Lester, was struggling with his bivouac. James noticed that he was favouring his right arm and cursed. He had forgotten. 'Sergeant Dawson,' he called out, 'your arm. Let me see it, please.' The sergeant let his blanket fall and hurried over. He rolled up his sleeve and held out his arm. The wound had not healed. It was red and swollen and oozing a yellow pus. Macdonell lifted the arm and sniffed it. No trace of gangrene yet, but it needed attention quickly. Without it, the arm would go and then the patient. 'You must have it attended to at once.'

'Oh no, Colonel. I hate hospitals and surgeons. Some of their weapons are worse than sabres. The arm will be good as new in the morning.'

'Nonsense, Sergeant.' He summoned Joseph Lester. 'Escort the sergeant to the nearest dressing station and stay with him until his wound has been stitched and dressed.'

'Yes, sir. If he tries to escape I'll shoot him. Come on, Sergeant, you're my prisoner now.' Dawson fired a furious look at his colonel and trudged off with Lester.

James turned to Harry. 'Brave as a lion in battle yet terrified of surgeons. In that he is not alone. Now, gin, I rather fancy, Harry. Would you care to take a foraging party to find a quartermaster who has some and tell him it's badly needed here? Exaggerate our numbers a little if you have to.'

'Delighted, Colonel,' replied Harry. 'And what else would you like for your supper?'

'Beef and potatoes would serve, but I'll settle for whatever you can find.'

'Very good, Colonel. Leave it to me.'

James had not yet caught sight of Francis Hepburn. Unless he had found himself a more comfortable billet, Francis should be there. His battalion left Quatre Bras well before the light companies and he should by now be safely bivouacked. He asked a corporal in the Foot Guards where Hepburn might be found. 'Gone to the hospital, Colonel,' replied the corporal. 'Said he would be back soon.'

'Is he wounded?' asked Macdonell.

'Don't think so, Colonel.'

'Then why has he gone to the hospital?'

'Couldn't say, Colonel.'

'And I do not imagine you know where the hospital is, Corporal.'

'No, Colonel, I don't.' Francis Hepburn's whereabouts would have to wait. A strangely disgruntled Macdonell returned to his duties.

So much for new uniforms. Mud-splattered, ripped, sopping. Ruined beyond repair. And still it was raining. If it rained all night, would they be able to fight? Would a single musket fire or cannon roar? Would heavy cavalry horses not sink into the mud and gun carriages stick fast? A bizarre image of chess pieces immersed in bloody water crossed Macdonell's mind.

The Grahams were still making no effort to erect a bivouac. 'Muskets and powder dry, if you please, Corporals,' he said, 'even if you are as wet as an Irish summer.'

'Dry as tinder, Colonel,' replied Joseph, holding up his oilskin-covered musket for inspection.

'And in Ireland the sun always shines,' added his brother. 'It's just that you can't always see it.'

A troop of engineers had been touring the countryside and returned with their wagons loaded high with fence posts, doors, window frames, furniture and farm gates. They dumped the timber in heaps around the camp. The reverse side of the ridge was soon lit by scores of fires fuelled by dry wood and strong enough to resist the rain. Away to their right, towards the farm, James had noticed through the trees a huge fire had been lit. He wondered what the Duke would make of it.

Something rubbed against his thigh. The bullet. He pulled it out of his pocket and examined it again. Definitely too big to be French. It was time he had a word with Vindle.

Private Vindle was cowering in his bivouac, as ever with his accomplice Luke. 'Up, both of you,' he ordered, peering under the blanket. The two of them muttered something he could not hear and slithered out of the bivouac. 'You might as well hear this too, Luke,' he said, standing so close to them that they had to strain to see his face. He held out the bullet in his palm. 'I found this in my pack. It is a British bullet and it knocked me down when we were feigning retreat in the wood. Fortunately for me the idiot who fired it did not use enough powder and it was almost spent by the time it hit my pack.' He stared at Vindle. 'Did you fire it, Vindle?'

Vindle wiped his few strands of greasy hair from his eyes and tried to look affronted. 'I bloody well did not, Colonel. If I had mistaken you for a frog and fired in error, I would have said as much at the time and taken my punishment like a man. Luke will support me in that, won't you, Patrick?'

'I will, Colonel. A good soldier is Private Vindle and not one to mistake a red coat for a blue one or to spill his powder on the ground.'

Macdonell's temper was rising. Vindle had tried to kill him but he could not prove it. 'He is also a troublemaker and a thief, Private Luke, as are you,' he snarled. 'I trust neither of you and nor do Captain Wyndham and Sergeant Dawson. Tomorrow we will face Buonaparte. If you survive the day, we will speak of this again.' Leaving them standing in the rain, he stormed off.

Francis Hepburn was still nowhere to be seen. Macdonell asked another guard about him and received the same reply. It was worrying. He would not put it past Francis to hide a wound from his men and only seek medical help when there was no fighting to be done.

He was wondering whether to visit the hospital himself, wherever it was, to find Francis, when Harry returned. Three of his foraging party had sacks slung over their shoulders, the other two carried a large wooden cask. All six of them looked as cheerful as if they had been promoted to generals. 'Miserable lot, quartermasters, Colonel,' said Harry as he approached. 'Nothing but stale bread and biscuit and took a deal of persuading to let us have a drop of gin. He'll have watered it, of course. Put it there, gentlemen, please.' They placed the cask carefully on the ground and threw the sacks down beside it.

Macdonell prised open the lid of the cask and peered in. It was full. He lifted a sack and tipped its contents out. Loaves of bread, cheeses and a roasted chicken fell out. 'Funny-looking biscuit,' he said, and looked suspiciously at Harry. 'Where did you get it?' In Wellington's army, theft from local people was an offence, although everyone knew that it happened all the time. Buonaparte, on the other hand, expected his troops to survive off the land by taking what they wanted. That was why they were better fed than the British.

Harry shuffled his feet. 'Local man selling his wares. I

happened to find a few shillings someone had dropped and used them to pay him.'

Macdonell believed him for not a second. Harry Wyndham had dipped into his own pocket, deep admittedly, to buy the food. 'A lucky chance, indeed, Captain. Doubtless your health will be drunk around many fires this evening.'

From the direction of the crossroads the captain of the Life Guards who had directed them to their division trotted down the lane. 'Colonel Macdonell, His Grace offers his compliments and requests that you send the light companies of the 2nd Guards to the chateau at Hougoumont, on our right.' He pointed down the slope to the woods Macdonell had noticed earlier. The Château Hougoumont must be there. 'His Grace asks that they go immediately. Lord Saltoun will be following with the light companies of the 1st Guards. You are to occupy and fortify the chateau, farm and grounds. When you have given the order to move, kindly attend His Grace. He awaits you at his quarters in Waterloo.'

That was a surprise. Why would Wellington want to see him in person? 'Kindly inform His Grace that I shall carry out his orders immediately.'

Immediately. Supper would have to wait.

CHAPTER NINE

'His Grace's timing is, as ever, perfect,' said Harry when the captain had gone. 'We will take our supper at the Château Hougoumont.' Adding to one of his foragers, 'See if you can find a handcart to transport it.'

'Harry, fetch the Grahams, please.'

The Graham brothers, not quite able to suppress 'told-you-so' smirks, arrived with their packs on their backs and ready to march. 'You sent for us, Colonel,' said James.

'I did, Corporal. We are ordered at once to the Château Hougoumont. Not all the company were as prescient as you. Their blankets will be wet and heavy and they were not expecting to have to move again today. There will be mutterings and grumblings. As Sergeant Dawson has not yet returned from the dressing station, I need you to organise the dismantling of bivouacs, repacking of blankets and collection of muskets. Do what you can to keep their spirits up. In the sergeant's absence, report to Captain Wyndham.'

The two giants exchanged a look. 'Depend on us, Colonel. We'll have them down at the chateau in no time,' said Joseph.

'That we will, Colonel, but what about Mister Gooch and Mister Hervey?' asked James.

'Show them how it's done. Politely, mind.'

'Politely it is, Colonel.'

'Better be off, James,' said Harry. 'The peer waits for no man, or so they say. Leave everything to us. The corporals will carry them down one at a time if they have to.'

Most of the senior officers were billeted in the town of Waterloo and the surrounding villages, each name marked in chalk on the door of the appropriate house. Macdonell was shown into the Duke's quarters in a hotel in the main street of the town by a lieutenant of the Life Guards and escorted to a room off the entrance hall. The four men sitting around an oak table in the centre of the room were studying a large map. Two were smoking cigars. He stood in the doorway, shako in hand, and waited. None of the four acknowledged him. He coughed lightly. The man whose aquiline looks and startlingly direct gaze were as well known as any face in England sat at the head of the table. He looked up. 'Ah, Macdonell,' said Wellington affably, 'here you are. You know, of course, Generals Cooke and Byng, and this is Colonel de Lancey of my personal staff.'

Macdonell knew of de Lancey, an unusual soldier in the British army in that he was American by birth and very young to hold the position of Deputy Quartermaster General. He inclined his head politely. 'Gentlemen. Your servant.'

'Had you a hard time of it at Quatre Bras?' asked Wellington.

'Not as hard as some, Your Grace,' replied Macdonell. The Duke, not above a little boasting himself, could not abide it in others. A tiny smile played around his eyes.

'And your strength now?'

'Two hundred and sixty officers and men, sir.'

The Duke tapped a finger on the bridge of his long nose. 'It will have to be enough.' The other three nodded their agreement. 'Now, Macdonell,' went on the Duke, 'look at this map.' Macdonell stepped forward to peer over General Byng's shoulder. 'I have deployed our forces across the Mont St Jean ridge. It is the very ridge which my illustrious predecessor the Duke of Marlborough recommended as the best place on which to mount a defence of Brussels, should one ever be needed.' He looked up from the map. 'And by God it is needed now. Buonaparte's advance guard is already arriving from the south and is taking up position here.' He ran a finger along an imaginary line running through the inn at La Belle Alliance. 'As you see, we have the advantage of the ground. However, there are three vital points which hold the key to our success. One is the farm on our left flank at Papelotte, which I have entrusted to Prince Bernhard's Nassauers. The second is the farm of La Haye Sainte, in our centre, which the King's German Legion will defend.' He pointed to the farm they had passed on their march up the slope. 'The third is the chateau and farm at Hougoumont on our right wing. Here,' the Duke paused, 'I have already sent companies of Hanoverians and Nassauers to Hougoumont with orders to occupy the farm and the wood south of it and Saltoun will be taking the light companies of

General Maitland's 1st Brigade down to occupy the orchard. Macdonell, your companies will occupy the chateau, farm and garden.' The Duke turned to Colonel de Lancey. 'I gather the garden is rather fine, de Lancey. Such a pity to ruin it but there it is. In addition, you will have overall command of the defence of the position. Any questions?'

'Are you expecting Marshal Blücher, Your Grace?'

'I certainly am. Blücher has promised to be here tomorrow. If we hold the three positions until he arrives, the battle will be won. If not . . .' The Duke let the thought hang in the air. It was clear enough. The Guards must hold Hougoumont. 'General Byng's main force will be positioned on the rising ground to the north of the chateau,' went on Wellington, pointing to the map. 'From there he will provide covering artillery fire. It might be the time to give Major Bull's howitzers a chance to show us what they can do, Byng, don't you agree?'

'I do, Your Grace,' replied Byng in his thoughtful way.

The Duke leant back in his chair. 'You know, Buonaparte once said that he never went into battle with a plan. He simply attacked in strength and then reacted to what his enemy did. Arrant nonsense, of course. Boney has a plan and it is to take Hougoumont. If he does, it will expose my right flank and give him the road to Brussels. That must not happen.'

For the first time, General Cooke spoke. 'Our intelligence is that Buonaparte has put his brother Prince Jérôme, under General Reille, in command of the attack on the chateau. That signifies how much importance he attaches to it.'

'I understand, General. Hougoumont must be held.'

'We will review your defences early tomorrow,' said Wellington, rising from his chair. 'Be about your business now, and may good fortune be with you.'

As Macdonell was leaving the house, he stopped for a moment in the hall to check his dress in a long mirror. While adjusting his collar he heard de Lancey tell the Duke that he had given a tired man with tired troops a fiendishly hard task. 'Ah,' came the reply, 'but you do not know Macdonell.'

CHAPTER TEN

He trotted the three miles back to the ridge and along the lane, where he found all but a handful of the company gone. 'Make haste, you men,' he urged the stragglers. 'There is little light left and we have work to do.'

'Our blankets are sodden, Colonel,' complained one of them. 'It is the devil's own job to get them into our packs.'

Macdonell was on the point of telling the wretched man to try harder when a flash of lightning streaked across the evening sky. It was followed by a deep, echoing roll of thunder. The weather, capricious and unforgiving, had yet to relent. 'There was a thunderstorm on the eve of our victory at Salamanca,' he told them. 'A good omen, to be sure.' Two horses, spooked by the thunder, bolted past them and galloped down the slope towards the French. 'There you are, even the horses cannot wait to attack the frogs. Make haste to the farm, now.'

The lane leading to the chateau ran along the crest of the

ridge for three hundred yards. Macdonell picked his way carefully along it and down the incline, already churned to mud by the coming and goings of men and horses and wagons. He joined a sunken lane which ran between thick thorn hedges separating it from a corn field to his left and a grassy slope to his right. The top of the slope would be where General Byng would place his artillery, complete with Major Bull's fearsome howitzers.

Once in the sunken lane he could see very little of his surroundings, but then very little would be seen of him. The lane ran for about a hundred and fifty yards before opening into a clearing in front of the north gate of the farm. It would make an excellent position for troops hidden in the hedge.

It was a thick oak gate, with two panels ten feet high and iron fixings, open to allow access to a constant flow of traffic. It was attached on one side to the wall of a long stable or cowshed and on the other to a small brick outhouse. A troop of Nassauers stood guard in the clearing. Inside the gates, a wagon parked in the yard alongside an ancient draw well was being unloaded by Nassauers and Hanoverians and its supply of ammunition moved into the farm grounds by a chain passing boxes of powder and shot from one to another. To Macdonell's surprise, the operation was being supervised by Sergeant Dawson. He dismounted and asked a private to take his horse to a stable. 'Sergeant Dawson, may I take it that you have attended a dressing station?' he demanded.

'I have, Colonel, and been passed fit.' Dawson rolled back his sleeve to reveal his arm, now covered by a well-used bandage. 'Stitched up nicely, it is. No need for the forceps, thank the Lord. I'd rather face a French lancer than a surgeon with forceps.'

'As would we all, Sergeant. Is there any water in the well?'

'A little, Colonel, from the rain.'

'Ration it carefully. Where is Captain Wyndham?'

'In the house, Colonel, seeing to the dispositions. There are two stables for the horses and a cowshed. Plenty of cover for us, too.'

'Good. Carry on, Sergeant.' Macdonell crossed the yard to the entrance of the house. It was a modest chateau, no larger than Glengarry, brick-built and, in parts, ancient. A tall tower, once perhaps a watchtower, stood on the north-east corner with a tiny chapel nearby. The entrance hall was dark and dusty and smelt of rats. There was no furniture and no decoration on the walls. It must have lain empty for some years.

A narrow flight of stairs led to the upper floor. Macdonell took them two at a time. In a bedroom facing south he found Harry Wyndham with Gooch and Hervey. They had opened the window shutters and were aiming muskets out towards the wood.

'Not much chance of hitting anything from up here,' said Harry, 'unless they break into the yard. Even then, we'd just as likely kill some of our own.'

James looked for himself. Harry was right. The chateau was high enough to afford a clear line of fire over the walls surrounding the farm, but only into the wood. An attacker between the edge of the wood and the wall of the farm would be safe. 'Two men at each window in case they do break in,' he ordered, 'and the lower floor will do for the wounded if we need it. We'll use the large barn by the north gate first for casualties. If you would see to that, Captain Wyndham, we will inspect the rest of our billet. Follow me, gentlemen.'

They retraced their steps and climbed a second staircase, this one narrow and spiral, to the top of the tower. There Harry had already stationed four men, who had heaved boxes of ammunition up the stairs and were busy preparing their position. One of them was Private Lester. 'Good evening, Lester,' Macdonell greeted him. 'Comfortable billet for you, I see. Should be able to land a few solid blows from here.'

'That we will, Colonel,' replied Lester. 'Fish in a barrel, they'll be. We can hardly wait to get started.'

'Watch the woods. That's where they'll come from and they'll have to cross open ground to get to the gate. Take care, though. If there is any risk of hitting a red jacket, hold your fire.' Macdonell looked out of the window. A house built above a gate on the south side blocked his view but he could see over the roofs of the two buildings either side of it and, to his left, over the garden and orchard towards the ridge at Mont St Jean. In the fading light he could just make out the fires of the troops stationed on the crest of the ridge. From here it was possible to shoot into the clearing outside the gate.

'Rely on us, sir.'

'Make haste, gentlemen. We must complete our inspection before dark.' Macdonell led the two ensigns back down the stairs and into a second courtyard, where the ammunition boxes were being opened and their contents distributed. Men were running in and out of the three buildings that formed the south wall of the enclosure.

'Small stable on the left, storage shed on the right, gardener's house in the middle over the gate, Colonel,' pointed out Gooch. 'No windows in the first two, so we're making loopholes in the brick, but the house is well placed to defend the gate. I have ordered some of the floorboards above the gate to be pulled up to make firing holes.'

'Have the gate opened, please,' said Macdonell. 'I must see it from outside, as the French will see it.' Unlike the north gate, this one consisted of a single oak panel.

'Colonel, French voltigeurs may be in the woods,' said Hervey. 'You might be better advised to stay within the walls.'

Macdonell stared hard at the ensign. 'Nonsense, Hervey. And when you are in command of a battalion, I trust you too will venture outside walls. Kindly open the gate.' Hervey mumbled an apology and ordered the crossbar lifted and the gates unlocked.

Ignoring the crack of musket fire, which they could now clearly hear, they stood in an open clearing about thirty yards long with their backs to the wood, and inspected the outside walls. They too were red brick, certainly not proof against round shot but adequate cover from muskets. The house had five windows on the upper level above the gate and three to one side below. The garden wall extended out at right angles from the house. 'This is where they will attack in force. As many muskets as you can in the windows,' ordered Macdonell. 'We shall need unbroken fire from the moment they show their faces. Who have we in the woods?'

'Hanoverians, Lüneburgs and Nassauer Jägers,' replied Gooch, as if he had ordered them there himself. The

Hanoverians and Lüneburgs were good troops – sharpshooters of whom many had been gamekeepers. The Dutch Nassauers were less reliable.

'Have either of you been in to take a look?' asked Macdonell. Neither of them had. 'Then you will wish to accompany me after our inspection.'

Back inside the walls, they made their way across the yard to a narrow gate leading to the formal garden of which Wellington had spoken admiringly. Surrounded by a brick wall about seven feet high, it had been laid out in four square parterres separated by gravel paths and each planted with flowers of a different colour. Adjoining the wall by the south gate, a small kitchen garden had been planted with cabbages, onions and peas. Until that day it would have been as fine a garden as any of them had seen. Now the beds were trampled and strewn with debris and the paths covered in soil and pitted with potholes and ruts. 'Quite a contrast to the chateau it must have been,' Macdonell said. 'And I fear it has little time left.'

'Someone has more love for the garden than the house,' agreed Hervey. 'Perhaps the gardener still lives in the house over the gate.'

Gooch laughed. 'Then let us hope he has retired to somewhere safer.'

Men scurried about fetching and carrying ammunition boxes and lengths of timber. Some were using their bayonets to fashion loopholes in the walls. Others hammered at loose bricks with the butts of their muskets. The timber they were hammering into makeshift fire steps set against the walls. James Graham had found a long wooden bench, which he was heaving into position at the far end of the garden. They walked over to him. 'Corporal Graham, how goes the work?' asked Macdonell.

Graham put down the bench and stretched his back. 'There is much to do, Colonel. We could do with some engineers with picks and hammers. And we haven't enough nails for the steps.'

'I will see what I can do. Meanwhile search the barns and sheds. Tear them apart if you have to.'

Beyond the garden wall was an orchard, reached by another narrow door. In the orchard Lord Saltoun's light companies were doing what they could to reinforce the hedge that ran round it. They had felled some of the fruit trees and were using them to plug holes. Alexander Fraser, Lord Saltoun, although only thirty, had already seen service in Spain and France, had a reputation for fearlessness and had caught the eye of the Duke. That, no doubt, was why he had been chosen to lead the defence of the orchard. He saw Macdonell and put down the axe with which he was felling an apple tree. 'James, I am pleased to see you in one piece. What is your strength?' Saltoun was not a man to waste words.

'Two hundred and sixty,' replied Macdonell. 'And yours?'

'About the same. Not enough to hold this position for long. The hedge is too patchy to be much use and they will attack in force. I propose that we hold on as long as we can and then withdraw into the lane or the garden. We might be able to defend the garden wall.' There was a crack of thunder above their heads. 'Heaven's artillery or French cannon?'

'The former, I trust. The orchard is yours, Alexander. I will command the house and garden. Between us we must keep the frogs out. The Duke insists.'

'In that case, we certainly must.'

There was a yell of warning from the far end of the orchard. 'Frenchies. In the field.'

'Infantry or cavalry?' called Saltoun.

'Infantry, Colonel.'

'If you can see them, shoot them.' They ran between the apple trees to the hedge where a line of men had poked their muskets through the branches and were firing on the enemy who had taken shelter behind the chestnut trees that dotted the fields beyond.

A corporal who was reloading turned to speak to them. 'Only a small patrol, sir. And a bit smaller now. Two or three down.' There was a short burst of firing from the field, then silence. 'Emptied their muskets and gone, I think, sir.'

'Good. Keep a close watch in case they return uninvited,' replied Saltoun.

'A look at the other entrances and then we will explore the woods,' said Macdonell, striding back to the farm.

The west gate, set beside the barn, was no more than a door – easily barricaded and defended. 'Whatever you can find to reinforce it and a small troup nearby,' he ordered.

The north gate, through which wagons were still arriving from the ridge, was a different matter. It was sturdy enough and unlikely to be struck by round shot or shell fired over the farm and chateau, but not impregnable. And it would have to be kept open or at least opened to allow men and wagons to enter. 'Twenty men here, if you please, Mister Gooch, and timber ready to reinforce the gate if necessary.'

'Yes, sir,' replied Gooch.

'May I command this position, Colonel?' asked Hervey.

'Why would you wish to do that, Mister Hervey?'

'A feeling, sir, that this gate will prove vital.'

'In that case, Mister Hervey, you may indeed command the position.' Macdonell turned to Gooch. 'And lest I am accused of being less than even-handed, Mister Gooch, you will command the south gate. Sergeant Dawson will be with you. The corporals will assist Mister Hervey. Is there anything else you can think of, gentlemen?'

'We will have men in the tower and the chateau, at all the gates and around the walls and the orchard. We shall be spread thin, Colonel,' replied Hervey.

'We shall. There is little I can do about it.'

'Wounded in the chateau and the barn, Colonel,' said Gooch, 'but we have no medical staff.'

'We will make do until we get some.' Sergeant Dawson was still supervising the unloading of supply wagons. 'May I borrow your musket, Sergeant?' he asked. 'We are taking a look in the woods while there is still enough light to see our noses.'

The sergeant handed Macdonell his musket. 'Take care, Colonel, you will be needed tomorrow.'

'I shall, Sergeant. Come on, gentlemen, and kindly remember that Nassauers wear green. In this light, green and blue are easily confused. Be careful at what you take aim.'

They left the farm by the open north gate, walked around the west side and entered the wood from the clearing outside the south gate, where hay had been stacked for the animals. The trees were mostly young oak – not dense – and evening light still penetrated the canopy. As he had in the wood outside

Gemioncourt, Macdonell immediately felt uneasy. He took several deep breaths and ordered himself not to be foolish. It was only a wood, not an African jungle full of wild beasts.

The wood sloped away from the chateau. They made their way cautiously down towards sporadic musket fire coming from deeper within the wood, until they saw the backs of green jackets crouching and kneeling behind trees. They could just make out the green plume and orange sash of a Jäger officer, his sword drawn, standing on a fallen tree. He was peering into the gloom and directing the fire of his troops. Macdonell called out to him. 'Captain, we are from the light companies of the British 2nd Brigade. We are coming up behind you.'

The captain turned and acknowledged them. 'As well you warned us, Colonel,' he said cheerfully. 'My men are nervous in here.'

'As are we, Captain. What is your situation?'

'We hold the wood but for the extreme southern edge. The French are camped in a shallow valley beyond and are keeping us at bay with musket fire. I sent a small troop to reconnoitre from the east. They report that the French have been receiving reinforcements and have brought up artillery.' It was not difficult to guess what the artillery would be firing at.

'I fear it will be a wet and miserable night for you and your men, Captain. We must hold the woods until the morning. Then we will see what the enemy's plans are.'

'I understand, Colonel. Wet and miserable is the lot of the Jäger. We are quite used to it.' He held out a hand to Macdonell. 'May tomorrow bring us glory.'

'I will settle for victory, Captain, glorious or not. Until tomorrow.'

So the woods were probably safe until dawn. But then the French would throw men into them and the Jägers and Nassauers would be forced to withdraw or they would need reinforcements. And unless General Cooke was willing to provide reinforcements, there would be none. The chateau and farm were thinly enough defended as it was.

Harry was waiting for them at the south gate. 'Relieved to see you, Colonel,' he greeted them, 'and you, gentlemen. How did you find the woods?'

'Unpleasant, thank you, Captain, but in good hands for now. Has any food been sent down?'

'Not yet, although we have a barrel of gin and the bits we foraged. And there is a pig in the barn.'

'So it's pork for supper and a cup of gin all round. Mister Gooch, see to the pig, if you please. Sergeant Dawson is handy with a butcher's knife. A piece for every man to go with the food Captain Wyndham managed to acquire for us. Mister Hervey, kindly take over from the sergeant. We may expect wagons to be coming and going most of the night. Captain Wyndham and I will make another inspection.'

'How will they do, James, do you think?' asked Harry when the ensigns had gone.

'Well enough, although this is likely to be the hardest fighting any of us have seen. The French are in a valley beyond the wood with artillery coming up. We will be bombarded and attacked on three sides. Only the west wall is anywhere near secure. And I gather that Buonaparte's brother Jérôme commands them. He will doubtless get all the men he asks for.'

They started with the farm buildings. The high points on the roofs of the cowshed and farmer's house had been made ready. Tiles had been removed and holes made for access. A man lying on his stomach on the cowshed would have a clear view of the area outside the north gate while being protected by the pitch of the roof. Men on the farmer's house would get some protection from the gable end and would be able to cover the garden. It was the same on the south side where the roofs of the gardener's house, the small stable and the shed adjoining it were being made ready. Stacks of muskets and boxes of ammunition had been placed inside the windows, and loopholes made in the brickwork. 'Good work, Harry,' said Macdonell. 'The question is, will it be enough?'

And there was still much to do. The garden was the best part of a hundred yards long and fifty wide. A loophole every five yards on three sides meant fifty loopholes, each one of which had to be hammered out of the brick. There was enough timber to build fire steps, but a dearth of nails. 'Have you looked in the store and the sheds?' asked Macdonell.

'We have. We found very little of use.'

Macdonell grunted. To lose Hougoumont for want of nails would be absurd. Not that it was likely to come to that. Round shot and shells from the French artillery on the other side of the wood would be their biggest worry. They would have to rely on General Byng's cannon and Major Bull's howitzers to protect them from those. 'Let us see how Colonel Saltoun is faring.'

In the orchard, the light companies of the 1st Brigade

were also struggling. The hedge still looked a hopelessly feeble obstacle against attacking infantry. A good cavalry horse might even jump it. Saltoun clearly thought so too. 'For God's sake, man,' he bellowed at a soldier working on the hedge, 'that wouldn't stop my old mother. Get some timber into the hole.'

The wretched man looked up from his task. His face and uniform were caked in grime and mud and he was barely able to speak from exhaustion. 'Haven't got any, sir,' he mumbled.

'Then go and find a dead frog and shove him in there. There are two or three in the field.' The soldier shambled off. 'About turn, Private. I was jesting. But for the love of God make a better job of it. There will be timber in the farm buildings. Go and get it.' He saw James. 'Thankfully there is a ditch on the other side of the hedge. Without it we wouldn't last ten minutes.'

It was nearly dark and the rain had started again. James took off his shako and looked to the heavens. 'Will it never stop?'

'Never. If Nelson were alive, Wellington would send for him at once. It is ships we'll need, not horses.'

'You know Harry Wyndham, of course, my captain?'

'I do, and pleased to have you with us, Captain.'

'I trust you will be able to say the same at this time tomorrow, My Lord.'

'Hah. Well spoken, Captain. How goes the work at the farm?'

'Well enough,' replied Macdonell.

'Good. In that case, James, I propose that we meet in the farmer's house at ten. There are matters to discuss.'

'Very well. Ten o'clock.'

In addition to supply wagons arriving at the north gate, a succession of officers had begun appearing, having ridden down the sunken lane from the ridge. They too knew that Hougoumont would hold the key to the battle and wanted to see for themselves how well defended it would be. Most offered a few words of encouragement and did not stay long. Being nearer to the French lines than their own made them nervous. A tiresome captain of Hussars insisted on riding around the entire perimeter and giving his opinion, loudly, on what should be done to improve their chances of keeping the French out. Very politely James suggested that he might like to dismount and lend a hand. The captain was soon gone.

It was dark when Francis Hepburn appeared. 'Francis,' exclaimed James, 'I had almost forgotten you. They said you were at the hospital. Are you wounded?'

Francis looked sheepish. 'No, no, unhurt. I merely thought to check on the medical arrangements. Every house in Mont St Jean is ready to take casualties and there is a hospital in Waterloo.'

'You were a long time. Is everything in order there?'

'Oh, yes, quite in order.'

'Then why so long? I was concerned.'

'Dammit, James. Can a man not be allowed a little privacy? If you must know, Daisy is in the village helping the surgeons. They are dealing with the wounded from yesterday. She travelled down from Enghien and arrived this morning. Clever girl managed to get a message to me.'

'I should have guessed. Brave and devoted. I do hope she knows what she has let herself in for.'

'Do any of us know, James?'

'Perhaps not. Now do inspect the premises if you wish.'

'I shall. Then I must return to my post. God be with you, James.'

'And with us all.'

Saltoun was waiting in the empty farmhouse, which had been stripped of its doors and furniture. There was neither table nor chair, nor even an upturned crate, but except where rain dripped through the hole made in the roof, at least it was dry. Laid out on a blanket on the floor were two bottles of claret, a loaf of bread and a small cut of beef. 'I thought we would eat while we talk, James,' said Saltoun. 'I daresay you are hungry.'

'Ravenous. As are my men. Fortunately, Wyndham acquired a little food from a trader and we found a pig in the cowshed.'

Saltoun cut a slice of beef with his bayonet and passed it to Macdonell. 'Try that, James. No glasses, I fear. We'll have to drink from the bottle.'

The beef was good and the wine better. 'Excellent, Alexander,' he said, raising his bottle in salute, 'but I must be about my business very soon.'

'Of course. And tomorrow will either of us be alive to finish our meal, I wonder? I am not entirely sure whether Wellington really thinks we can hold out or whether we are merely a diversion intended to lure troops away from the French centre. Either way, even with the Hanoverians and Nassauers we are no more than eight hundred or so.'

'We are outnumbered everywhere, Alexander. The Duke will send reinforcements if he can spare them. He expects Blücher's

Prussians to arrive sometime tomorrow. Our task is to hold Hougoumont until they do.'

Saltoun tipped wine into his mouth. 'To do that, some of us must stay alive. That is what will be difficult. The orchard is our weakest spot. I will hold it only as long as we are not in danger of being wiped out. There is no point in sacrificing men unnecessarily for the sake of it. We will withdraw when we have to.'

'I agree. As long as we hold the garden and the house and farm, the frogs will not be able to attack the Duke's right flank. That is his main concern.'

For a while they were silent, each alone with his own thoughts. Suddenly, Saltoun jumped up. 'Frogs, always the frogs. Ever since the Normans arrived, it's been the frogs. Now and again we fight the Spanish or the Dutch, even the American rebels or ourselves, but it doesn't last long. We always go back to the frogs, damn them. Why?'

'I am but a humble soldier, Alexander,' replied James with a smile. 'Such questions are for politicians. Now, if you would excuse me, I must be gone. We will be using the large barn for the wounded. There is dry straw in there. I am hoping for a surgeon and an assistant or two. Send your wounded there.'

'Thank you, James. Until tomorrow.'

Despite the rain a fire had been lit in the yard over which the pig was being cooked on a makeshift spit. While Sergeant Dawson kept a line of hungry soldiers at bay, the Grahams were hacking chunks off the beast. Two men were fighting over a scrap of meat that had fallen on the ground. One of them was the weasel-faced Patrick Luke. Another was complaining loudly that he had been given only a bit of pig's head, barely cooked and foul-smelling. 'If you had waited until the bloody thing was cooked,' yelled the sergeant, 'it would have tasted a sight better.' He was ignored. The aroma of roasting meat was too much for men who had eaten almost nothing for two days. They stuffed whatever they could get into their mouths and tried to swallow it whole. Some retched and coughed their prize into the dirt, others managed to wash it down with a cup of water or gin. Macdonell, who had enjoyed several slices of well-cooked beef, could not help feeling a little guilty.

'It's a full-grown pig,' he told Dawson. 'Enough to go round, and do not forget the guards in the orchard.'

In the chateau, the men stationed at the windows were sitting with their backs to the wall, leaving just one to keep watch. They had seen nothing outside the south gate or in the wood. It was the same in the tower, where Private Lester was playing a tune on a child's whistle while his comrades sat or lay on the floor. Macdonell told them to send a man down to fetch their share of the pig and to get what rest they could.

Inside the south gate, Ensign Gooch's troop was standing to arms, ready to act if a warning came from the gardener's house above it. They had used thick timbers as props for the gate. 'Have them rest in the house, Mister Gooch,' Macdonell ordered. 'As much rest as possible for every man. Including yourself.'

Ensign Hervey at the north gate had already sent half of his troop to the barn, while he kept watch with the remainder. 'It will be light at four, Colonel,' he said. 'I intend two hours on guard and three hours rest in the barn for each man.'

In the garden Harry had placed a man at every loophole and sent the rest to find shelter. 'How did the meeting with Lord Saltoun go?' he asked. 'I looked in on the farmer's house to make sure all was well but you had finished.'

'It did not take long,' replied Macdonell.

'No, indeed. Surprising choice of claret, though.' They must have left the empty bottles there.

'Would you believe me if I told you that we found the bottles in the house?'

'No.'

'Then I won't. Have you managed to build sufficient fire steps?'

'Barely. We have a shortage of nails, not to mention carpenters. Some of the steps look like the bell tower in Pisa. Have you seen it?'

'Never, although I know it is still standing, despite being crooked. Have faith, Harry. And don't forget to get some rest yourself.'

The faint sound of singing reached them from the direction of the wood. 'There, James, can you hear them?' asked Harry. 'They've been at it for an hour. Singing away like choirboys.'

'They are camped without shelter in a narrow valley beyond the wood. They're singing to keep their spirits up. As long as they don't keep us awake, let them sing.'

For the first time, Macdonell realised how tired he was. Until then the need to keep going had driven him on. Now, suddenly, his eyelids were drooping and an irresistible urge to sleep took over. He found a place in the barn, kicked straw into a pile and lay down. Around him, exhausted men snored, scratched and grunted. Their colonel heard nothing. Within seconds he too was asleep.

He was woken by someone gently shaking his shoulder. He struggled briefly back to consciousness. There was an urgent voice in his ear. 'Colonel, General Byng is here.' It sounded like Hervey. His eyes closed and he was asleep again. The voice was insistent. 'Colonel, General Byng.' With a huge effort he pushed himself up. He shook sleep from his head and stood up. Stupid oaf, he thought, I should never have allowed myself to lie down.

'Where is the general?' he croaked. Hervey passed him a canteen of water.

'At the north gate, Colonel.'

He tipped water down his throat and splashed a little on his face. It helped. 'Brush me down, if you please, Hervey.' Hervey used his hand to sweep straw from Macdonell's jacket and trousers. 'What is the time?'

'Two o'clock. It will be light in two hours.'

Byng had ridden down from the ridge and was waiting in the small yard inside the north gate. An aide was holding his horse. 'Ah, James, getting some rest, I trust.'

'I was, sir. At least here we have some cover from the rain.'

'You do. Bivouacs are little use in these conditions. Our only consolation is that the French must be just as wet.'

'What are their movements, General?'

'They have been bringing up troops during the night. Their front line is centred on the inn at La Belle Alliance. The Duke is convinced that Buonaparte will try to take Hougoumont before launching his main attack. Reille will of course have artillery and cavalry as well as infantry. You may expect all three.'

'We will be ready, General, although the orchard is vulnerable.'

'I know. Saltoun will keep them out for as long as he can. Above all we must hold the farm and chateau. Take no risks. You will need every man you've got. Patch up the wounded and send them back to work.'

'We could do with medical staff, General. We have none.'

'None? An oversight, I imagine. I will find you a surgeon. Anything else?'

'Nails, General, please. For the fire steps. We asked for more but they haven't come.'

Byng laughed. 'That's the first time I've been asked for nails. I'll see what I can do.' He turned to his aide. 'Nails and medics, Thomas. Don't forget.'

'I will not forget, General.'

'My artillery is in place on the hill behind us,' went on Byng. 'Major Bull's howitzers will be joining us when it is light. We will do everything we can to support you.'

'Thank you, General.'

'It is you whom I look forward to thanking tomorrow night, James. *Bonne chance.*'

CHAPTER ELEVEN

18th June

Dawn was breaking and the rain, at long last, had stopped. For James Macdonell there had been no more sleep. He had spent the two hours since General Byng's visit checking and rechecking their defences, trying to think of anything more they could do, and searching for words of encouragement for five hundred weary, miserable men.

From the top of the tower there was a cry of 'cavalry'. He ran through the garden gate to the wall and climbed onto a fire step. Two hundred yards away a squadron of cuirassiers, the rising sun glinting off their breastplates and helmets, had appeared from behind the wood. He watched them come closer until they were just within musket range, where they halted. A cuirassier officer took out a glass and ran his eye over the garden wall and the hedge around the orchard. 'Hold your fire,' shouted Macdonell. The chances of a correct shot were slim and there was no point in revealing their firing positions. The cuirassiers soon turned their mounts and cantered back to their lines.

Harry Wyndham appeared beside James. 'Fortunate that a box of iron nails came down in an ammunition wagon last night, James,' he said, 'otherwise that step would not have held your weight.'

James stepped down. '*Bonjour*, Harry. Let us hope the general sends down a surgeon as well as the nails. How was the night?'

'Uncomfortable, but quiet. Those are the first frogs we have seen today. Most of us managed a little rest. I have ordered fires. If there is any food, it would be welcome. No more of that pig, though. It was foul.'

'We should get some food soon. The supply wagons are back and forth like flies.' He looked up at the sky. It was clear. 'No more rain, I think. Order powder and flints checked and barrels cleared.'

'There will be some beyond help,' replied Harry. 'Their springs will be wet and useless.'

'Replace them from the spares in the chateau.' A thought occurred to him. 'Is it not Sunday, today?'

'It is, James. The Duke has chosen a Sunday for his battle. And I think I shall have a shave. I might be too busy later.'

James strode back to the chateau. The tiny red-brick chapel beside its south face could not have accommodated more than a dozen worshippers.

He thought at first that it was completely empty. No altar, no lectern, no seat of any kind. He knelt on the stone floor with his back to the door and recited the Lord's Prayer. He could think of no other. He longed to stay there but there was much to be done.

He rose to leave and glanced up. The chapel was not quite empty. Above the door a wooden carving of Christ on the cross had been attached to the wall. It was almost life-size and undamaged. He bowed his head. It was a good sign.

In the barn, in the chateau, in the houses and sheds and the stables, those who were not standing to arms were eating whatever they had – biscuit, a scrap of meat, a lump of bread – writing letters, and checking their weapons. No food or drink had arrived from the quartermaster's stores behind the lines on the ridge. In the yards and the garden, they sat around fires, or stretched their backs and legs to rid them of the night's stiffness. Here and there, Macdonell heard a prayer being recited. Very soon every man would be standing to arms.

The south gate, under Henry Gooch, was closed and barricaded. A rusty iron bedstead had been wedged against the timbers. It was a single-panel gate, perhaps eight feet wide and ten feet high. The French would move heaven and earth to force it. The guards would defend it with tooth and nail and fist and foot.

The north gates, where James Hervey commanded twenty men, were open for the wagons still trundling down the sunken lane. As Macdonell watched, a wagon carrying medical supplies arrived. In it sat three men – a scarlet-coated surgeon and two bandsmen to act as assistants. They jumped out and presented themselves. The surgeon introduced himself as Sellers. He carried two saws, his assistants held canvas bags in which there would be a variety of probing tools, pliers, needles, thread, knives and dressings. There was a small pile of blankets in the wagon. 'We have set aside the lower floor of the chateau and the barn to your right for the wounded,' Macdonell told them. 'Is there anything you need?'

'We have the tools of our trade, Colonel,' replied Sellers, holding up a saw. 'No opiates or spirits, I'm afraid, but the locals have donated blankets. If you have gin it would be welcome.'

'If we have, it will be delivered to you. And there is a little water in the well. The Duke's orders are to minimise casualties and to throw any man who can fire a musket back into the fray. Put them back together, sir, if you please, and send them out.'

Sellers nodded. 'We will, Colonel.'

The sun had risen and the French might attack at any time. It was time to close the north gates. Macdonell gave the order and left Hervey to carry it out. Bring in the guards, bar the gates and defend them from the wall and the roofs. No French foot must be allowed to enter the yard. Open the gates only for a supply wagon or reinforcements and close them again at once.

From the shed in the south-west corner of the enclosure came the sounds of voices raised in anger. Macdonell strode over. 'I don't give a bucket of shit if you have a bellyache, you foul worm. Get up and take your place on the roof.'

'Have a care, Sergeant. I can hardly stand for the pain, never mind climb onto the roof.' The voice was unmistakeable. Vindle.

Macdonell entered. Vindle was cowering in a corner, his

knees tucked up under his chin. Sergeant Dawson stood over him. 'I'll count to three, Private,' bellowed the sergeant, 'and if you are not on your feet and on the ladder by then, I will shoot you. Is that clear? One . . .'

Vindle saw Macdonell in the doorway. 'You know me, Colonel. I'm not one to shirk a fight. Tell the sergeant.'

'Two . . .'

'Do as Sergeant Dawson has told you, man, or I will shoot you too. And with a full measure of powder.'

Dawson unslung his musket and cocked it. 'Three.' Vindle was on his feet in a trice and on the bottom rung of the ladder. Two seconds later he had disappeared through the hole in the roof.

'Cowardice?' asked Macdonell.

'No, sir,' replied the sergeant. 'He's a thief and a liar, but he's not a coward. Probably ate too much pig. But we need every man we've got.'

'I believe he might have tried to shoot me in the wood at Gemioncourt. Luckily the shot was weak and lodged in my pack. He denies it, of course.'

'I'd better keep an eye on the evil creature, sir. If he so much as thinks of trying it again, I'll shoot him.'

'Thank you, Sergeant. Apart from bellyaches, is all well and prepared here?'

'It is, sir. Mister Gooch has kept us busy most of the night. No frog will get past us.'

'Where are the Grahams?' asked Macdonell. 'I haven't seen them this morning.'

'They asked permission to visit the chapel, sir, it being a

171

Sunday. They will be there.' Like himself, the Graham brothers were Catholics. They too would take comfort from the wooden carving above the door.

The two men sitting upright on their mounts, heads steady and eyes forward, who walked slowly down from the ridge and around the outside of the orchard and the garden, appeared impervious to the enemy not many yards away. Macdonell, looking out from the tower, recognised one of them instantly. Wellington, almost casual in blue coat, white buckskin breeches, white cravat and cocked hat, had come to see Hougoumont for himself. His companion wore the uniform of a Prussian general. Macdonell did not know him.

The two riders made their way around the hedge to the south gate, oblivious to the danger of tirailleurs or voltigeurs in the woods. In the clearing outside the gate they halted briefly before retracing their steps back up the slope. A little piqued that the Duke had not sought him out, Macdonell watched the two men go. Then it occurred to him. The Duke had not sent for him because he would not have wanted to divert attention from the preparations going on within the enclosure.

In the orchard, Saltoun's men were already standing to arms. At intervals of no more than five yards, clusters of Guards prepared to meet the first attack. When it came, the French would be subjected to continuous musket fire through and over the hedge. When they broke through, as they would, they would be met by the needle-sharp points of the Guards' bayonets.

Saltoun himself was in fine spirits. 'Good morning, James,'

he yelled from the far end of the orchard. 'Are you rested and ready for the day?'

'Well enough, I trust. Did you see the Duke?'

'I did, with General Müffling, Blücher's liaison officer. I thought they had come to wish us a good day, but it seems not. Just taking a look.' Saltoun pulled out a gold pocket watch. 'It is nine o'clock. When do you suppose the first attack will come?'

'When Boney's had his breakfast and judged the ground firm enough for his cavalry, I imagine. Mind you, the longer he waits, the better the chances of the Prussians arriving.'

From the sunken lane to their left came the sounds of rattling muskets and marching men. Through the hedge they caught glimpses of shakos hurrying down towards the north gate. 'It seems that the peer's visit was not merely social. He has sent us reinforcements. Just in time, I daresay,' said Saltoun.

The Nassauer staff officer who strode up to them saluted smartly. 'Major Sattler, gentlemen. I have a battalion of six hundred of our men and a company of Hanoverians waiting outside the gates. We have been sent from Papelotte to take over the defence of the orchard and to reinforce the troops in the wood,' he told them in heavily accented English. 'Lord Saltoun is to take the light companies back to the ridge to rejoin the 1st Guards.'

James and Alexander exchanged a look of astonishment. 'On whose orders, sir?' asked James.

'My orders came from General d'Aubremé of our 2nd Brigade, and his from the Duke of Wellington,' replied the major. 'His Grace also orders that half the company of the 3rd

Guards who are in the garden should be moved to defend the west side of the chateau.'

That at least made sense. If the west side of the farm was held, the enemy would not be able to get around the chateau to attack them from the north or go on up the slope in their rear where General Byng had placed his artillery. But why would Wellington replace the experienced 1st Guards with Nassauers and Hanoverians?

'Are you quite sure of this?' asked Saltoun, his handsome face flushed with anger.

The major looked affronted. 'Entirely sure, sir. I am not in the habit of misunderstanding orders.' It was absurd. Reinforcements would of course be welcome, but to send Saltoun's companies back to the ridge after they had spent the night fortifying the orchard made no sense at all. Yet the major was adamant. He was to replace them with his own troops.

'Do you have your orders in writing, Major?' asked James.

'I do not, Colonel. General d'Aubremé seldom commits his orders to paper.'

Saltoun exploded. 'Dammit, James, there is something amiss here. This is where we are most needed. Why would Wellington move us now?'

'Doubtless the Duke has his reasons, although I am damned if I know what they are,' replied James. 'But if Major Sattler is certain of his orders you had better do as you are bid.'

Saltoun swore and trudged off to give the orders. Within a few minutes two hundred disbelieving men had left their carefully prepared positions and set off through the garden gate and back to the ridge. God alone knew what they were thinking. As soon as they had gone, Major Sattler sent the Hanoverians into the wood and led his Nassauers into the orchard, where he began placing them around the hedge. James left him to it.

In the barn, the surgeon and his two orderlies had laid out their instruments on one table and cleared another for their work. One of the orderlies was busy sharpening the knives and saws that would be used for amputations, the other was using a nail to scrape blood off the probes and forceps they would use to extract musket balls and giving them a polish on his sleeve. Sellers patted his operating table and greeted Macdonell with a confident grin. 'All ready, Colonel, and we'll have them sewn up and back to work just as quick as we can. The minor wounds will take priority. Stomachs and limbs will have to wait their turn.'

'Today, sir,' replied Macdonell, 'you will be busier than you have ever been. Have you everything you need?'

'Ten more orderlies would be welcome, Colonel, but I doubt I'll get them. We'll manage as we are.'

It was mid-morning. The bands of both armies had been doing their best to lift the spirits of their men for over an hour, yet still no shot had been fired. Carried on the wind from the ridge came the drums and flutes playing 'Lilliburlero' and 'The Grenadiers' March'. The bandsmen were working hard, although they would work harder tending to the wounded when the battle started. James climbed the stairs to the top of the tower again and stood at a window.

To his right he made out the inn at La Belle Alliance and the blue of French infantry brigades on the low ridge running westwards from it. Beyond the inn, hidden by the rise of the land, there would be cavalry and Buonaparte's fearsome artillery – rows and rows of howitzers, mortars and cannon, the largest of which could hurl a twelve-pound ball a mile.

To the left, troops and artillery pieces were visible on the south side of the long ridge that straddled the road to Brussels and behind which most of the Allied army had spent the night. The wretches within sight of the French guns were in for a bloody time. If James's guess was right, they would be the first to be bombarded by the guns before the cavalry charged up the hill to cut whatever was left of them to shreds. Wellington would sacrifice them to show that he was inviting battle but keeping his main force hidden and protected by the ridge. It was exactly what he had done so successfully in the peninsula and he would do it again. Buonaparte might suspect it, but there was little he could do about it unless he attacked from the flanks. That was why Hougoumont must be held.

He descended the stairs and stood in the yard inside the south gate. On every roof, at every window and over the walls, muskets pointed out at the woods, where the Jägers waited for the first of the French infantry to attack. He wondered how long the Jägers would hold out before being forced back behind the walls. Not long, probably, and then the French would sweep through the wood and hurl themselves at the south wall. Prince Jérôme, desperate to win his brother's praise, would take no account of casualties. He would blast the farm and chateau with his artillery and drive his troops forward and forward again until they stormed the gates and claimed victory.

To hold them off, Macdonell had four hundred men of the light companies in the chateau and farm, six hundred under Major Sattler in the orchard and about the same number in the wood. He checked his watch again. It was fifteen minutes past eleven o'clock. From the direction of the valley beyond the wood a cannon roared and round shot screeched over their heads.

It had started.

CHAPTER TWELVE

There was no foreplay, no caress, no gentle exploration. In their dozens, the French guns thundered, their teams reloaded and they thundered again. It was sudden and brutal and for Macdonell's Guards there was no respite and no escape. The first of them went down, struck by bouncing round shot or stabbed by splinters of timber and brick ripped from the walls of the chateau and the farm buildings. In no time the yard was a swamp of blood, mud and debris and the air full of the cries of the injured.

The wounded who could walk to the barn did so; those who could not were helped there by comrades. The dead were carried to a corner of the yard near the tower. For an infantryman this was the very worst time. Against cavalry he could form square, against infantry he could fight with musket and bayonet or his bare hands. Against artillery fire he could do nothing but pray. Like them, Macdonell hated it.

In the yard he stood and listened and watched. He was watching his men, assessing their spirits, observing their reactions to the onslaught. He had known good men crumble in the face of round shot or canister and he knew the signs. Here there were none. And he was listening. Listening for an end to the artillery bombardment that would signal the advance of the infantry.

From the hill behind them General Byng's cannon returned fire. Their height gave them an advantage and, ignoring the Duke's standing instructions never to engage in long-range artillery battles, they fired over the wood and into the valley behind. The French Gunners immediately altered their aim and the Guards in the garden and the farm and the Nassauers and Hanoverians in the orchard found themselves watching shot hurtling over their heads from both front and rear.

The spark that had ignited the fire of battle at Hougoumont soon did the same in the fields and lanes beyond. Great twelve-pound cannon sent death into the sky to rip heads and limbs from brave men who might see and hear it coming but were expected not to move, not even to flinch. That was a matter of honour for all from the loftiest general to the humblest private. Yet any man who had stood in square and faced an artillery attack knew that it was impossible to stand entirely still in the face of round shot and canister exploding all around, ripping heads from shoulders and limbs from bodies. Macdonell had experienced it himself. He knew what it was like. Terrifying, ear-splitting, blood-soaked hell.

The farm and chateau were enveloped in foul smoke. Everywhere men coughed and spluttered and screwed their eyes shut. Macdonell yelled an order. 'Eyes on the wood. Watch the wood.' A shot crashed against the chapel wall, showering the dead with brick dust but leaving the chapel standing. He ran into the gardener's house and up the stairs to a window. He strained his eyes to peer through the smoke until tears ran down his face. In the wood, muskets fired and men screamed, but he could see nothing. Perhaps the Nassauers and Jägers were holding the French at bay.

They were not. As he watched from the window, green-jacketed men began to emerge from the wood into the clearing outside the gate. They were firing back into the trees as they withdrew, covering each other as best they could. A man went down clutching his knee and was dragged to the wall by a burly sergeant.

Macdonell could not risk removing the barricade and opening the gate to let the retreating men in. He yelled at them to run for the orchard hedge. The Hanoverians and Lüneburgs did so, but some of the Nassauers sloped off into the fields behind the farm. A night in the woods and an attack by French voltigeurs had apparently been enough for them. Macdonell shrugged. There was no point in trying to stop them. A man whose heart was not in the fight would be worse than useless.

Behind the retreating Hanoverians, voltigeurs and tirailleurs poured out of the wood and ran for the gate, firing as they went and shouting the name of their Emperor. It was not what skirmishers were for and little more than foolish bravado. They were met by a storm of musket fire from the roofs and windows and fell in their scores. The few who managed to reach the garden wall were clubbed or hacked down as they tried to climb it. They carried no ladders. Macdonell barely suppressed a grin as James Graham reached over to grab a Frenchman by the neck and heaved him bodily over his shoulder to be dealt with by the Guards behind.

The attackers faced a hopeless task. They could not hope to hit targets protected by walls and hidden behind windows, or to survive the merciless fire rained down upon them. Yet they kept coming, the skirmishers soon being joined by regular infantry and to their right facing the garden, by Dragoons.

Macdonell dashed round the chateau to the north gates. They were secure, guarded by James Hervey's men on the roofs of the sheds and behind the wall. In the garden, Harry Wyndham's company was picking off Frenchmen through the loopholes and from the fire steps. Macdonell climbed onto a step for a better view. The private beside him fired and a French shot whistled past his shoulder. The man had found his target in the nick of time. Macdonell clapped him on the shoulder and jumped off the step.

All around the garden, in the farm, at the walls and gates, men died with the crack of muskets and the screech of round shot in their heads. And then a new sound, subtly different from the roar of cannon. Now that the wood was clear of Allied troops, Major Bull's battery of howitzers had joined the fray. Their shells rose high into the sky, dropping steeply to explode above the trees and rain down a storm of shrapnel on enemy heads. There was no soldier in any army in the world who was not terrified at the mere thought of shrapnel. Iron shot and evil shards of hot metal caused wounds more terrible than any other.

More Frenchmen poured from the wood. But the Guards had had time to reload and picked them off like rabbits. Singly and in groups, the French braved the deadly fire of the Coldstreams, charged across the clearing and threw themselves at the gate and the walls. Dead or dying, they fell there in their dozens and in no time the ground was littered with bodies. Yet they came on and on again. It was hard not to admire the courage of these men but it was futile courage. And the only real damage to the defences or the defenders had been caused by the French artillery. Their infantry were achieving next to nothing. The hundred men of the 3rd Guards Light Company now stationed in and around the lane on the west side of the farm were not even engaged. The French could not reach them.

Macdonell made his way into the garden where yet more French infantry were attacking the wall. Despite their numbers, they were faring little better than their comrades at the south gate. The loopholes afforded almost complete protection to Harry Wyndham's men shooting through them, and the brave men who did reach the wall were smashed brutally back by the butt of a musket or the thrust of a bayonet. All manner of objects were being put to use – lengths of timber, bricks and stones, even kettles. A kettle jammed into a moustachioed French face appearing above the wall did the job as well as anything.

Harry Wyndham, mounted on his fifteen-hand grey and sword in hand, was in the middle of the garden watching for signs of weakness and shouting for more ammunition or more men where he judged they were needed. From where he was,

Harry had a good view of the whole garden and was directing its defence with calm skill while deliberately exposing himself to enemy fire. Wellington himself would have approved.

In the orchard, it was a different story. Major Sattler's battalion, protected only by the ragged hedge, were suffering. Even reinforced by the Hanoverians who had been driven out of the wood, they would not be able to hold the position for much longer. French Dragoons had already dismounted and broken through the hedge on the east side and were streaming through the gap. The defenders were being driven remorselessly back, yard by yard, towards the garden and the lane leading up to the ridge. If the French occupied the lane, reinforcements would be unable to reach Hougoumont.

The Hanoverians fought ferociously with sword and musket, but they were increasingly outnumbered. Watching from behind the garden wall, Macdonell knew it could only be a matter of minutes before the whole orchard was in French hands.

In fact it was less. Major Sattler, realising the hopelessness of his task, called for a withdrawal to the lane. Leaving the orchard strewn with bodies, his Hanoverians managed to work their way to the lane where they re-formed on the bank and in the hedge alongside it. It was a skillful manouevre which not only saved lives but also kept the lane open.

But the French now had the orchard, from where they would attack the garden wall and pepper the farm and chateau with case-shot. Light case fired at close range from small four-pound guns could do terrible damage, as

Macdonell had seen for himself at Salamanca, where he had watched in horror as ranks of advancing guards were ripped to shreds by the iron balls that exploded out of the case and into their bodies and faces.

Without reinforcements, they could not hope to retake the orchard. Macdonell cursed. His defence of Hougoumont looked like being short-lived. He rushed back into the garden and shouted for Harry. 'The French have the orchard, Harry,' he yelled. 'Every man you can spare to the east wall. They must not get into the garden.' Harry heard him, immediately gathered fifty men and ran to the wall. James picked up a discarded musket, gave the flint a cursory glance, made sure it was loaded and ran to join them. For all the heaped fortifications around it, a crumbling section of the wall on the east side was their most vulnerable point and where the French would probably try to break through.

The French Dragoons were working their way steadily through the orchard, sheltering behind the fruit trees and using the mounds and hollows in the ground for cover. They were fighting like voltigeurs – fire, move, reload, fire – hard to see in the smoke and even harder to hit. Each Guard was getting off three or even four shots a minute, but they were firing almost blind. And at any moment, the French light guns might start spitting their lethal charges over the heads of their own men and into the garden and the farm.

James and Harry heard them before they saw them. A thundering of hooves and feet down the sunken lane, followed by the light companies of the 1st Brigade, Alexander Saltoun, mounted on a grey charger at their head, bursting out of the cover of the hedge and into the orchard. Major Sattler's Hanoverians, screaming their ancient battle cries, followed behind.

Taken by surprise, the French Dragoons turned to face the new threat and exposed their backs to fire from the garden wall. Through the thinning smoke, Macdonell saw a number fall, killed by musket shot or skewered by a bayonet. He exchanged a glance with Harry, grinned and jumped down into the orchard. Harry and his company were quick to follow. They ran at the Dragoons, bayonets ready to strike, and yelling with glee. The enemy, hemmed in on all sides, had nowhere to hide and, bravely as they fought, were doomed. A few managed to break through the hedge and escape. Most went down, sliced, hacked or disembowelled by bayonet or sword.

A Dragoon captain was one of the last to fall. He stood with his back to an apple tree, using his sword to parry and thrust. He was a courageous man and a skilful one. The bodies of two Guards lay beside him, a third staggered off with an arm hanging by threads of skin. A Guard raised his musket and aimed at the captain's head. 'Hold your fire, man,' yelled Macdonell. 'We will make the captain our prisoner.' He was too late. The Guard fired and the captain fell, a bullet in his brain.

Saltoun gave orders for the dead to be heaped in a corner of the orchard, the wounded to be taken to the barn while Major Sattler's men set about patching up the hedge. It would not be long before the French returned to recover the ground they had held so briefly.

'Well, James,' said Saltoun, 'I do not know what you are doing in my orchard but I am pleased to see you.'

'And I you. Was there a change of orders?'

'I really do not know. On our way back to the ridge we met Wellington who told us he knew of no order for us to leave Hougoumont and that we should stay where we were. A little later he rode down again and ordered us back into the fray. I can only think that the excellent General d'Aubremé, whose English is less than perfect, mistook the order to reinforce for one to replace.' Saltoun looked about. 'Just as well the Duke met us when he did, I'd say.'

From the direction of the chateau came more sounds of battle. Muskets fired and men screamed. Without another word, James turned and ran back through the yard and into the gardener's house. He elbowed aside a Guard and looked out of a window. The French were attacking the south gate again.

For all the losses they had already suffered, their general had thrown them back at the gate. Out of the woods they came like sheep driven by their shepherd, firing, shouting, falling and dying. They climbed on and over the corpses of their comrades, apparently fearless and determined to smash their way through the gate. It was madness. Why did Jérôme not bring up his light artillery and blast a way through the door? Thick as it was, the oak would not stand many direct hits from four-pound cannon.

In the yard, the same thought had plainly occurred to Henry Gooch. He had ordered his company to keep away from the door and had concentrated his strength at the windows and on the roofs, from where they had clear lines of sight into the clearing. Gooch had taken a horse from the stable and, like Harry Wyndham, chosen to fight mounted. This gave him the advantage of height but made him an easy target for a French musket fired over the wall. So far, there had been none of those and Gooch was unharmed.

Macdonell walked over and took hold of the horse's bridle. 'You might wish to spend the remainder of the day on foot, Mister Gooch,' he shouted over the crack and clamour. 'I would not want to lose you so early.'

'As you wish, Colonel,' replied the ensign, dismounting. 'I merely thought to follow His Grace's example.'

'You may do that when you are a general, Mister Gooch. For now, kindly stay alive and hold this gate.'

A shout came from the upper floor of the gardener's house. Macdonell looked up to see Sergeant Dawson's face at a window. 'The frogs are in the lane,' he called out, pointing to the west side of the farm. 'A company, at least.'

Thank God Wellington had sent orders for the lane to be defended and James had moved a hundred men of the 3rd Guards there. They were light company men, well trained, tough and disciplined. And they were led by Charles Dashwood, a veteran of Maida and Toulouse.

Unless he left by the north gates and entered the lane in the rear of Dashwood's company, the only way for Macdonell to see what was happening was to look over the top of the small west gate. There were no windows in the west walls of the barn or stables.

The men guarding the gate had found old crates and ammunition boxes on which to stand. Six of them were shoulder to shoulder, firing into the lane while another six reloaded. Macdonell stepped up onto a crate and looked down. Dashwood's company had been pushed back halfway up the lane towards the north gate. The lane itself was narrow and defined by the farm walls and a four-foot bank on the other side. It was not difficult to defend but beyond it was open ground, over which the French had extended their line, forcing the light company to do the same. Without reinforcements they would not hold the lane for long.

Macdonell jumped down and ran to the north gates which, so far, had not been threatened. James Hervey, unlike Henry Gooch, was on foot. 'Mister Hervey,' shouted Macdonell, 'Colonel Dashwood's company will soon be outside the gates. Make ready to let them in and to close the gates immediately after them. Not a Frenchman must enter.'

'Not one, Colonel,' replied Hervey. 'You may count upon it.'

'Good. Send someone to fetch Captain Wyndham and Mister Gooch and anyone else who can be spared. Now.' For the first time the north gates were about to come under attack. They too must be held.

A guard on the roof of the shed on the west side of the gates was the first to sound a warning. He filled his lungs and bellowed. 'Open the gates. Colonel Dashwood's company approaching. Open the gates.'

It took two men to lift the heavy cross-beam from its housings. They threw it to one side and joined the others pulling the doors open. Macdonell stood at the open gate, urging the retreating Guards inside. They began to withdraw to safety, backs to the farm and trying desperately to keep the pursuing French at bay. Muskets empty, they fought with broken butts and with their fists whilst trying to manouevre backwards through the gates. A Guard slipped in the mud and tripped the man in front of him.

Both died at the point of a French sword. Charles Dashwood, at the front of his men, yelled at them to make haste. He took a blow to the shoulder from a musket, dropped his sword and fell to one knee. A Frenchman raised his own sword to strike at the colonel's unprotected neck and let out a brutal cry of triumph. Two seconds later he was dead, killed by a shot from the roof of the cowshed. Above the clash and clamour, the shout could be heard clearly. 'Got the bugger, filthy frog bastard.' Macdonell looked up in surprise. Patrick Luke, of all people, had saved the life of Colonel Dashwood.

Dashwood had been dragged inside and almost all the Guards were safe when Macdonell climbed onto the cowshed roof to see whether the French were preparing for another attack or had withdrawn to the safety of the lane. A French colonel, mistakenly sensing the moment of victory, came galloping down the lane, sabre raised. He yanked on the reins, turned his mount sharply and aimed a cutting stroke at one of the few Guards still outside the gates, a sergeant named Fraser. The sergeant, a small, wiry fellow, avoided the stroke and seized the Frenchman's arm. He pulled the colonel off his horse, jumped into the saddle and to a loud cheer rode it triumphantly through the gates. The colonel was left defenceless on the ground and at the mercy of a row of muskets trained on him from the cowshed roof. 'The man is helpless,' shouted Macdonell. 'Let him go.' The muskets did not fire and the colonel rose, saluted, and walked slowly back to the lane. The remaining Frenchmen followed him.

The last of Dashwood's Guards were inside the gates, which were hastily pushed shut. The Graham brothers lifted the cross-beam and replaced it in its housings. The north gates were secure. 'Come on, Harry,' called out Macdonell. 'Time we inspected the garden.'

But they had barely reached the garden gate when there was a splintering sound not unlike that of a tree falling, followed by cries of alarm. They ran back to the gates. The two panels had not quite shut fully, and through a narrow gap between them, an axe was making short work of the cross-beam. The axeman must be a goliath. The beam was solid oak and the gap allowed him to raise his axe only a foot or two. Yet before they could react the beam split and the gates were pushed open. Thirty or forty Frenchmen, led by a bearded sous-lieutenant – a giant several inches taller than either of the Grahams – had turned back and smashed open the gate.

The French charged into the yard. The lieutenant was uttering blood-curdling threats, brandishing a long-handled axe and looking ready to take on an entire battalion by himself. He swiped at a head, missed, reversed the axe and sliced into the head from behind. Faced with the swinging axe, the Guards with empty muskets backed away. A Hanoverian private ran for the farmer's house and got his hand on the door handle. He was just too late. The axe fell with brutal force and removed his hand at the wrist. The giant ran through the archway and past the chateau towards the south gate. A dozen of his comrades followed him.

Blue jackets were pouring in through the gates and filling the yard. The Guards could not hold back the tide. They fired into the mass of bodies and defended themselves with bayonet and musket, but were being swiftly overpowered.

Macdonell put his head down and charged at the intruders like a bull. They must close the gates immediately. Leave them open and hundreds of cheering Frenchmen would sweep through the farm, the chateau and the garden. And Hougoumont would fall.

Almost simultaneously, Harry Wyndham and the Graham brothers followed, hacking and slashing their way through the melee. A handful of Guards, led by the two ensigns, joined them. The rest formed a line to block the route to the south gate.

'The gates,' yelled Macdonell, over the clash of steel and the crack of muskets. 'Close the gates.' Ignoring a sharp sting on his left arm he jabbed his sword into the eye of a Frenchman, shouldered another aside and kicked a third in the knee. Beside him, James and Joseph Graham, shoulder to shoulder, were also carving a bloody path. The enemy were all around them yet it was French blood that spurted from heads and stomachs and Frenchmen who fell dying. The three of them reached the left gate and put their weight on it. For all their strength, it was blocked by the crush of bodies outside and barely moved. Straining for purchase in the mud, they tried again. This time it moved a few inches, and, gradually, painfully slowly, gathered momentum.

The right-hand gate was still wide open. Harry and the Guards had not been able to reach it and were fighting with their fists and feet. More blue jackets ran into the yard. One, a corporal, turned back and aimed a slash at James Graham's back. His brother saw the strike coming and yelled a warning. Just in time, James swivelled, grabbed the corporal's wrist, twisted it and kicked him in the groin. The man dropped his sword, fell like a sack of flour and lay gasping in the mud.

Without Graham's weight behind it, the French had pushed the left gate open a little. A private slipped around it. Graham picked up the corporal's sword and pierced the private's windpipe. The man fell back, blood gushing from the wound. Graham dropped the sword and put his shoulder to the gate. Immediately it moved again, creaked and groaned and was closed.

On the other side Harry was still struggling. James Hervey stood beside him, smashing his musket into French faces, but making no progress towards the gate. Henry Gooch and a handful of guards were fighting to reach them. The gate was open and the French were still coming in.

Macdonell made a decision. 'This one's yours, gentlemen,' he gasped, taking his weight off the gate. He stepped over a body and launched himself at a French back. The man fell like a skittle. Macdonell jumped over him and fought his way to Harry.

The muskets on the cowshed roof were firing into the French outside, barely taking aim, just firing and firing again into the mass of bodies. Men fell, blocked the path of those behind and had to be dragged out of the way. The flow of Frenchmen through the gates slowed.

Macdonell reached the gate. He put all his weight on it, slipped in the mud and lost his footing. He was up in a trice with Hervey at his shoulder. Harry landed a punch in a French face and was with them. They leant on the gate. It began to move, slowly at first, then under its own momentum, faster. The French too were finding it difficult to keep their footing in the mud. The gap was little more than a foot wide when, out of the corner of his eye, Macdonell saw a tiny figure slip through it and run into the yard. He had no time to dwell on it. One more heave and the gates closed. It took two men to lift a timber and drop it in the housings but he could not spare two men. He called for a Guard to take his place, dashed to the cowshed, squatted to get his forearms under a timber, straightened his legs and back, rose unsteadily and staggered back to the gates. With a huge groan, he dropped it in place. The gates were closed.

But the fight was not over. Three Frenchmen had managed to climb onto the wall. Two fired and jumped back to safety. The third took careful aim at Harry Wyndham, doubled over and trying to catch his breath. At the moment the Frenchman fired, a bullet from James Graham's musket exploded into his mouth. His own shot went wide and he died instantly. Barely able to stand, Harry leant on James Graham's arm until he could breathe. 'My thanks, Corporal,' he gasped. Graham grinned but did not reply.

Ignorant of the struggle at the gates, Major Bull's howitzers were sending their exploding shells to rain havoc on the French in the valley and Prince Jérôme's heavy cannon were blasting away at General Byng's 2nd Brigade on the hillside. Below them, while the guns thundered and their deadly missiles flew overhead, eardrums were battered by the blasts and eyes rendered red and weeping by the smoke. Breathing was difficult, swallowing was agony. Throats burning from the taste of powder were scraped raw. And there were at least thirty Frenchman still inside the walls.

Macdonell wiped sweat from his forehead, picked a musket from the ground and ran for the south gate. If the intruders opened that, the French would pour in from the woods. He was almost too late. In the south yard, the crash of cannon and howitzer had drowned the clamour of the struggle at the north gate. The intruders had taken Sergeant Dawson's troop by surprise and fired into their backs, killing a dozen instantly. The giant sous-lieutenant had used his axe to carve a path to the gate while his comrades fought with sword and musket to protect his back. Bloody bodies lay outside the chapel and the gardener's house, from where Guards had rushed out to join the fight.

The lieutenant was within touching distance of the bricks and timber piled up behind the gate. His comrades had surrounded him and were taking the Guards' musket fire themselves. They were brave men, intent upon their purpose, and they had very nearly achieved it.

The Guards who had followed Macdonell into the south yard had had time to reload their muskets. On his order, they raised them and sent twenty bullets into French faces. They fell, all of them but the giant lieutenant, who had put down his axe to lift a length of timber from the barricade. He turned to face them, threw the timber to one side and defiantly picked up another. Macdonell charged at him, shoulder down, and knocked the timber from his grasp. The giant reached out for his attacker's throat. Macdonell ducked down to pick up the axe, slashed at his knees and rose to bury it in his chest. Astonishingly, the man did not fall. His huge hands were on the axe handle when a musket fired. A hole appeared over his eye and he collapsed face down into the mud.

Macdonell stood for a moment to regain his breath. Harry put a hand on his arm. 'Was that wise, James?' he asked quietly. 'We could have shot him.'

'It was necessary, Harry. Some things just are.' He filled his lungs and shouted over the cannon fire. 'Clear the dead, wounded to the barn. Check muskets and flints.'

'And what shall I do with this, Colonel?' asked a voice behind him.

He turned. Sergeant Dawson was holding a boy of about twelve by the collar of his tunic. He was a drummer boy, the boy who had slipped in while the north gates were closing.

'*Tu es très brave, mon garçon,*' said Macdonell. '*Mais pourquoi?*'

The boy pointed to a dead Frenchman. '*Mon père,*' he replied.

Macdonell nodded. '*Ton père était brave aussi.*' And to Dawson, 'Put him in the barn. Ask the orderlies to keep an eye on him.'

Dawson glanced at Macdonell's sleeve. 'Perhaps you should visit the barn yourself, Colonel.'

Macdonell looked down. His left sleeve was ripped and dripping blood. The sting he had felt must have been from a musket ball. He pulled back the sleeve. It was no more than a graze. 'If you would fetch me a bandage, Sergeant, I will not trouble the surgeon.'

'Very well, Colonel,' replied Dawson doubtfully. When it came to surgeons, the colonel apparently did not care to take his own advice. 'Come on now, boy, let's get you out of the way.' The boy, who was unlikely to speak a word of English, took the sergeant's meaning and went off with him.

'How are we faring, Harry?' asked Macdonell. 'Casualties? Have you counted?'

Harry nodded. 'I have. Seventeen dead, two officers wounded. Colonel Dashwood's shoulder is broken. And you, of course.'

'A scratch. Get Colonel Dashwood to the chateau. He can wait there for the surgeon. And other casualties?'

'About forty, half serious. The rest can hold a musket and near enough see a target.'

'Perhaps Prince Jérôme will give us time to lick our wounds and prepare for his next visit. Have we enough water?'

'No. The well is all but empty. There's gin, but it scorches like fire down a raw throat.'

'Then let us hope General Cooke takes pity on us and sends down a supply wagon loaded with water and bullets and powder. If he can, that is. Are the frogs in the sunken lane yet?'

'I don't know. They might be.'

The sound of the howitzer was unmistakeable. Instinctively, they both looked up. A shell passed over the trees and landed in the orchard. It had come not from the slope behind them but from the woods. Far from allowing them a rest, the Prince had called up his own howitzer battery.

CHAPTER THIRTEEN

When their sighting shots had given their teams the range, the deadly howitzers began their bombardment on the orchard. Saltoun's tired and miserable troops could do little but seek meagre shelter from the shards of burning metal exploding over their heads. If they ran for the garden, the French would be into the orchard instantly, so they crouched behind apple trees and in the hedge, while the shells rained down like lethal hailstones, killing and wounding and maiming. Macdonell saw ten men carried to the barn, most with terrible wounds to the head, and ten more killed instantly. The awful howitzers were doing their duty and he expected them at any moment to turn their attention to the farm. Yet they did not. It soon became clear why.

From around the woods to the south galloped a company of Dragoons and, at the same time, several companies of infantry emerged from the trees beyond the gate, outside which scores of French bodies had lain since their last attack. Prince Jérôme, it seemed, had decided that the defenders' strength was sufficiently depleted and their ammunition low enough for another attempt to be made.

He was right. Saltoun's troops were pinned down in the orchard, Wyndham's were defending the garden and the barn was filling up with the wounded. The farm was under threat at both north and south gates and ammunition supplies were already dangerously low. Only the chateau itself was secure. At least until the French turned their heavy cannon on to it. Then its ancient walls would surely crumble and fall.

Macdonell ran to the garden, climbed on a wooden crate and peered over the south wall. The Dragoons had formed in line facing the wall, ready to charge the moment they saw a breach. The infantry were gathering behind them and on the edge of the trees beyond the gate. Drums sounded the advance, orders were shouted, and muskets raised. Under cover of their fire, French light troops dashed to the south walls of the garden and farm. Through loopholes and windows, the guards fired back, picking their targets and killing them with ease. So many fell that their bodies filled the clearing and obstructed the advance of those behind.

Yet they kept coming. For every man who died, two more ran out of the woods. They grabbed the burning hot barrels of muskets sticking out of loopholes, fired through the gaps and, still without ladders, climbed on each other's backs to reach the top of the garden walls. In the clearing a mounted French colonel, impervious to the Guards' fire, exhorted his troops forward. When his horse was shot from under him he walked briskly back to the trees and returned on another one.

By sheer force of numbers, the French would breach the walls and take Hougoumont. Jérôme's divisions would sweep through and around the farm and up the slope to attack the Allied army's right wing. At the same time, his brother, the great Buonaparte, would continue to blast the Allied centre and left wing with his heavy cannon before unleashing his fearsome cavalry. If Wellington's right wing was exposed, Buonaparte's army of tough professional soldiers would destroy the Allied ragbag of Dutch militia, Belgians, Germans and raw British recruits without pausing to draw breath. It would be slaughter. Buonaparte clearly thought so too. He would take Hougoumont whatever the cost.

A French face appeared over the wall. Macdonell smashed the hilt of his sword into it and heard bones snap. All along the wall and at every window, individual battles of life and death were being fought. An attacker fired at a defender's head and saw him fall. A defender thrust his bayonet into an attacker's stomach and heard the life sucked out of him. The attackers, exposed to fire from every vantage point behind the walls, were taking enormous losses. Their dead piled up like sacks of grain, their wounded – those who could – limped and crawled back to the woods, pursued by fire from the chateau and the tower. As many as ten Frenchmen were dying for each Guard. But on they came, more and more of them, heedless of the unceasing fire, climbing over their bloody dead, most not even reaching the walls, those that did dying there.

Then everything changed. The French withdrew to the trees and brought up a pair of four-pounders, placed them just inside the treeline and began firing over the heads of their own troops into the gardener's house and the yard beyond. Unlike the gun teams behind the wood, these could see where they were aiming. And the Gunners were skilled in their work. Their first salvo crashed through the upper windows of the gardener's house, the second blasted the roof of the stable.

Macdonell ran back to the farm. He had been expecting this. Indeed, if he had been in Jérôme's shoes, he would have brought up his light cannon as soon as he had possession of the wood. It can only have been the Prince's pride that led him to believe he could take Hougoumont without destroying it. To win the praise of his brother, the man had been prepared to sacrifice hundreds, even thousands of French lives. Now he had been forced to change his tactics.

The cannon fired and fired again. It could not go on. A single breach in the wall and the French would be inside. Worse, enough direct hits and the south gate would be blasted into firewood. Macdonell found Sergeant Dawson and asked for a man to take a message to General Byng. The man must be quick and nimble. The sergeant handed him a blood-soaked bandage for his arm and went to find a man suitable.

The cannon roared again and the stable wall took two more hits. The horses had been moved to the cowshed by the north gate, but that was scant comfort. Muskets fired from the gardener's house and the roofs. They had no effect. The gun teams went busily about their work, making ready the cannon, loading, aiming and firing.

Macdonell was struggling with the bandage when there was a quiet voice behind him. 'You sent for me, Colonel.'

He turned. It was Joseph Lester. Dawson had made a good choice. 'I did, Private. Slip out of the west gate and through the woods behind us. You will find General Byng on the ridge near the Nivelles Road. Ask him if we might have a little assistance.'

'Yes, Colonel. Can I help with your bandage?'

'I'll manage. Quick as you like, Private.'

Macdonell hated seeking help but there was nothing else for it. If he led an attack on the guns from the farm, the gate would have to be opened. That was too big a risk. If he did nothing, there would soon be no gate. Help it would have to be.

A round shot whistled over the roof of the gardener's house and exploded against the wall of the chateau, sending bricks and debris flying across the yard. A man screamed and grasped his stomach. Another, struck on the head by a brick, fell to the ground without a sound. The French heavy artillery had started up again. Howitzers, light cannon, and now heavy cannon. Jérôme was taking the risk of killing his own men. But he would kill a thousand Frenchmen with his own hands if it meant taking Hougoumont. *C'était la guerre.*

In the garden, Harry Wyndham's troops still lined the walls, desperately beating back every French assault with musket and blade and fist, while the Dragoons waited and watched from the safety of the treeline.

Seeing, hearing, speaking, even thinking, became harder with each round shot, each shell, each musket ball. They brought not only death and disfigurement but mind-numbing, ear-shattering noise and smoke so foul and dense that a man could barely keep his eyes open or take a breath without retching.

On both sides of the walls men died. The luckiest were dead before they fell. Many lay helpless and pleading for release from their agony. Some of the French even called on their enemies to shoot them. One heap of bodies grew so high that a fearless Frenchman, ignoring the screams of pain under his feet, clambered up it to get to the top of the wall. He leant over to take aim only to fall back onto the heap with blood pouring from his throat.

And on it went. Somewhere in the valley of smoke, now invisible even from the tower of the chateau, the battle for Hougoumont was being replicated a thousand times. Cannon fired, men died and very soon Buonaparte would unleash his cavalry. Macdonell forced that persistent and intrusive thought from his head. Hougoumont must be held.

The bombardment ended suddenly. One minute round shot was crashing into the walls of the chateau and the farm buildings, the next the guns were silent. Despite the noise of the battle being fought away to their left, for the newest of the guards it was an eerie moment of relief. For the veterans, the silence was a warning.

Miraculously, the gate was still standing. Its thick oak timbers had stood up to French cannon. Now it would have to stand up to another attack by French muskets. The assault was coming.

Macdonell yelled for the barricades to be strengthened, all muskets to be checked and a cup of gin issued to each man. Sergeant Dawson, his face black from powder and smoke, supervised the distribution. Harry Wyndham, in the garden, went from man to man with a few words of encouragement and warning. For all his lack of experience, he too knew what was coming.

Henry Gooch, his mouth bloody from a French fist, had his men collect more broken timbers and rubble and use them to strengthen the south gate. In the chateau, the farm, the garden and the orchard, some seven hundred exhausted, filthy, parched men made ready. From the top of the tower came the sound of singing, hoarse and rough, but more or less in tune and accompanied by a child's whistle. 'Lilliburlero' again. Joseph Lester was not the only musician at Hougoumont.

The faces of the troops who advanced from the wood were unmarked by powder or smoke and their uniforms were clean. Fresh men – perhaps a full battalion – as many as Macdonell had under his command. In extended line from the western edge of the wood, along the walls of the farm and garden as far as the Dragoons opposite the orchard, officers mounted, infantry poised with muskets primed and loaded, they waited for the order to charge.

Inside the walls, every man stood ready. A musket peeped from each loophole, the fire steps were manned and every roof and window hid three or four of the light companies' best sharpshooters. Macdonell had instructed them not to expose themselves to the first French volleys and to fire only when the enemy were at the walls.

He did not see or hear the order. Without warning, the French charged forward, firing at windows and loopholes, allowing those behind them to pass, reloading, advancing and firing again. The manoeuvre was well executed and met with little resistance. Very few of the defenders panicked and fired too soon. The front rank of the French had reached the walls and those behind them were in the middle of the clearing before the Guards opened fire. Their first volley, from muskets carefully cleaned and loaded, found scores of targets. The second found even more, piling yet more dead and wounded onto the heaps outside.

But every musket had to be reloaded and the Guards were tired. Shaking fingers fumbled with cartridge and ball, eyes half-blinded by smoke missed their aim and the French came on. Henry Gooch was beside Macdonell, firing over the corner of the garden wall where it turned towards the house, from where they had a good view of the clearing, the woods and the south gate. 'Eight hundred, at least, Colonel, do you not think?' he spluttered through his swollen mouth.

'I do, Mister Gooch. Eight hundred fully occupied here, so not available elsewhere.' He took a loaded musket from a private behind them, cocked it, aimed quickly and fired. Another Frenchman died. 'Subtlety was never Boney's strong point. Men, men and more men is his motto.' He took another musket and fired again, wincing from the jolt to his wounded arm. 'All the more targets for us.'

'Shall we be reinforced?' asked Gooch, taking another loaded musket and firing.

Macdonell wiped a sleeve across his eyes. 'That will depend upon what is happening elsewhere. No doubt General Byng will send them if he can.' A shot fizzed past his ear. 'Meanwhile, we keep them out of Hougoumont.'

Such was the weight of fire thundering into them that

Macdonell expected the attackers' discipline to collapse into chaos. Yet, for all their losses, it did not. There was no sign of panic or retreat. Man after man reached the gate or the walls, fired through the loopholes and windows and climbed up to shoot down into the yard. They hacked at the gate with picks and axes, searching for a weak spot, while in the clearing behind them their officers sat tall in their saddles, inviting shots from the tower and the roofs and diverting fire away from them. Many fell. They were soon replaced and more attackers emerged from the wood. Jérôme had decided that this would be his final, successful attack.

Inside, the Guards too were falling. No longer was there a man to step forward when another fell and there was little time to reload. Where once there had been two men on each step, now, more often than not, there was one. The line was spread alarmingly thin. Macdonell looked to his left, wondering whether he dare leave his position to find out what was happening in the garden and orchard, when the butt of a French musket caught him a blow on the temple. He fell back, scrambled to his feet and smashed the hilt of his sword into the face that appeared over the wall. He put his hand to his temple. There was no blood but he could not focus his eyes and his head felt as if it had been stuffed with straw. He bent double, hands on knees, and breathed slowly. Gradually his vision cleared but the straw did not. Muskets, cannon, howitzers, the cries of dying men and terrified horses close by and far off piled one on top of the other inside his head.

He had a mouthful of water in his canteen. He managed

to open it and tip the contents down his throat. It helped a little. A hand holding a tin cup appeared in front of his face. Unthinkingly, he took it and drank. It was gin. 'I thought you could do with it, Colonel,' said a voice. Macdonell tried desperately to focus his eyes. It was Sergeant Dawson. He nodded his thanks and climbed back onto the step. The straw was disappearing. He took a musket and fired at a French head. It exploded in a fountain of blood. That too helped. He could still kill Frenchmen.

A private, black from head to toe and nursing a broken right arm, arrived at the wall. He tapped Macdonell on the shoulder. 'Beg pardon, Colonel. Captain Wyndham's compliments and he says he will not be able to keep the French out of the garden much longer. The buggers are in the orchard again.'

'Thank you, Private. Can you still fire a musket?'

'No, sir, but I can load one and I can piss down a barrel to cool it.'

'Good. Tell Captain Wyndham that I have asked for reinforcements. Until they come, he must hold the garden.'

Now what? Sacrifice the garden and bring Harry's men back to the farm? What then about Saltoun? He would have to withdraw too, or make for the sunken lane. Macdonell could certainly not reinforce either of them.

From somewhere in the wood a howitzer barked. Its shell flew over the south gate and exploded over the yard, hurling sixty iron balls from its thin case. The balls struck with the strength of a musket shot at short range, killing six Guards outside the chateau and wounding more in the yard. Another bark and another explosion and more men fell. Jérôme, still careless of the safety of his own troops, had lost patience. Knowing that the Guards could not seek shelter from his guns and defend the walls at the same time, he had decided to blow them to bits – bits of bone, bits of flesh, bits of bodies. The yard was splattered with them.

From the slope behind them, General Byng's cannon and Major Bull's howitzers returned fire but they were firing blindly into the wood, hoping for a lucky shot. They could not pinpoint exactly where the French guns were nor could they risk firing into the clearing. Round shot or even shells landing short might do the French the favour of breaching the wall.

An axe thudded into the gate. Through the storm of noise Macdonald heard it splinter. He looked over the wall. A hole had appeared in the planking and the French were elbowing each other aside in a race to break through it. Two blue jackets had clambered onto the roof of the shed and were wrestling with a Guard. The Guard managed to push one of them off but the other flattened him with a punch to the jaw. He too fell into the melee below. The blue jacket raised his arms and bellowed in triumph before a musket shot tore into his back and he fell.

Cannons roared. Round shot crashed into the chateau and the farmer's house and more men died. An eight-pound ball bounced into the base of the tower, tearing a great chunk out of the brickwork. Another landed on the stable on the west side, ripped through the roof and sent Guards dead and alive flying into the yard.

Along the walls, the Coldstreams were fighting a brutal battle for survival – shooting, hacking, smashing, skewering.

But the French numbers had started to tell. Inside the farm and garden, bodies lay strewn in the yard and on paths and flower beds. It could not be much longer.

Behind Macdonell, another voice spoke. 'They are on their way, Colonel.' For a moment, Macdonell, still dazed, thought the man was talking about the French. 'Reinforcements, Colonel. On their way. General Byng says so.' The fog cleared. It was Lester.

'Thank you, Private.' Battalions of reinforcements, hopefully, and without a minute's delay. Hougoumont was held, but by a thread.

The attackers had found their way around the west side of the farm and were threatening the north gates again. James Hervey was there with the Grahams and his troop. The French would not find it easy to break through those gates for a second time but that would not stop them trying. If nothing else, it tied up Guards who could have been used elsewhere.

The three companies which charged down the slope from General Byng's position were led by Charles Woodford. Outside the north gates they drove into the enemy, hurtling them back down the west lane past the large barn. At the south wall, Macdonell heard the cheers and could not stop himself rushing to see what they were for. The French were disappearing into the woods and taking their cannon with them. He found the small west gate open and Woodford's troops pouring into the yard.

'Hard fighting we've had, Charles,' said Macdonell by way of greeting. 'You are not a moment too soon.'

'I know,' replied Woodford. 'We could see some of it from

the hill. The general was wondering whether to send us down when your man arrived. Good fellow, did well to get to us.'

Charles Woodford, colonel of the 2nd Battalion of the Coldstreams, was Macdonell's superior. 'Would you care to take over command, Charles?' he asked. It was the proper thing to do.

'Certainly not. You will remain in command. Where would you like us?'

A little surprised, Macdonell took a moment to gather his wits. 'Harry Wyndham is under pressure in the garden. Two companies there, if you would. The other along the south wall.' A shell exploded overhead, scattering its contents like lethal hailstones. 'It's safer by the walls.'

'Very well. I will join Harry. General Byng is sending Francis Home with two companies from the 2nd Battalion to clear the frogs out of the orchard and the hedges around the lane. Two supply wagons have tried to reach you. Both were destroyed.' Woodford gave the orders and led two of his companies to the garden.

Three hundred fresh men made an immediate difference. The French could not withstand the force of their fire and were driven back into the woods. Lt Colonel Home, easily recognised on his white horse, led the attack on the lane and the orchard from north of the Nivelles Road. His two companies took the French by surprise and soon chased them back to join their comrades in the woods. Once again, the whole enclosure, including the orchard, was in their hands.

Like two exhausted prizefighters, both sides paused for breath. Even the French artillery, perhaps awaiting ammunition supplies, was silent. It was as if Prince Jérôme, his every attempt on Hougoumont so far having come to naught, was considering what to do next.

James Macdonell, however, knew exactly what to do. Clear the dead from the yards and buildings, get the wounded to the barn, check muskets and ammunition, repair defences. Before the French came again.

CHAPTER FOURTEEN

To the east, all along the low ridge that straddled the Brussels road, Buonaparte's heavy cannon had been blasting away since soon after his brother had opened fire on Hougoumont. Having given his orders, Macdonell climbed the steps to the top of the tower. His glass had long since been lost but from there he would still get some view of the battlefield, albeit only through breaks in the foul smoke that filled the valley between the ridges. It was smoke so dense that a man might think he could reach out and grab a handful of it.

The four men at the window were cleaning their muskets and replacing their flints. They had had a relatively easy time of it so far, the nearest round shot having passed by the tower and over the north wall. Macdonell told them to ignore him and carry on with their preparations.

Over the wood, so many of its oaks now leafless and broken

by Major Bull's howitzers, he looked out towards the inn at La Belle Alliance – the inn they had passed on the retreat from Quatre Bras less than twenty-four hours earlier, although it seemed like months ago. Squadrons of French artillery lined the low ridge as far as he sould see. Black smoke erupting from a gun barrel signalled yet another heavy shot on its way to the Allied lines where it would kill and maim the miserable troops standing or crouching in square against the threat from the Lancers and cuirassiers hovering below the ridge and dashing up to harass them. Artillery, cavalry, infantry. It was the order of battle.

There was very little response from the Allied artillery. Wellington abhorred what he called 'long-range duels' and the commander of an artillery squadron fired back at his own peril. The Dutch and Belgian battalions stationed on the south side of the ridge had disappeared – withdrawn perhaps but more likely destroyed. How long would the Duke allow this to go on? His infantry were doing no more than provide the French Gunners with target practice. Surely he would counter-attack soon.

To the north the fields beyond the orchard were seething with voltigeurs and tirailleurs, no longer hidden by the corn, which had been entirely trampled and flattened. They would be in the hedgerows, too, around the sunken lane and in the woods to the east. When Jérôme gave the signal, they would attack again.

Macdonell was about to leave the tower when, from beyond the Brussels road, he thought he caught the faint sound of drums beating the *pas de charge*. He could not see over the rise in the ground as it neared La Haye Sainte but the road was a good half-mile away and the wind blowing from the west. If he was right, there were hundreds of drums beating, which meant thousands of troops. Wellington's line was about to be attacked by columns of infantry. He hurried back down the steps.

Sergeant Dawson was at the south gate with Henry Gooch, whose face was now so swollen that he could not speak at all. They had nailed a plank across the hole in the gate and found more timbers to reinforce it. 'No frogs coming in this way, Colonel,' said Dawson cheerily. The little man looked like a chimney sweep.

'Any problems, Sergeant?'

'None, sir. Poor Mister Gooch is lost for words, so I am doing all the talking.' Gooch shrugged and nodded.

It was the same in the chateau, where the wounded now occupied the hallway, and in the garden, where Charles Woodford's men, still recognisable as Guards, had joined Harry Wyndham's around the wall. Harry, too, looked as if he had been wallowing in mud. 'Grateful for the help, James,' said Harry, 'but we're very short of ammunition. Don't suppose there's much chance of getting any more, is there?'

'I doubt it, Harry,' replied James. 'The frogs are all around the lane. Have you recovered what you can from the casualties?'

'We have but it will not last long. Is there anything else to hand? Crossbows, javelins, slingshots?'

Macdonell laughed. 'Afraid not. You'll just have to hope that the frogs take fright and run away when they see you.'

'I thought I heard the *pas de charge*.'

'You did. Boney's infantry are on the move. Best be ready for another attack.'

'We are ready, James. Let them come.'

With a twinge of guilt, Macdonell realised that apart from his brief sleep, he had not yet visited the barn, where most of the wounded had been taken. He left the garden and made his way to the north yard.

In the barn at least a hundred men stood, sat and lay on straw soaked with blood, urine and excrement. As good as his word, the surgeon and his assistants were attending first to those with minor wounds. Cuts from bayonets or swords were stitched and bandaged. With their fingers or a pair of forceps, they probed for musket balls in stomachs and chests, being careful to keep the patient as near as possible to the position he was in when he was shot. Most balls were safely extracted and many of the wounded went straight back to the battle. Arms and legs from which a ball could not be extracted had been removed and thrown onto a heap in the corner. The little French drummer boy sat beside it, his head on his knees, sobbing quietly. The surgeon glanced up from removing a shattered finger and saw Macdonell looking at them. 'It is my practice to amputate as soon as I can,' he said. 'It reduces the chances of suppuration and gangrene. That and the generous letting of blood saves many lives.' The finger came off and joined the pile in the corner. Macdonell nodded. He knew nothing of medical matters and was content to put his trust in those who did.

'There you are, Private,' said the surgeon. 'Mrs Osborne will bind it.'

216

'Mrs Osborne?' demanded Macdonell. 'I was not aware that a woman was here.'

'Were you not, Colonel? Two women, in fact, Mrs Osborne and Mrs Rogers.' Sellers did not look up from examining a chest wound. 'And we are grateful for their help, are we not, North?'

'We are, sir,' replied the bandsman, who had had the good sense to cover his uniform with a length of sacking tucked into his collar. The sacking was streaked with blood and decorated with bits of flesh.

Macdonell looked about. 'Where are they? I do not see them.'

'They are in the chateau, Colonel,' replied North. 'We are sending the minor wounds to them for dressing. It speeds things up.'

Macdonell shook his head. He had seen no women in the chateau and for all that they were useful, he wanted to know how the devil they had got there without his knowing. He would pay them a visit.

He let his eye wander over the faces waiting their turn. Many he knew by name or by sight. Most stared back blankly. Some – the lucky ones who expected to survive – managed a weak smile. Few spoke, fewer still made any sound of distress. It was as if each man had withdrawn within himself to concentrate solely on bearing his pain without complaint. Even soldiers given to grumbling about the smallest inconvenience had the capacity to suffer stoically. Private Vindle, his face a gruesome mess of bone and flesh, sat quietly, eyes closed and arms crossed. Beside him, Joseph Graham saw Macdonell and smiled. He was holding his right thigh with both hands, trying to stem the flow of blood. Macdonell hoped it was no more than a sabre cut. If it was a musket ball he might lose the leg.

From the yard outside the barn came the sounds of desperate fighting – musket fire and voices raised in alarm. Macdonell dashed out. To his horror, the north gate was open again and James Hervey's troops were outside, their muskets pointing up the lane. As he ran to the gate, a cheer went up and a wagon pulled by two horses and driven by a single, hatless man, thundered down the lane and in through the gates. The Guards followed it in and secured the cross-beam.

Both horses had been wounded by fire from the voltigeurs hidden in the hedgerows but the driver, miraculously, was unhurt. He jumped down and called for help in unloading his wagon. When he saw Macdonell, he saluted smartly. 'Private Brewer, Colonel, Royal Waggon Train.'

'Do you bring us ammunition, Private Brewer?' asked Macdonell.

'I do, sir.'

'Good man. Now you are here, you'd best stay here. Mister Hervey will find you a musket.'

'Very good, sir.'

A brave man, Private Brewer, and a fortunate one to have survived his dash down the lane. 'Distribute the ammunition at once, Mister Hervey. Captain Wyndham in the orchard would appreciate it and so would Mister Gooch.' Macdonell barked the order. There was no time to spare.

Almost immediately, the howitzer in the wood fired and a

shell flew over the wall. It did not explode above their heads but landed in the yard and shattered. Its contents, burning clumps of pitch, gunpowder and turpentine, spilt into the yard, where they spluttered and died in the mud.

Macdonell swore. Mrs Osborne and Mrs Rogers would have to wait. The French had turned to carcass shot.

CHAPTER FIFTEEN

The man who invented carcass shot was certainly spawned by the devil. A plain canvas sack, strengthened by iron hoops and filled with a hellish mixture of turpentine, tallow, saltpetre and pitch, it burst on impact, creating fires which were nigh on impossible to extinguish. As James Macdonell knew all too well.

More carcass landed in the yards and on the roofs of the farm buildings. The guards stumbled from one shell to another, slipping in the mud and on the bloody cobbles in their haste to put out the fires. They tried urinating on them, stamping on them and throwing blankets over them. Nothing worked. The terrible things would burn until they expired and they did not expire easily. It was only a matter of time before the flame from one of them caught dry timber and Hougoumont was on fire.

It did not take long. A stack of hay had been piled against the wall of the cowshed and covered by a canvas sheet. Until then Macdonell had given it no thought. But when he saw the stack engulfed in flames, he cursed himself for not having done so. The canvas had kept the hay dry and it burnt fast. The flames caught the shed and spread inside, where they were fuelled by straw and timber. Three Nassauers on the roof jumped off, landing awkwardly in the yard but avoiding the flames.

Men ran to help but there was little to be done. Even if there had been water in the draw well it would not have been much use. The fire was too strong. Within minutes the farmer's house, where James and Alexander Saltoun had shared beef and claret, was alight. Blazing timbers fell into the yard and around the garden gate, shooting sparks into the sky and setting fire to the barricades. Burning men ripped off their jackets and rolled in the mud. In the stables and the cowshed, the horses caught the smell of fire and screamed in terror. Several charged into the yards and ran around in blind panic. One forced his way through the gate and into the garden where he was caught by a brave Nassauer. The rest, hopelessly confused, ran back into the stables.

Macdonald yelled at Sergeant Dawson to ignore the fire and keep his men at the south wall, where the French were launching another attack. At the north gate he found Hervey making a futile attempt to put out the fire which was now scorching the tiles on the cowshed roof. 'Leave it, Mister Hervey,' he bellowed. 'Concentrate on the gate. Do not allow the gate to burn.'

Once it had taken hold, the fire spread with astonishing speed. The smoke was everywhere – thick, black, suffocating. Eyes streamed, lungs filled with soot and men fell choking. Sparks caught hair and flesh and melted them. A box of cartridges exploded, killing four men nearby. The flames crossed the yard and threatened the chateau. The French were attacking from north, south and east and Hougoumont was burning. The French had seen the smoke and flames, known that the fire was out of control and changed back to round shot. The shots thundered over the walls, killing, wounding and hammering into stone and brick. The tower took a shot about halfway up. Many more like it and the tower would fall.

Macdonell ran through the chateau door, jumped over the wounded men lying in the hallway and dashed up the stairs. Private Lester and three other guards were at the top windows, firing at the enemy emerging from the wood. 'Hold this position, Lester,' shouted Macdonell. 'Do not leave the house on any account.' Without waiting for an acknowledgement he ran back down the stairs and into the yard. Even if they lost the orchard, the garden and the farm buildings, they must hold the chateau. From there, they would be able to continue harrying the French and perhaps prevent them sweeping up the slope towards Byng's artillery.

The garden, although safe from the fire, was again being attacked on every side. In the clamour and confusion Macdonell could not make out much of what was happening but through the smoke he saw that in places the walls had collapsed, leaving gaps through which faceless blue jackets were trying to fight their way, while equally faceless red ones stood and knelt in the gaps, firing volley after volley into them and hurling back those who managed to reach the wall. The bloody bodies of Frenchmen and Englishmen and Germans lay heaped together without distinction in the dirt, not only at the wall but also among the parterres and on the paths. So some Frenchmen had got inside and had died there.

Harry had abandoned his horse and was at the wall where it met the gardener's house near the south gate – the place Macdonell had chosen for himself earlier in the day – slashing and cutting with his sword at any face that appeared over the wall. As the wall there was over seven feet high, the French must have been climbing on each other's shoulders to get to the top of it. Macdonell had not yet seen a ladder being used. There was no time to check the orchard. He turned to go back to the farm. As he did so, an eight-pound shot landed behind him, spewing up earth and stones from a parterre. The soft ground took most of the shot's momentum and it bounced only once before embedding itself. A garden that had once bloomed with flowers was now littered with ugly iron balls.

In the few minutes Macdonell had been in the garden, the fire had spread. Flames were playing around the stables, the sheds and the chateau itself. Again he bellowed at the Guards at the south gate not to leave their positions. That was what the French were counting on. The fire would have to take its course. Sergeant Dawson was standing on a step, firing down into the clearing. A private was handing him up musket after musket. Over the gate and along the wall, the men worked in pairs – firing, reloading, firing again. The crack of muskets had become a continuous barrage of noise and smoke. Macdonell climbed onto a crate. The clearing had become a graveyard, filled with French bodies from the treeline to the gate. Yet still they came on. Hundreds of them, shrieking for their emperor, for France, for victory. Prince Jérôme had set light to Hougoumont and now he was pounding it with round shot and throwing troops at the gates. And he would go on doing so until he took it. He could not disappoint his brother.

Henry Gooch was on his knees, struggling to get up. Macdonell reached down and pulled him to his feet, wincing when the wound in his arm protested. The ensign's face was a bloody mask, his mouth absurdly swollen, his eyes almost closed and one cheek sliced to the bone. He could scarcely breathe. 'To the barn with you, Mister Gooch,' ordered Macdonell in a rasping voice. Gooch shook his head. 'Do as I say, sir, or you will be disobeying an order.' Gooch tried to speak, but his mouth was too dry. Instead, he gestured with an arm to the dead and wounded lying in the yard. 'I know, Mister Gooch, we need every man we have but you are in no state to fight. Go now. Tell the surgeon I want you back sharpish.'

Macdonell's head was throbbing and his throat on fire from the smoke and powder. He craved water but there was none. His canteen was dry, the well was dry. Their casualties were mounting with every French attack. Harry Wyndham in the garden was under ferocious pressure. Alexander Saltoun can only have been hanging on to the orchard by his fingertips. And Hougoumont was burning.

From beyond the chateau an arrow of flame shot skywards. He ran back to the north yard. The barn was alight. The fire had leapt from the cowshed across the yard to the barn. As he watched, the roof collapsed and burning timbers fell inside. Many of the wounded inside could not walk and would be trapped in the inferno. Their terrified screams could be heard over the crackling of timber and straw.

The barn door had disappeared and the entrance was a wall of flame. The fire had taken so quickly that very few had got out. Sellers and his assistants emerged, coughing and retching and each carrying a wounded man. They set them down in the yard and went back into the barn. A tiny, filthy figure followed them out. At least the drummer boy had escaped. A voice at Macdonell's side spoke. 'Permission to fall out, Colonel, if you please.' It was James Graham.

'Why, Corporal? You are needed at the gate.' It was a surprising request from a soldier as dutiful as Graham.

'My brother is in the barn, Colonel. He took a bullet in the leg.'

Macdonell remembered seeing him inside. He clapped Graham on the shoulder. 'Then be quick, for his sake and ours.' Graham ran straight through the flames at the entrance and disappeared into the blazing barn.

The surgeon staggered out again. He was carrying no one and his jacket was on fire. Macdonell leapt at him, pushed him to the ground and rolled him in the mud. The fire died and the surgeon rose unsteadily to his feet. 'Your assistants?' asked Macdonell. Sellers shook his head. The barn was collapsing and James and Joseph Graham were in there and so was Henry Gooch.

The stench of burning flesh was overpowering. Macdonell ripped off his jacket, held it over his face and crashed through the flames into the barn. Even without a roof it was full of smoke. He could see almost nothing. He blundered blindly forward. God willing, there was someone still alive whom he might be able to carry to safety. A huge figure loomed out of the smoke and stumbled past him. The figure seemed to be carrying a body over his shoulder. Macdonell groped his way forward. A spark caught his hair, making it crackle. He managed to smother it with his jacket and pressed on. A blazing timber fell from the roof. He tripped over it and landed on the stone floor. The heat of the stone scorched his hands, forcing him back to his feet. He fell again. This time his hands met not stone but flesh. A body, and one that was alive. It grunted and moved. Macdonell hoisted it onto his shoulder and made for the entrance. At least he hoped he was making for the entrance. In the heat and smoke he had lost his sense of direction. He took a dozen unsteady steps, saw a glimmer of daylight, threw himself and his burden through the entrance and fell into the yard.

His eyes opened when earth was thrown over him. A stab of pain shot through them and he quickly closed them again. He lay in the yard trying to breathe. Someone pulled off his boots. Someone else tipped a few drops of water down his throat. Gradually his mind cleared and he could open his eyes. The crash of musket fire and the screams of wounded men and burning horses filled his head. The north gate was again under threat. He pushed himself to his knees and looked about. The barn was a smouldering heap of wood and flesh and bone.

Henry Gooch was sitting with his back to the draw well, bare-chested and bootless. Joseph Graham sat beside him, his leg twisted and bloody. Both were the colour of tar. 'Corporal Graham, so your brother found you?' growled Macdonell.

'He did, Colonel. I am a lucky man, though the surgeon thinks my leg beyond saving.'

'And you, Mister Gooch, how did you get out?'

Gooch could only whisper. 'I believe you carried me, Colonel.'

'Then I am glad of it. Help Corporal Graham to the chateau. Take the boy. There are wounded there.'

'Should you not be there yourself, Colonel?' asked Graham.

'Later, Corporal.' Another tower of flame shot into the sky. The roof of the chateau was alight. 'On second thoughts, stay here. It's as safe a place as any.'

The barn, the stables and cowshed and now the chateau. All burnt or burning. If the fire reached the gardener's house or the shed beside it, the south gate would burn too. There was no water with which to fight the fire and nowhere to hide from the round shot still thundering over the wood and into the farm. Macdonell looked at his pocket watch. It was just after three o'clock. They had held Hougoumont for four hours. If General Blücher and his Prussians did not arrive very soon, the next hour would be their last.

CHAPTER SIXTEEN

On the hill behind them, General Byng and Major Bull were doing their best to keep the French artillery quiet. Cannon blasted ten-pound shot over the wood while the howitzers sent a stream of their deadly shells into it. For the attackers, just as for the defenders, there was little respite. Yet the French guns were far from silenced. The Gunners in the valley were loading canister as well as round shot, battering the chateau and the farm and raining death and mutilation onto the Guards in the yards and in the garden.

Macdonell made a decision. He would hold the chateau and defend the gates for as long as possible. Only when he had to, he would withdraw all his troops into the garden from where they would fire on the French entering the farm. Alexander Saltoun would hold the orchard behind them. He would move the wounded from the chateau to the garden immediately. They would be safer there and the surgeon would just have to do what he could for them. He had lost his bandsmen but the women, hopefully, were unharmed.

Almost without a break, the French infantry attacked the south gate and the walls. Wave after wave charged forward, screaming for their emperor, ignoring the losses they were taking, and forcing the Guards to expose themselves to French fire. The best soldiers could fire three or four shots a minute. The Guards were firing at least that.

But the pressure was beginning to tell. Shaking hands spilt powder. Barrels overheated. Flints failed to spark. Muskets misfired. Lungs craving air filled with smoke. Mouths craving water struggled to bite off the end of yet another cartridge. Stomachs heaved and threw out what little contents they had. Sharpshooters in the woods and the clearing picked off heads that appeared over the wall. Men screamed and died. By force of numbers alone, the French would eventually break down the gate or destroy the wall. The Guards could not resist for ever.

It was the same in the garden. Harry Wyndham's troops, supported by Charles Woodford's two companies, were on the fire steps, at the loopholes, and even sitting astride the walls, in their efforts to keep the French at a distance. Macdonell could not see either of them through the smoke. One blackened uniform was much like another.

He made his way carefully into the middle of the garden, stepping over bodies and closing his ears to the cries of the wounded. The French canister had done its terrible work, cleaving open heads and tearing flesh from bodies. The dead lay everywhere. Without Woodford's help, Harry's company would already have been wiped out. And the canister kept coming and coming, hurling its fearful contents into faces and limbs.

Charles Woodford was at the orchard end of the garden, firing over the wall into the field. 'By God, James,' he croaked, wiping powder from his mouth, 'this is terrible work. There's no end to them. The more we kill, the more they come. And we're losing too many men to the canister. I see the fire is still raging. How much longer can we hold on?' A shell exploded nearby. Instinctively, they ducked their heads as iron balls and shards of red-hot metal flew past them. Hidden by the smoke, a man cried out for his mother.

Macdonell had to shout. 'The chateau is on fire. I will have the wounded brought into the garden. We will hold the house and the farm as long as we can and then join you here. Saltoun will hold the orchard.'

'Saltoun's gone. Francis Hepburn has taken over the orchard with the 3rd Guards. They cleared the lane to get there.'

Macdonell shook his head in surprise. He had no idea that Saltoun had been replaced. In the confusion, he had seen nothing and no word had reached him. Women, Saltoun, what else did the officer in charge of the defence of Hougoumont not know? Yet it was hardly surprising. The 1st Guards in the orchard had had the very worst of the fighting and must have been exhausted. 'Then we shall be in Francis's hands and if we hold the lane there is a chance of reinforcements.'

'A chance. Your plan is sound, James. You have my support.'

'Thank you. Please tell Harry, wherever he is.'

'I will.'

At the north gates, the foul stench of burning flesh still hung heavy in the air. The roof and walls of the barn were no more, exposing its gruesome contents for all to see. Among the ashes and embers, the fire had left blackened, scorched, twisted reminders of the terror and agony it had brought.

James Hervey had lost the advantage of the cowshed roof, now a heap of smouldering timbers, but the gates were still intact. Macdonell stood on a half-barrel and looked over the wall. His arm throbbed and the palms of his hands were raw. He ignored them. French bodies covered the clearing. He stepped down and told Hervey his plan. 'You will remain here until I send orders to withdraw into the garden,' he said. 'Bring with you all the muskets and ammunition you can carry. French or British, either will do. Make two trips if you have to, but be quick. The order will come only at the last minute.'

Hervey nodded. 'I understand, Colonel.'

A shout came from a man at the wall. 'Single rider coming down the lane, sir. Uniform of a major.'

'Let him in,' shouted back Macdonell. A single rider was unlikely to be a French trick.

The gates were briefly opened and the major ushered in. He did not dismount. 'Major Andrew Hamilton,' he introduced himself. 'I have an order for Colonel Macdonell from His Grace.'

'I am Macdonell. What is the order?' The major handed him a rolled sheet of goatskin. The order was in the Duke's hand and written in pencil. Macdonell read it twice. 'Thank you, Major. Please assure His Grace that I shall do exactly as he orders.' Hamilton saluted and turned his mount to leave. 'Before you go, Major,' called out Macdonell, 'what news can you give us?'

'The artillery bombardment continues, as you can hear. French cavalry threaten our squares. The farm at La Haye Sainte is barely held. His Grace believes the battle will be decided here at Hougoumont.'

'And the Prussians?'

'An hour away at least. Good luck, Colonel.'

'Well, well,' said Macdonell, when the major had gone. 'His Grace orders us to hold the chateau, being careful to avoid falling timbers, and to retire to the garden when we have to. A happy coincidence, don't you agree, Hervey?'

Hervey grinned. 'I do, sir. No room for doubt or dispute.'

'Quite. But remember. Only when I give the order and then at the run.'

The flames had reached the chapel and were playing around the door. The roof of the chateau was on fire and the top of the tower had disappeared. Henry Gooch, still unable to speak, had returned to the south gate. Macdonell gave him his orders and returned to the chateau. From there he would get the best view and would know when the moment to withdraw to the garden had come.

The hallway where the wounded had lain – those lucky enough not to have been in the barn – was, for the moment, intact. He remembered the women. He found them in the dining room, tending to rows of wounded men lying on the floor. One was dressing the stump of an arm, the other bandaging a head. 'I am surprised to find you here, ladies,' he shouted over the cannon and muskets, 'although you are not unwelcome. The barn has gone and the roof of this house is on fire. I have ordered the wounded taken to the garden and treated there. You must go there yourselves. The surgeon's assistants are dead.'

'As you wish, Colonel,' replied the younger woman. 'Osborne – my husband – is in the orchard.'

'And mine,' added the other. 'Tom Rogers, private.'

'Go at once. The house is not safe. These men will be carried there.' The women nodded.

He climbed the stairs, also intact but unsteady under his weight, and reached the upper floor. Private Lester and his three comrades were still there, firing from the windows into the wood and the far end of the clearing. Above their heads, the roof timbers were spitting and crackling in the flames. With hardly a break, the four men had been there for over four hours, relatively safe from enemy muskets but at the mercy of cannon and now from fire.

Macdonell repeated his orders to Lester. 'We will hold the house to the last minute before withdrawing to the garden. I have ordered the wounded taken there. Is that clear, Private?'

Joseph Lester straightened up from ramming a ball into the barrel of a musket, his back to a window. In the fury of the battle outside, Macdonell did not hear the shot. It could only have been a lucky one, aimed in the general direction of the chateau. Lester fell forward, blood spurting from his shoulder.

Macdonell sighed. 'I cannot spare another man. You must manage as you are.' He was gone before any of them could reply.

To reach the orchard he ran back through the garden and clambered over the wall. As Charles Woodford had said, Saltoun had returned to the ridge and left the orchard and the lane in the hands of Francis Hepburn and his 3rd Guards. Beyond the hedge, so ragged it was more like a broken row of scrubby bushes, and the ditch, now a common grave, Lancers milled about in the field, preparing for their next attack. The orchard had changed hands three or four times that day and there was no saying that it would not do so again.

Francis was supervising the cleaning of muskets and distribution of ammunition. He saw James making his way between what was left of the fruit trees and waved a hand. 'You come at a good time, James,' he shouted. 'A lull in the fighting, brief no doubt, and we're in need of every man we can get.'

Macdonell came up to him. 'As are we all. I was not aware that you had replaced Saltoun.'

'The message probably went astray. Saltoun's men were out on their feet and could do no more. The peer sent us down to take over. We've seen off one attack and we're expecting another.' He pointed at the Lancers in the field. 'Look at the devils getting ready.'

'I see them. Francis, I came to tell you our orders. We are to hold the chateau for as long as we can and then withdraw into the garden to join Charles Woodford and Harry Wyndham. You will be at our back.'

'I do hope so. At least that will mean we are still alive.'

There was a huge explosion from the farm. A box of ammunition must have gone up. 'We cannot fight the fire and the French at the same time, Francis,' said James, 'whatever the peer expects of us.'

'I know you, James. You will find a way.' He paused. 'Do you know, I rather think that this might be the first battle ever in which there are no survivors at all. The carnage on the ridge is beyond words.'

'The carnage everywhere must be beyond words. We have hundreds dead. I fear Lester is among them, your champion. I saw him fall.' Macdonell looked over Hepburn's shoulder. 'It seems your Lancers are leaving.'

Francis turned to look. 'So they are. Ah, there's the reason.' Down the slope from the ridge, marching steadily in line, was a battalion of green-jacketed infantry. They were followed by a second battalion. Nearly two thousand men in all. 'King's German Legion. Excellent troops. Now your rear will be secure, James.'

'Good. But much of the farm has been destroyed and the chateau is on fire. I will leave the Germans to you.'

They were fighting not one battle to defend Hougoumont, but four – in the orchard, the garden, the farm and the chateau. Hold Hougoumont, the Duke had said, and the battle will be won. From the ridge he would have seen enough to know what was happening there. He knew the chateau was on fire and the farm and garden under bombardment. He probably knew or could guess that they had no food or water. He knew they were exhausted. He would have a good idea of their depleted numbers. He had sent two battalions of German veterans to reinforce the orchard. And he had sent down clear orders. Hougoumont must be held.

The latest attack on the south gate, like the others, had failed. The French had withdrawn to lick their wounds before trying again. In the distance cannon roared and muskets fired, but around the farm there was a strange quiet. Not silence – in battle there was never silence – but the sounds of voices and movement rather than guns.

Sergeant Dawson was sitting in the mud, his back to the wall, trying to open a cartridge of powder with his teeth. It was something he had done hundreds, thousands of times. But he could not do it. His mouth was too dry. Macdonell took the cartridge from him and bit off the end. Although he had fired less than half the number of rounds that the sergeant and his men had, his mouth too was like tinder. Dawson nodded his thanks.

There was no water. Those who could, emptied their bladders down the barrels of their muskets to cool them. Those who could not, threw their gun down and went in search for a replacement. Bleeding lips were dosed with drops of gin. Sweat and dust were rubbed from streaming eyes. Hands and fingers rubbed raw were wrapped in scraps of cloth. Macdonell inspected his own hands. They were red and sore from the barn floor. He forced a drop of saliva into his mouth and spat on them. That would have to do.

Henry Gooch, now barely recognisable, was on his feet, moving painfully from man to man, patting shoulders and shaking hands. 'Seriously wounded to the garden, Mister Gooch,' ordered Macdonell. 'Everyone else to make ready for the next attack. It won't be long coming.' Gooch raised a hand in acknowledgement.

The roof of the chateau was still blazing but had not yet fallen in, nor had the fire spread below the top floor. The chapel and the gardener's house were alight. The tower had gone.

At the north gates, James Hervey was bustling about,

inspecting wounds and checking muskets. James Graham was on a step at the wall. From the slump of his shoulders, even he looked exhausted. His brother was propped against the draw well. His eyes were closed but his thigh had been strapped and he was losing no more blood.

Macdonell called up to Graham. 'Take your brother to the garden, Corporal Graham. The surgeon will do what he can there. Be quick now.' Graham stepped clumsily down and stumbled to the well. 'Mister Hervey, I rather think we are in for another dose of angry Frenchmen and this one even nastier than the last. Are you prepared?'

From a face streaked with powder and dirt, Macdonell saw a tiny glint of teeth. A man who could smile or even try to smile after fighting for nearly six hours deserved to survive. 'We are, Colonel, as best we can. Primed and loaded.' The words rasped in his throat.

'Very well. Colonel Woodford and Captain Wyndham are in the garden. I shall be at the south gate. God be with you.'

'And with you, Colonel.'

They both knew that the next French attack would be the last. With his two thousand Germans, Francis Hepburn might hold the orchard but if Jérôme was calling up yet more troops, Hougoumont was surely doomed. A few hundred tired men could hold it no longer. They would be forced to withdraw to the garden.

The fire was still raging. The barn was gone, and the cowshed, and the stables. The chateau roof had finally collapsed, dropping timbers on to the floor below and setting it alight. The chapel was burning, the farmer's house was burning. Round shot had destroyed the tower and reduced the yards to piles of rubble. The dead lay among bricks and timbers and ashes. There was no time to move them. Carnage, Francis Hepburn had said. It was the right word.

The captain who trotted down the lane from the ridge at the head of three companies of black-clad Brunswickers and led them through the north gates into the farm was tall and fair. Macdonell recognised him at once. 'Captain Hellman, we meet again.'

The captain grinned and handed him a canteen of water. 'It is my pleasure, Colonel. I have five hundred men. Where would you like them?'

Macdonell tipped water into his mouth and swilled it around before swallowing. 'A hundred at the north gate, Captain, two hundred in the garden and the remainder here in the south yard, if you please. Do you have enough water for all?'

'Two canteens each.'

Another volley of four-pound balls crashed into the wall. 'Make haste, Captain. The enemy are at the gates.'

With Captain Hellman's Brunswickers, there were now about a thousand men in the farm and the garden. Francis Hepburn, reinforced by the Germans, would have over two thousand in the orchard. How many would Jérôme hurl at them?

It did not take the light cannon much longer. Jérôme had lost patience. He wanted the affair over. Volley after volley struck the south wall, smashing holes in the brickwork and breaking it open. The holes soon became gaps large enough for one man to get through, then two, then three. The gate hung loose on its hinges. Macdonell stood with the Guards and the

Brunswickers waiting for the moment. He had ordered every spare musket loaded and stacked by the fire steps along the wall. The Duke had sent reinforcements and must now be expecting them to fight on in the farm. Perhaps the Prussians had at last arrived. If so, they would be threatening the French right wing. If the Guards and Brunswickers could keep Jérôme's troops at the burning Hougoumont, it would reduce Buonaparte's options. Now there would be no withdrawal to the garden.

The first warning came from the men on the fire steps by the gate. Prince Jérôme might well have demanded more men but he had decided, as if to atone for not having done so earlier, to blast what remained of Hougoumont to dust. He had brought up a fresh artillery team with four-pound guns – the very guns he had used to good effect before Woodford arrived and that Macdonell himself would have gone on using. Why the Prince had not done so was a mystery.

The first volley smashed into the gardener's house. The second into the wall. There was no point in returning fire – there was nothing to aim at. The French Gunners crouched behind their guns and in the trees. Better to save ammunition for the attack that would come the moment the wall or the gate were breached. Macdonell watched and waited.

The surgeon was directing the transfer of the wounded to the garden. Those who had lost legs or suffered serious leg wounds were carried on stretchers fashioned from jackets slung between two muskets. The stretcher-bearers scuttled back and forth between the chateau and the garden gate, closing their ears to the sobs and screams of the wounded and eager to get the job done. Mrs Osborne and Mrs Rogers were in the garden, doing what little they could.

James Graham appeared at Macdonell's side. 'Are you not meant to be at the north gate, Corporal Graham?' he asked.

'With your permission, sir, I would like to be here,' replied Graham. The big Irishman was a fearful sight – the dye from his jacket had run down his trousers, turning them pink, and he was covered from collar to boot in streaks of blood, mud and grime. His hands and face were black.

'You have my permission, Corporal.'

Jérôme's light cannon were still battering the walls and the gaps in them were widening. Through them they caught glimpses of the French near the woods. It would not be long now. A round shot flew over their heads and crashed into the chateau. Another destroyed the garden gate. The gardener's house where Macdonell had posted more men to shoot down into the clearing was battered and crumbling. He looked about. There was little left to defend. But his strange company of black Brunswickers and filthy, hollow-eyed Guards were ready.

Sergeant Dawson, at the gate, gave the signal. Macdonell bellowed the order to charge and ran. Every man in the yard followed him and did what he had been told to do. He screeched and howled and screamed. At the wall they jumped over bricks and bodies and met the French head on. They fired their muskets into French faces, reversed their weapons and smashed the butts into mouths and eyes and noses. Macdonell had hoped to take the French by surprise, and he had.

Slashing and skewering, he bludgeoned a path towards a mounted French captain armed with a long cavalry sabre and desperately shouting orders. Around him, Guard and Brunswicker killed and wounded and maimed, pressing home their advantage while they could.

Macdonell reached the captain, ducked under his slash, grabbed a stirrup and tipped him off his mount. The captain lay on the ground, his sabre raised in defence. A musket fired over Macdonell's shoulder and the captain's eye turned to mush. 'Easy pickings,' snarled a voice behind him. It was Luke. Macdonell could not reply. The point of a French sword appeared under the private's ribs, twisted brutally and withdrew. Eyes wide with shock, he fell forward, blood gushing from his back. His killer turned and disappeared into the melee.

The clearing had become a battlefield. Muskets fired, swords slashed and men died. A head taller than anyone else, James Graham towered over the crush. He hammered his musket butt down onto French shakos, crushing them into skulls and splintering cheekbones and jaws. A group of Frenchmen surrounded him. Holding his musket by the barrel and swinging it like a scythe, he scattered them.

Captain Hellman's Brunswickers had worked their way around both sides of the clearing and trapped the French like fish in a net. They were merciless. Blue jacket after blue jacket fell and died. The Brunswickers shrugged off their own losses and clawed their way into the body of the enemy.

The French fought bravely. Despite the furious charge that had taken them unawares, they did not lose their discipline, nor did they turn and run. Rallied by their lieutenants, they began to fight back. Coldstreams fell, Brunswickers fell. The surprise had gone and the fight was in the balance. More French came out of the trees, firing as they ran and shouting for their emperor. They tipped the scales. The Guards found themselves being pushed back towards the farm.

At what remained of the wall around the gate, Macdonell called for a stand. 'Hold the wall,' he bellowed. 'Keep them out. Coldstreams with me. Brunswickers inside and on the wall.' Captain Hellman led his Brunswickers through the gate and the wall. They climbed onto the fire steps and took up the muskets stacked there.

Outside the wall, a line of Coldstreams blocked the gate and the gaps in the wall. Some of them fell to French muskets, but the French could not break their line. They stabbed and sliced, punched and kicked, and gouged French eyes and mouths with their hands. Macdonell, in the centre of the line, drove the hilt of his sword into a lieutenant's face and saw his nose disintegrate in a fountain of blood.

In the clearing the French were packed tight, elbowing each other aside in their haste to reach the farm. From behind the wall the Brunswickers poured fire into them, yet they came on, stepping over comrades' bodies, ignoring the wounded, screaming for France and for Buonaparte. This time, at last, they would surely take Hougoumont.

Above the crack of muskets and the clash of steel and the cries of triumph and pain and death, Macdonell did not hear the howitzer fire. Major Bull had seen his chance and taken the risk. And he knew his business. The shell flew high over the wall, seemed to hover for a second above the clearing and crashed down into the very middle of the French troops. Its lethal charge of iron shot and scalding metal cut a swathe of death through them. Dozens fell, maimed or dead, shrieking in agony, uncomprehending. Without warning, death had rained on them from the sky.

More shells fell, more French died. The Coldstreams backed up against the wall, hoping that the Gunners' aim would not falter, while the Brunswickers added their bullets to the mayhem. For the attackers, it was too much. The howitzers had their range and would go on blasting their shells until every one of them was dead. A French trumpet sounded the retreat.

The Guards slipped back into the yard. The Brunswickers jeered and hooted at French backs. Macdonell left them in the hands of Dawson and Gooch and went quickly to the garden. The gate and part of the farm wall had been destroyed by round shot and the garden was no longer recognisable. Not a blade of grass or a plant to be seen. Instead, corpses, mud, bricks, timbers and discarded muskets lay singly and in heaps. Along the wall lay the wounded, among them the huge figure of Joseph Graham. They were tended by the two women, Mrs Osborne and Mrs Rogers. Macdonell wondered fleetingly if their husbands were still alive.

Brunswickers and Guards stood and sat in clusters, attending to their muskets and sipping water from canteens. Harry Wyndham and Charles Woodford were at the far wall, from where there was a clear view of the orchard.

'What news?' called out Macdonell.

'Hard fighting, James,' replied Harry, wiping his mouth with a sleeve. 'They came at us in droves. Thank God for the Brunswickers.'

'As long as the wall is standing,' added Charles, 'we can hold the position. For now, we have enough men. What of the farm?'

'Still burning, as you can see. The gate is broken and the south wall wrecked. Bloody work keeping them out. Bull's howitzers rescued us. The frogs will try something else next time. And Francis? Has he held the orchard?'

'Colonel Home now commands the orchard.'

'Is Francis wounded?'

'I do not know. They have twice had to face cavalry. It's a wonder they still hold the ground.'

'Ammunition?'

'Getting low.' From the field beyond the garden a round shot smashed against the wall. It was followed by musket fire. 'Here they come again, James. *Bonne chance.*' Macdonell raced back to the farm.

All four entrances to Hougoumont were under attack: Charles and Harry in the orchard; the north gates where James Hervey, without the advantage of the cowshed and stable, had men on steps, barrels and crates, firing down over the wall; the small west gate, which a French platoon were trying to set alight; and the south gate, the most vulnerable.

A quick look at the north and west gates and Macdonell ran past the smouldering chateau and back to the south yard. Hervey's troop would have to fend for themselves. Gooch and Dawson were at the wall. Graham was encouraging the men, checking their muskets and ammunition and doling out gin from a small cask. Where he had found that, Macdonell had no idea.

Outside the wall, there was no sign of the French. Not a blue jacket in sight, except for the dead in the clearing. 'Taken fright,

Colonel, and hopped off back to Paris, I shouldn't wonder,' said Dawson.

'Would that you were right, Sergeant. Alas, I fear not. Although I confess I do not know what they are up to. The other gates are under attack and so is the garden, yet this is our most vulnerable spot and the frogs know it.'

The answer came almost immediately. Cantering around the wood came a troop of Dragoons. Macdonell counted – there were fifty. Their mounts were jet black with a blaze of white, their black-tasselled helmets gleamed in the evening sun, their green jackets were spotless, and they were armed with short-barrelled carbines and straight-bladed swords. Not for them the awkward curved swords of the cuirassiers and the Lancers. Dragoons were cavalry, but as ready to fight on foot as on horseback. These Dragoons were fresh and drawn from Buonaparte's elite reserves. France's finest. Behind them, a column of infantry emerged from the shattered wood.

Forming square would be fatal. The Dragoons would simply race past the squares and into the farm. The troops at the north and west gates would be slaughtered like pigs. Having disposed of them, the Dragoons would turn back to the south gates to join their infantry. The infantry who had failed and failed again to take Hougoumont. Their mood would be murderous.

'Sergeant Dawson,' yelled Macdonell, 'every step manned and ready to fire the moment they come. Aim for the horses. And muskets behind every door, wall and window with a clear view of the yard. Hurry.' Captain Hellman was in the garden. There was no time for the niceties of command. 'Brunswickers with me at the wall. Hold your fire until I give the word. If they get in we'll hit them from the rear. Corporal Graham, by the chateau, if you please. They must not get through the yard.' Between the chateau and the smouldering remains of the barn, a mounted man might get through to the north gate.

He ran into the gardener's house and up the stairs. The Dragoons were gathering on the edge of the wood. Their captain sat a pace ahead of the line, his gaze fixed on the wall. The infantry had formed up behind them. It was the same as far as he could see along the garden wall – a line of Dragoons, supported by infantry. The garden wall was still intact. They would find it more difficult to break in there. The farm and chateau were another matter.

He dashed back to the yard and took a place with the Brunswickers. A private offered him a musket. He shook his head and withdrew the heavy sword from its scabbard. The sword had met cavalry before. It knew what to do with them.

In less than a minute they were ready. James Graham was by the chateau wall with six men. He raised a hand to Macdonell and smiled. Sergeant Dawson, on a fire step, adjusted his shako and stood as tall as he could. Henry Gooch checked that his sword would come free from its scabbard. A Brunswicker lieutenant shouted something in German. Two hundred men lined the walls and waited.

The charge came without warning. Hooves thundered over the ground and the French captain galloped through the broken gate and into the yard. His Dragoons took the wreckage of the wall like steeplechasers and flooded in behind him. Not one fell to the muskets at the wall. Suddenly the yard was full of horses, perhaps thirty of them, the rest forcing their way in behind.

If they found a way through to the north gate, Hougoumont would be lost. Macdonell gave the order and muskets fired from every door and window. Half the horses in the yard fell, their riders crushed under them or thrown into the melee.

Caught in the trap and half their number killed or wounded, the remaining Dragoons should have surrendered or been swiftly despatched. But these were elite troops, proud and disciplined. Their carbines spat bullets into enemy faces. The private who had offered Macdonell a musket screamed and fell. The Dragoon captain barked an order. His men drew their swords. He barked another order and the Dragoons hurriedly formed themselves into a rough square among the dead in the middle of the yard. Macdonell shouted and the Guards charged.

The Dragoons were brave men and sold their lives dearly. When the last of them fell, nine Guards had died. Macdonell's sword dripped blood and his arm ached from wielding it. Injured horses were despatched with a single shot, the few which had escaped injury were herded back through the gate.

The Brunswickers at the wall had held their fire. Now they turned it on the French infantry who were waiting for a signal to advance. The French saw the frightened horses and knew what had happened. They quickly disappeared back into the wood.

Sergeant Graham organised the clearing of the dead. The Dragoons joined the pile by the chapel, their horses were dragged to the wall. Macdonell checked the west gate and the north gates again. They were secure.

So was the garden. The French cavalry had been blasted by Major Bull's howitzers and been driven off. Charles Woodford and Harry Wyndham were unhurt. Captain Hellman was dead, struck in the chest by a musket ball. Mrs Osborne had also been wounded. A shot had entered her breast and lodged in her shoulder. She lay beside her husband whose left eye had gone.

In the yards and the farm buildings, not one of them untouched by fire or cannon, in the garden and at the walls, men lay spent among the dead. Blue jackets, black, red and green sprawled in a macabre embrace of death. Idly, Macdonell pulled out his pocket watch. It was twenty minutes after seven o'clock.

Then he heard it. Even half a mile distant it was unmistakeable. The booming, threatening, unrelenting roll of drums that announced the advance of Buonaparte's Imperial Guard. In the centre of each column of marching guards, drummers beat out the rhythm of the advance. The Emperor sensed victory. He only released his beloved Guard when the enemy were on the point of defeat. That, in part, was why they were known as *Les Immortales*.

The Guards had defended Hougoumont for over eight hours. All day they had held the chateau and the farm and the garden. They had faced artillery, cavalry and infantry and refused to be beaten. Yet now the Imperial Guard was on the move. The French had won. It had been in vain.

CHAPTER SEVENTEEN

Harry Wyndham had left the garden and found James leaning against the chapel wall. 'Can you hear it?' he asked. James nodded. 'Does it mean what I think it means?'

'I fear so.' He could barely get the words out.

'What's to be done?'

James pushed himself upright. His legs shook and the wound in his arm throbbed. He could not see out of his blood-caked right eye and his throat was on fire. 'Until we are ordered otherwise, we will stay here,' he croaked. 'If the frogs come again, we will kill as many of them as we can. After that . . .' The thought hung in the air.

'Woodford said you would say that. He wants you to know that he agrees. We will hold the garden until we receive word.'

'Tell him that we will do the same.' He waved a hand around the yard. 'Not that there is much left to hold.' He held out the hand to Harry. 'Your first battle, Harry, and you will never fight a tougher one.'

Harry's filth-covered face lit up in a grin. 'I certainly hope not.'

In the distance, apart from the drums, it had gone strangely quiet, as if the French Gunners were leaving the stage to their emperor's Imperial Guard. Few muskets fired, even fewer cannon. The drums beat out the march and, in his mind's eye, Macdonell saw the solid blue columns advancing up the slope. He was almost tempted to go to the orchard to watch them. The rhythm of the drums quickened. The Guard was charging. He swallowed hard and tried to shout. 'Mister Gooch, all muskets at the wall and eyes on the woods, if you please. Corporal Graham, kindly take a look at the north gate. Mister Hervey might be in need of assistance. Sergeant Dawson, distribute whatever ammunition we have left.' He paused. 'And gin if there is any.'

With the Guard on the ridge, Jérôme might well decide that he had one last chance to take Hougoumont. He had been trying all day and with a final attack by his rampaging, exultant infantry he would expect finally to succeed.

James Graham had returned from the north gates. 'The gates are secure, Colonel,' he reported. 'Mister Hervey has seventy men but is short of powder.'

'Can't do much to help there, I fear. James, if the Guard is on the ridge, we are likely to face another attack. I do not want it to end inside the walls. When the frogs appear, you and I will lead a charge. Every man we've got, Brunswickers and Guards. Colonel Woodford will defend the garden.'

'A fine plan, Colonel. One more go at them it shall be.'

The small west gate had never seriously been threatened and with the north gates secure under Mister Hervey, he would throw every man still standing into the charge. There was no point in a roll-call. At a rough guess, he had one hundred and fifty light company men and one hundred Brunswickers. The rest he had sent to the garden. Two hundred and fifty against whatever Jérôme sent against them – five hundred? A thousand? More? They were very low on powder and shot, worn out and in dire need of food and water. The French would be rested and fed.

'I doubt it will be much of a fight, James,' replied Macdonell. 'We shall squash the French like ants.' General Byng's artillery had stopped firing over them. The Duke must have moved them to their left, from where they would be able to fire on the advancing French columns. The threat of an attack on his right flank had been superseded by the threat to his centre. 'Mister Gooch, Sergeant Dawson, gather all the troops save those at the north and west gates in the yard.' Hougoumont could be held no longer but there was one last fight to be won.

The chateau and chapel were still burning. The barn and farmer's house and stables were little more than heaps of smouldering ashes. There really was very little left to defend. Macdonell absently brushed ash from his jacket, and yelped. His palms were agony. He would not be able to hold a sword. The body of a jacketless French corporal lay on top of the heap by the chapel. Being careful to use only his fingers, he ripped open the corporal's shirt. 'Allow me, Colonel,' said a voice behind him.

Macdonell looked round. 'Thank you, James. I was just trying to work out how to do it without crying like a baby.'

James Graham used his bayonet to cut two strips from the shirt. 'Hands out, if you please, Colonel.' It was embarrassing, but he had no choice. Macdonell held out his hands, palms up, and watched Graham tie a strip of cloth around each one. 'Try that, Colonel,' said Graham, holding out his own hands. Macdonell grasped them and grimaced. Holding a sword would be possible but not easy.

'You would have made a fine surgeon, Corporal,' he said.

Graham laughed. 'Now there's a thought, Colonel. When I go back to Ireland and I'm too old for soldiering, I might just take to studying medicine. I'd be the first doctor in the family.'

There was a shout of warning from the window of the gardener's house, followed by a long roll of drums. They were coming. 'Every man in the yard. Muskets checked and ready,' yelled Macdonell. 'On my order, we will advance. There will be only one shot each, so aim well. Our task is to kill as many of them as we can.'

The Guards watching from the gardener's house ran down the stairs to join them. The yard was full. Macdonell made his way to the gate. The wood was full of blue jackets, spilling out into the clearing. Among the leafless trees, mounted officers stood ready to join the attack. It was the same as far as he could see to his left. For the length of the garden and beyond, lines of French infantry awaited the order to charge.

But James Macdonell would not allow them to charge. The Guards would beat them to it. He turned to face them. 'Fill your lungs, aim well and hit hard,' he shouted. 'With me, now.

Charge!' He hopped over the broken wall, the Guards and Brunswickers screaming and shrieking behind him.

The leading Guards had almost crossed the clearing before they put their left shoulders forward and fired. The Brunswickers did the same. Dozens of blue jackets fell. Dozens more returned fire and ran forward to receive the Guards' charge. Once again, the clearing was a battlefield.

Macdonell felt a surge of energy flow through him – that special energy of battle, which could give a man the strength to go on however tired he was. He raised his sword and hacked down on a French head. Blood spurted and the man fell. He smashed the hilt into a face and thrust the point into a stomach. All around him Guard fought Frenchman and Frenchman fought Brunswicker. The clearing was a heaving, struggling, bellowing crush of bodies. Muskets slammed into noses and chests, swords hacked at heads and limbs and bayonets sliced into flesh and bone. Whatever was happening on the ridge was forgotten. Each man could think only of his own battle to kill and survive, or die.

The energy that gave strength also dulled pain. The bandages had gone from his hands yet Macdonell felt nothing. Again and again he used his sword to thrust and slice and his height and reach to defend himself from the butts of muskets and the points of bayonets.

Two Frenchmen were falling for every Brunswicker or Guard, but bravely as they fought, the Guards could not hold back the tide of Frenchmen for ever. Gradually, inevitably, they were forced back towards the wall, leaving their dead and wounded lying in churned, blood-soaked, guts-splattered earth. Macdonell found himself beside the towering figure of James Graham who had appropriated the axe of the giant sous-lieutenant and was using it to fell any Frenchman who came within striking distance. Twice, Macdonell stepped back sharply to avoid the arc of its blade and twice saw a French head fly from a French body as cleanly as if its owner had met his end on the guillotine.

Some of the French had managed to slip round the west wall and up the lane towards the north gates. If they breached the gates and attacked the Guards from the rear, the battle would be over. Macdonell could only trust that Hervey and his small troop would keep them out. He had no inkling of what was happening in the garden or the orchard but as no French had yet appeared behind them, hoped that they were still held.

Their backs were now hard against the wall of the house and the shed beside it. Macdonell stood beside the portly figure of Sergeant Dawson under the arch of the gate. They could retreat no further without surrendering the farm and the chateau, so they would stand where they were. James Graham was still swinging the axe with brutal force, Dawson was thrusting his bayonet into stomachs and groins, every Guard and every Brunswicker was smashing, cutting and gouging at whatever he could.

And so was every Frenchman. Their commander had only to call his men back to allow his muskets a clear sight, and they would drop the Guards like a row of skittles. But the French attackers were not to be called back. They had suffered grievous casualties and would not allow them to have been in vain.

Neither order nor threat would deter them. They would have the glory of taking Hougoumont.

Sergeant Dawson thrust his bayonet at another French groin, lost his footing and fell face down in the mud. The butt of a musket smashed into the back of his head and he lay still. Macdonell grabbed the musket, tore it free and jammed it into its owner's face, which dissolved into a mess of blood and bone. He stooped quickly to put a hand to Dawson's neck. The sergeant was dead. As he rose, a blow slammed into his shoulder, sending a stab of pain down his wounded arm. He lashed out with his sword, felt it strike bone and lashed again. A Frenchman fell with blood spurting from his thigh. A thrust into his windpipe and he too was dead.

The first cries came from outside the orchard. At first Macdonell could not make out even if the voices were English or French. But as they increased, he thought he could hear what they were saying. It was not possible. He must be mistaken. The cry was taken up outside the garden. He listened harder. '*La Garde recule, La Garde recule.*' Was it possible?

The French in the wood and the clearing heard it too. The Imperial Guard, Buonaparte's *immortales*, never defeated in battle, were in retreat. Yet it could not be. The Emperor only sent forward his Guard when victory was assured. It was a perfidious British trick. They did not believe that the Guard were retreating and they would not be denied their victory. They launched themselves at the defenders with desperate fury. They would take Hougoumont.

The Guards and the Brunswickers stood firm. They knew what the cry meant and if it was true, there was still hope. Try as they might, the furious French could not break their line.

Now the woods echoed with the cry. *La Garde recule. La Garde recule.* And suddenly the Guards were facing French backs. It was as if the realisation that it was true had drained every ounce of courage from them. If the mighty Guard really had been put to flight, what hope was there for them? They ran back to the woods. The tiny figure of the drummer boy jumped out from behind a pile of bricks and sped after them.

'Let them go,' croaked Macdonell. 'Where is Mister Gooch?' Henry Gooch, blood streaming from his nose and mouth, raised his sword. He could not speak. 'Mister Gooch, hold this position, if you please, until I order otherwise. Assume that the frogs will be back. Water and gin, muskets ready.' Gooch nodded. 'Corporal Graham, Sergeant Dawson is dead. You will take his place.'

The Irishman rested his huge hands on the axe handle and breathed deeply. He might have killed twenty Frenchmen. 'Very good, Colonel.'

All along the garden wall, in the fields and the orchard, there was barely a blue jacket to be seen other than those lying dead or wounded. It was not until Macdonell reached the far end of the orchard that he could see what was happening. The entire French army was in full retreat. As he watched, squadrons of British cavalry set off in hot pursuit. He shuddered. A man with his back to charging cavalry would be lucky not to be sliced in half. But the retreat was total. He saw no attempt to stand and fight, no attempt to form square, certainly no counter-attack.

Down the slope the cavalry galloped, whooping and bellowing and brandishing their sabres. Somehow the wily Duke had kept them hidden for just this moment and they were going to make the most of it. All along the ridge behind them, the infantry and artillery teams cheered them on. And the French were running. The first of the cavalry reached them and the slaughter began. Macdonell turned away. He had seen enough blood spilt that day.

He could only guess at what the Duke had done but he would wager a hundred guineas he was right. Once again, the old fox had chosen his ground, concealed his strength and awaited his moment. And once again, the French had fallen for it. Having bombarded the ridge with his cannon and believing the battle as good as won, Buonaparte had sent his Imperial Guard forward to finish it off. They had been met first by artillery and then by cavalry they did not know existed. They had panicked and run, taking the rest of the French army with them.

'Now that,' said Harry Wyndham, who had left the garden to watch the spectacle, 'is something I did not expect to see today. The Guard have indeed *reculed*, and so have the rest of them.' James did not reply. The energy of battle had drained from him and he was too exhausted even to whisper. 'Are you hurt, James?' asked Harry. James shook his head. 'I am happy for it. I too have been lucky. I dread to think how many were not. Did the Prussians arrive?' James shrugged. He wanted only to lie down and sleep.

But he could not. There was still work to be done – the roll-call, the wounded to be taken to the dressing stations behind the ridge, food and water to be found. He put a hand on Harry's shoulder, smiled weakly, and returned to the farm.

He had seen hundreds die that day, and many more wounded. He had killed a dozen himself. Yet he had survived with little more than burnt hands and a scratch on the arm. The capricious fortunes of war.

Outside the south wall, a Brunswicker corporal offered him a canteen of water. He tipped it down his rasping throat and managed to splutter his thanks. As instructed, Henry Gooch and James Graham had kept the troops at their posts. 'Stand them down, Mister Gooch,' he croaked. 'It is over.' Gooch, still unable to speak through his swollen mouth, nodded to Graham, who gave the order. A ragged cheer went up and every man sat or lay where he stood.

Hougoumont was a smoking ruin. The clearing outside the south gate was a graveyard. The remains of the barn were a charnel house. In the yard heaps of bodies lay awaiting burial. They would have to wait. Macdonell would order burial pits dug the next morning. In the garden Sellers was doing his best for the wounded. Macdonell found Mrs Osborne, her dress soaked in blood from her wound. Mrs Rogers was with her. 'The battle is over, ladies,' he said, 'and we are victorious. Do your husbands live?'

'They do, Colonel,' replied Mrs Rogers. 'Both safe, thank the good Lord.'

'And you, Mrs Osborne, how do you fare?'

'A bullet through my breast and into my shoulder, Colonel. The surgeon says he will extract it and I will live to be an old lady.'

'I am glad of it. How did you get to Hougoumont without my knowing?'

'We slipped down with the men when you were with the Duke, Colonel. We wanted to be with them,' replied Mrs Rogers with a grin.

Macdonell nodded and moved on. He exchanged a word or two with each wounded man until he came to Joseph Graham. His thigh had been bandaged with a pair of trousers. He was deathly pale. 'Corporal Graham?' whispered Macdonell. The Irishman opened his eyes briefly. He showed no sign of recognising his colonel. Macdonell left him to sleep.

James Hervey and his troops were in the north yard, inside the gates. 'I think we may open the gates now, Mister Hervey,' said Macdonell. 'We must get the wounded up to the dressing stations.'

Two guards lifted the cross-beam off its housings and pushed open the gates. Outside them, the lane was full of French bodies. 'Check for wounded, Mister Hervey. If there are any, send them up too.'

'I will, Colonel.'

'And send a foraging party up to the ridge. Food and water, whatever they can find.'

Darkness was falling and the clash of battle had been replaced by the cries of the wounded. Macdonell found James Graham in the south yard. 'James, we need wagons for the wounded. Send a party to fetch some. Your brother is in the garden. Make sure he and Mrs Osborne are on the first wagon. Are you hurt?'

'Me, sir? Good Lord, no, sir. Not a scratch. But I fear for Joseph.'

'He has lost much blood. Get him to a surgeon, James.'

From the corner of his eye, Macdonell saw two figures emerge from the gardener's house – a broad-shouldered man in a leather jerkin and a battered old hat and a blonde girl of about five in a dirty white smock. They were holding hands and, despite the failing light, were blinking as if they had emerged from a cave into bright sunlight. 'Who the devil are you?' he called out before collapsing into a fit of coughing. The two figures came towards him and the man held out a bottle. James took a mouthful and coughed again. It was brandy. He handed back the bottle. 'Thank you. *Merçi.*'

'*Mon plaisir, monsieur. Je m'appelle van Cutsem, le jardinier. Voiçi ma fille.*' Macdonell shook his head. The man claimed to be the gardener and the little girl to be his daughter. Where had they come from?

With mounting astonishment, he discovered that Monsieur van Cutsem and his daughter had spent a night and a day in the cellar under the gardener's house and had emerged only when the sounds of battle had died. They did not know which way the battle had gone until they climbed the stairs and saw red uniforms in the farm and the garden. The gardener did not trust the French and was relieved that they had been defeated. Best of all, he had food and wine in the cellar, and would be happy to share them with the British soldiers. Macdonell advised him not to visit the garden with his daughter until it had been cleared of bodies. He did not tell them that they were fortunate not to have been burnt alive or buried under a ton of rubble.

More than half the remaining Guards did not wait for the

foraging party to return. They simply found a place to sleep and something with which to cover themselves and lay down. They lay in the gardener's house and the shed, among horses burnt to skeletons by the fire and among their own dead comrades in the yards and the garden. Wagons trundled down the lane to take the wounded up to a dressing station or the makeshift hospital in the village.

When the last of the wounded had gone and such food and water as the foragers could find had been distributed, Macdonell went to the chapel and crept inside. The fire had destroyed the door, the walls were scorched and blackened. He looked up to where the wooden carving of Christ had hung over the door. It was still there. The flames had reached his feet and no further. The rest of the carving was intact.

Macdonell found a place in the gardener's house, spread a filthy blanket on the stone floor, lay down and slept.

CHAPTER EIGHTEEN

19th June

It was an hour after dawn and the sun was rising into a cloudless sky. After the recent storms, it would be another scorching day.

The two men sat on their horses under the elm tree at the crossroads at Mont St Jean from which Wellington had conducted the battle. Behind the slope of the ridge to their right, where he had concealed the main body of his army, tired men lit fires, grubbed about looking for food and sipped tea or gin. There had been no issue of rations. Some nursed wounds, all were battered, numb, starving. They were the lucky ones.

In the valley below them, as far as the eye could see to their left, to the Château Hougoumont on their right and as far as the inn at La Belle Alliance on the far side of the valley, the fields were piled with the bodies of men and horses and the detritus of war. Some still lived, pleading pitifully for help but too weak to stand or walk unaided. Most were dead. Friend and foe together, they lay entwined, heaped one on top of another, under broken artillery pieces and beside upturned wagons. They lacked arms and legs and stomachs and heads.

Grotesquely injured horses wandered aimlessly, heads down, exhausted, dying. One by one the wretched beasts were put out of their misery with a single pistol shot. Some were hacked into bloody chunks and carted up the slope in carts. And while the butchers worked, so did the blacksmiths. The saddles and bridles of cavalry horses were valuable and horseshoes could be hammered back into shape and reused. The chipping of the smiths' hammers rang out in the still air.

Clouds of carrion crows filled the sky above the fields, squawking their hateful warnings and swooping to fight over a scrap. Silent figures in peasants' smocks and strange long-eared hats moved among the corpses, hands slipping under jackets and into packs in search of coins or tobacco or a silver watch. Grubby children crawled in the dirt, looking for treasures. Dogs sniffed and licked and lifted their legs. Muskets and swords and boots were loaded into handcarts. Earrings were ripped from the ears of the Emperor's guards, gold buttons from officers' uniforms. Bodies were stripped even of the uniforms themselves, leaving them cruelly naked and exposed. A coat or a shirt not too bloodstained might fetch a few pennies.

Among the women and children and dogs, soldiers too searched for plunder. As survivors they thought it their right and knew that their officers would turn a blind eye. Red uniforms rifling the packs and pockets of their comrades and enemies alike made a gruesome sight, but in the eyes of a soldier it was no more than justice. He had fought, he had won and he would take the spoils. The dead did not need them any more than dead Imperial Guardsmen needed their pigtails. They too were cut off and stuffed into packs.

Most shocking, perhaps, of all, a tall figure in morning coat and black top hat picked his way carefully among the bodies, a handkerchief pressed to his nose. Now and again he prodded a body with his cane. The first of the sightseers had arrived.

Outside the ruins of the farm at La Haye Sainte, a company of bare-chested pioneers hacked at the earth with picks and shovels. They were digging the first of the many huge graves that would be needed before the dead were finally put to rest. There would be no distinction – officers, private soldiers, cavalry, infantry and artillery, British, German, Dutch, French, Catholic, Protestant and heathen – all would share the same graves. There were too many of them to do otherwise.

Here and there a fight broke out. Wives and sweethearts who had been sent to the rear before the battle started were beginning to arrive. They too wandered among the dead, hoping to find a husband or a brother or a sweetheart. They waved their fists and shrieked insults at the looting Belgian women, who stood and stared dumbly back until they were shoved aside and forced to slouch off in search of easier pickings elsewhere.

Neither of the mounted men at the crossroads wore jackets or shakos. Their trousers and shirts were bloody and ragged. Their boots were streaked with mud and gore.

'Is there an artist or author who could do justice to this?' asked James Macdonell. He was dirty and unshaven and black rings drooped under his eyes.

'There is not,' replied Alexander Saltoun. 'And even if there were, he would not be believed.' A livid bruise from the hilt of a French sabre ran from his ear to his chin.

'Yet it was a victory. Buonaparte was beaten.'

'He was, and has fled to Paris, I hear, chased by the Prussians.'

'So he lives. How many do not?'

'Tens of thousands,' said a quiet voice behind them. General Byng had ridden from the town of Waterloo and seen the two of them at the tree. 'Can there be a more melancholy sight than a field of battle after the battle is done?' He paused. 'But you gentlemen are alive and I rejoice for it.'

'We are obliged, General,' replied Macdonell. 'And rejoice also for you.'

'The fortunes of war, James. Picton and Ponsonby are dead, Somerset may not live, Cooke is wounded, Uxbridge has lost a leg, Fitzroy and Harris have one pair of arms between them. Yet the Duke, astonishingly, is unharmed. He was seldom out of danger and four of his aides fell around him. At one time he found himself without an aide to hand and had to send a civilian down to General Kempt to warn him to form square. A button salesman who had come to watch the battle, the Duke says. The man got rather more than he had bargained for. The fortunes of war.'

'I had four horses shot from under me yet I too have not a scratch,' added Saltoun.

'You know,' went on Byng, 'the young frog ordered me to evacuate Hougoumont when he saw the fire. He did not believe it could be held. I ignored the order. He, too, is wounded, although not seriously.'

'One trusts there will not be ramifications, General.'

'There will not. The Prince was proved wrong and in any event will have forgotten the matter or possibly even remembered that his orders were to hold the place.' He gazed out over the valley. 'Look at the poor devils. Brave men who fought and died and are now robbed and stripped and will be dumped in unmarked holes.'

'Was it not ever the lot of the soldier, General?' asked Macdonell.

'It was, of course, James, yet I pray never to look on anything like this again. I doubt if the Duke is yet aware of the scale of his victory or of its price and I shall not be the one to tell him. I do not have the words. It was a desperate affair, was it not? And your own efforts will not go unnoticed, gentlemen.'

'Others would have done the same,' replied Macdonell, a trifle gruffly. He had never been comfortable with compliments.

'Perhaps,' replied the general. 'Old Blücher did arrive, although late in the day, and I thank God for it. His Prussians kept two French divisions occupied around Planchenois. Their losses were high, but without them, the outcome might have been very different.'

'And what now, General?' asked Saltoun. 'Will Buonaparte try again?'

'Good God, Alexander, I pray not. Can you imagine another day like yesterday? No, his invincible Imperial Guard proved anything but, and their reputation, and his, have been destroyed. Surely the French will not rise for him again.'

'I recall hearing similar words when he escaped from Elba, General,' said Macdonell quietly.

'It will not be Elba this time, James, if the Duke has his

way, which, of course, he will. Somewhere very much more distant and inhospitable will be found for him. If the royalists do not get their hands on him first, that is. Looking at what lies before us, I for one rather hope that they do.' For some minutes they sat in silence. 'Gentlemen, the Duke sent his preliminary despatch to London last night. He intends to send another, more complete, within a day or two and has asked me for my report. To write it, I shall need yours.'

'You shall have mine this evening, General,' replied Macdonell, dreading the prospect of having to sit down and write it.

'And mine, General,' added Saltoun.

Byng nodded. 'It was a terrible day. I thank God it is over.' He turned his horse and trotted back up the road to the village. Macdonell and Saltoun did not move. For all its horror, the battlefield had a mesmerising effect. They sat and stared at it.

A carriage rattled down the road towards them. The driver reined in his huge black carthorse and came to a halt at the crossroads. He wore the grey trousers of the Royal Waggon Train. The door of the carriage opened and a crimson-jacketed surgeon with a large bag of instruments stepped out, followed by three women in floral dresses and pink bonnets. Each of them carried a basket of bandages. All four were so bloodstained and filthy that their own mothers might not have recognised them. They took no notice of the two mounted men under the elm tree but walked a little way along the ridge and looked down into the valley.

A single rider had followed the carriage. 'Good morning, gentlemen,' he said as he approached. He looked down on the battlefield. 'Well, perhaps not good, but for us at least better than it might have been.'

'Good morning, Francis,' replied James. 'Have you ever set eyes on a more desolate sight? I certainly have not. Did you find a billet for the night?'

'No. I slept in a haystack in the village. A trifle prickly but not too bad. The surgeons and their assistants were at work all night. I came down with Daisy. She's exhausted.'

'Is that Daisy with the surgeon?' asked James. 'I did not recognise her.'

'It is.'

'There were two women with us at Hougoumont, wives of privates helping with the wounded. One was wounded, a shot to the breast.'

'I am sorry for it. Now I shall attend the ladies. Daisy has taken to calling me general, the impertinent child, although I have told her not to.'

'General?'

'When General Cooke was wounded, General Byng took his place and I in turn took General Byng's place. A temporary state of affairs only but it amuses Daisy to think otherwise.'

'Yet you remained in the orchard.'

'I did.' He grinned. 'From there I could stand in for the general whilst keeping an eye on you. My new role made no difference. The orchard had to be defended.'

'Yet you might have told me,' replied Macdonell. 'I should have been happy for you.'

'Tush, James, you were much too busy.'

'There,' said the surgeon loudly, 'the battlefield. It is as we were warned, is it not? Let us waste no time. Miss Brown, Miss Westfield, kindly make your way down the slope to the left. Take great care where you step. Call out if you find a man living. Miss Box, if you would, accompany me. We will do what we can for them.'

Francis dismounted and led his horse along the path to where the little party stood. He called out. Daisy turned. Tears ran down her unwashed cheeks but her eyes were blank. Francis put his arms around her shoulders and embraced her. It was no time for convention.

'Time I went to work,' said James quietly. With a flick of the reins he set off down the path towards Hougoumont, leaving Saltoun on the ridge.

He passed groups of haggard soldiers, sitting, squatting and lying around their fires or in roughly constructed bivouacs. The men glanced up but looked quickly away again when they realised he was not an officer in their battalion and was not there to give them orders. Soldiers need orders and they had none. Until orders came they would have to stay where they were and fend for themselves.

Behind the rows of bivouacs, Gunners sat propped against the wheels and carriages of their artillery pieces, smoking their pipes and sipping from their canteens. Their carriage horses, hobbled together, searched in vain for tufts of grass in the narrow strip of mud between the guns and the wood.

At the top of the ridge the path was still stony and hard. Lower down, the earth had been churned to mud and they had to go slowly. Twice Macdonell's mount slipped and he only just avoided a fall. The ground was littered with discarded packs, shakos and blankets. The dead had been cleared to one side to await burial or burning. The looters would find them soon.

In the field outside the orchard that Saltoun and Hepburn had defended all day, half a dozen soldiers were going from body to body. At first Macdonell thought they were checking for signs of life but soon realised that they too were looting. He spurred his horse and cantered towards them. When they saw him, they ran off towards the woods. None of them wore jackets. It was hard to be sure but he thought three were British and three French.

Smoke was still rising from the ruins of the chateau and the farm. He entered through the north gates, battered but intact and standing open. Bodies filled the yard, many, to his fury, already stripped naked. The looters had been at their foul work during the night. What had been the barn was a smouldering heap of debris. Fragments of bone and skull lay flensed and charred in the ashes. The cowshed and the farmer's house were gone, the draw well was a hellish tangle of bricks and bodies, the garden wall was barely standing.

The walls of the chateau and the tower – what remained of them – were pitted with bullet holes and still warm to the touch. The chapel door had gone – burnt to cinders – but the chapel itself still stood. Macdonell bowed his head and went in. The walls and floor were scorched black. He turned to look at the place above the door where the carving of Christ on the cross had hung on the wall. It was still there. The flames that had destroyed the chateau, and the farm which had brought death to so many, had reached Christ's feet but no higher.

Macdonell crossed himself. The Grahams had been right. God had watched over them.

In the south yard, where the worst of the fighting had been raging no more than twelve hours earlier, a party of men under James Hervey had begun the task of collecting the dead and carrying them outside. Hervey, too, was blank-eyed and exhausted. 'I thought before the looters find them, Colonel . . .' he began.

'Quite so, Mister Hervey,' replied Macdonell. 'The scavengers must have been here all night. Let us bury them as quickly as we can. Where are you digging?'

'Near the woods, Colonel.'

'Good. Use every man you can find and do not forget the wretched souls in the barn.'

The gardener's house, where the gardener and his daughter had hidden in the cellar for the whole day, was still standing. The south gate under it had been destroyed by the French light guns, as had much of the south wall. James left the yard through the arch of the gate.

The wood was no longer a wood. Such trees as were still standing had not a leaf upon them. Every trunk was black and every branch broken. He walked around the garden wall. Unlike the woods and the farm it had stood up to the assault remarkably well. The loopholes were there of course, in places there were gaping holes and barely a brick was unmarked by bullet or shot, yet it stood. Outside the wall the dead were being cleared and taken to what would be their grave near the wood. A large figure was pushing a handcart on which three bodies had been loaded.

'Corporal Graham,' called out Macdonell. 'How is your brother?'

Graham put down the cart. 'He lives, Colonel, but his leg has gone. The surgeon took it last night.'

'Were you with him?'

'I was, sir. He is in the farm at Mont St Jean. Many of the wounded are there. A young lady named Daisy held his hand while the surgeon worked. She helped him bear it. Joseph says he will live.'

'Then I am sure he will.'

In the garden, piles of bodies had been heaped against the south wall. In the middle of what had been a parterre a fire had been lit. Five men sat around it, using upturned French cuirasses as seats and another as a cooking pot. One of them was Harry Wyndham.

'Breakfast, Harry?' asked James. Whatever was in the cuirass flooded his mouth with saliva.

The men jumped up. 'Pigeon,' replied Harry. 'They obligingly arrived this morning from the wood. Nests blown to bits, I daresay. Would you care for a mouthful? I am sure we would not mind.' The soldiers shook their heads.

'Thank you, Harry, I would. And you have found new uses for French armour.'

Harry skewered a piece of pigeon on a bayonet and passed it to James. James took a bite and raised his eyebrows in surprise. It was good.

'I found an unwanted bottle of claret. Just the thing for pigeon stew,' said Harry. 'We've grim work before us and we need a good breakfast.' The four privates grunted their agreement. 'It was hard fighting, James. The roll was difficult last night. It was dark and I may have missed some, but we lost at least five hundred. More in the orchard.'

'Have you stood on the ridge?'

'Not yet.'

'There might be fifty times that and as many French.'

'Good God. So many?'

'I fear so.'

For some moments, Harry was lost in thought. Abruptly, he stood up. 'But we held Hougoumont.'

Macdonell too rose. 'Seeing it now in ruins, it is hard to believe, but we did.'

AFTERWORD

James Macdonell

There are various spellings of 'Macdonell'. Wellington, bizarrely, refers to him on at least one occasion, as 'Macdonald'. I have used the spelling Macdonell himself used when signing the regimental order book on the morning of 16 October.

He was awarded, among other honours, a knighthood and the Order of the Bath for his gallant service at Waterloo and, not surprisingly, went on to a distinguished career in the army, becoming commander of the Brigade of Guards in Canada and being appointed a general in 1854. He died in 1857, aged 76.

'The Bravest Man at Waterloo'

There is more than one version of the story but the likeliest seems to be this. In August 1815, the rector of Framlingham, in Suffolk, one John Norcross, late of Pembroke College,

Cambridge, offered an annuity of £10 to the man nominated by the Duke of Wellington as the most deserving of it for his gallantry at Waterloo. Wellington demurred and suggested that the choice should be made by Major General Sir John Byng. Perhaps advised by James Macdonell, Byng jointly nominated James Graham, who had been promoted to sergeant and had already been awarded a special gallantry medal and Joseph Lester, his boxing opponent. (Sergeant Ralph Fraser, the man who pulled the French colonel off his horse and rode it triumphantly through the north gates, was another to receive the medal. The unlucky colonel was named Cubières.) They received the annuity for two years but when the rector was declared bankrupt, it ceased.

The rector's fortunes must have recovered because when he died twenty-two years later, his estate was sufficient for him to leave £500 (about £23,000 in today's money) to the man nominated by Wellington as 'the bravest man in England'. This time, Wellington agreed and nominated James Macdonell. More than once, Wellington, who was not given to extending praise, expressed the view that the outcome of Waterloo turned on the successful defence of Hougoumont and, in particular, on 'the closing of the gates'. He was referring to the heroic closing of the north gates when the attackers might easily have overrun the enclosure and opened the south gates, allowing their waiting comrades to pour in. He wrote, '*The success of the Battle of Waterloo turned on the closing of the gates at Hougoumont. The gates were closed in the most courageous manner at the very nick of time by the efforts of Sir J. Macdonell. I cannot help thinking Sir*

James is the man to whom you should give £500.' Macdonell accepted the award only on condition that it be shared with James Graham. Every British soldier who fought at Waterloo was awarded The Waterloo Medal.

Not only was Macdonell a man of great personal courage, renowned for always being in the thickest of the fighting, he was also an exceptional leader of men. In scorching heat, his light companies marched twenty-seven miles from Enghien to Quatre Bras, were thrown straight into the battle there, spent a wet, miserable night in the open, conducted a fighting retreat for the twelve miles back to Mont St Jean, were sent down to Hougoumont without food or water, spent another wet night there, and, finally, fought for over eight hours in its successful defence. James Macdonell led them through all of this.

Casualties

Estimates naturally vary but the consensus seems to be that at Quatre Bras the Allies lost nearly 5,000 killed and injured and the French about 1,000 less.

At Waterloo, on a single day, some 15,000 Allied, 7,000 Prussian and 25,000 French troops died or were injured. It took weeks to bury and burn the dead.

Hougoumont

In the story James Macdonell wonders whether Wellington really expects the Guards to hold Hougoumont or whether they are merely intended to draw French troops away from Napoleon's centre. General Müffling certainly did not think Hougoumont could be held and said so. Wellington took pleasure, after the battle, in pointing out his mistake.

It seems likely that Wellington hoped the Guards would hold the chateau and farm all day but, if not, that they would do so for long enough to be a serious thorn in Napoleon's side. Napoleon, on the other hand, hoped that Wellington would have to reinforce the Hougoumont garrison, thereby weakening his own centre. In fact, the relatively few reinforcements Wellington sent came from his right wing and did not weaken his centre.

The French may have committed as many as 14,000 men at different times to the attacks on Hougoumont, the Allies perhaps 3,500 (including Hanoverians, Brunswickers and Nassauers) to repulsing them, so Napoleon's plan did not work. French casualties in and around Hougoumont of 5,000 were more than three times those of the Allies.

Hougoumont is often described as 'a battle within a battle'. In some ways, it was. Macdonell and his Guards could not have known much of the progress of the battle raging in the valley and on the ridge beyond the orchard other than what little could be seen from the tower before it was destroyed. The whole battlefield would have been shrouded in smoke, information coming down the hollow lane would have been sketchy and unreliable and it would not have been easy to distinguish between the report of an Allied cannon and a French one. Fighting in a vacuum cannot have made the Guards' task any easier.

The chateau and farm were situated about equidistant from Wellington's right wing and Napoleon's left. If Hougoumont had fallen, the French would have been able to use it as a springboard from which to attack the Anglo-Dutch forces on the slope behind it, which would have forced Wellington to reinforce his right wing, thereby weakening his centre.

That is why Wellington reckoned that Hougoumont held the key to the battle and why he chose James Macdonell to command the garrison there.

Fact and Fiction

On 17th August 1815, Wellington wrote, '*It is impossible to say when each occurrence took place, nor in what order.*'

Hougoumont was attacked at least five times during the day, and the orchard more often. Within the framework of the battle, I have simply tried to give the reader an idea of what it must have been like for both attackers and defenders – unceasing, terrifying hell – rather than try to recreate the exact sequence of events.

The incident of Lord Saltoun leaving the orchard and meeting Wellington on the way up to the ridge is well recorded, but odd. The explanation I have suggested is my own invention, but seems to me to be plausible. In the notorious 'fog of war', such things can happen.

The name of the giant, axe-wielding French sous-lieutenant was, appropriately, *Le Gros*. He was known to his comrades as *L'Enfonceur* – 'The Smasher'. The drummer boy's name is not known, or even whether he survived. I have chosen to believe that he did, and that he managed to run back to the French lines at the time of the general retreat.

Stories of the gardener, Monsieur van Cutsem, and his daughter vary. At least one contemporary account denies their existence altogether. Some histories suggest that van Cutsem took an active part in the battle, others that his presence came as a shock to all when the fighting was at last over. I have chosen the latter. The brave Mrs Osborne, happily, survived.

The gallant button salesman who carried a vital message down from Wellington to General Kempt disappeared after the battle. It was only some years later that, by chance, Wellington learnt of his whereabouts and was able to reward him for his service.

There is a painting by W. Wollen, entitled by the artist – I respectfully suggest, mistakenly – *The First Shot at the Battle of Waterloo*. It looks to me much more like the French cavalry officer at Quatre Bras who was so furious at his horse being shot from under him that he brandished his sabre at the Guards in the wood who had done such an unchivalrous thing. The officer did not survive. I mention this as an example of how stories of Waterloo so easily changed with the telling and became confused. There are many other such examples.

Wellington's remark, 'Ah, but you do not know Macdonell', is well documented but did not, as I have suggested, take place at the house in Waterloo. It was more probably said to General Müffling when they rode down on the morning of the battle to inspect Hougoumont.

Of the hundreds of other incidents, such as the carving of Christ on the cross which, apart from his feet, survived the fire, the bloody water and the obliging pigeons, that occurred at Quatre Bras and Waterloo, I have selected a few, sometimes with a little licence, that fitted my story.

ACKNOWLEDGEMENTS

For excellent histories and accounts of this period, the humble novelist is spoilt for choice. I would mention, in particular, Alessandro Barbero's *The Battle*, Mike Robinson's *The Battle of Quatre Bras 1815*, and *Hougoumont* by Julian Paget and Derek Saunders. All these I found invaluable, as were Gareth Glover's comprehensive *Waterloo Archive* series, Private Matthew Clay's personal account of the battles, first published in 1853, and Sergeant Major Cotton's *A Voice from Waterloo*, published in 1849.

My grateful thanks are also due to:

Rhydian Vaughan of Battlefield Tours, www.battlefieldtours. co.uk, who expertly guided us around the battlefields and acted as unofficial researcher and corrector of errors.

Colonel Simon Vandeleur, Regimental Adjutant Coldstream Guards at Wellington Barracks, for kindly allowing me access to the regimental archives.

Robert Cazenove, Regimental Archivist, Coldstream Guards for his help with uniforms, musical instruments and proper forms of address.

My agent David Headley, of DHH Literary Agents, for his encouragement and support and Susie Dunlop of Allison & Busby for hers.

And to all others who were kind enough to read my drafts and offer advice.